JORDAN'S
DELIVERANCE

JORDAN'S DELIVERANCE

ALLEN STEADHAM

Ambassador International
GREENVILLE, SOUTH CAROLINA & BELFAST, NORTHERN IRELAND
www.ambassador-international.com

Jordan's Deliverance
The Jordan of Algoran Series, Book Three

© 2020 by Allen Steadham

ISBN: 978-1-64960-025-7
eISBN: 978-1-64960-026-4

Scripture taken from the King James Version. The Authorized Version. Public Domain.

Cover Illustration by Christopher Jackson
Cover Design & Typesetting by Hannah Nichols
Edited by Daphne Self

AMBASSADOR INTERNATIONAL
Emerald House
411 University Ridge, Suite B14
Greenville, SC 29601, USA
www.ambassador-international.com

AMBASSADOR BOOKS
The Mount
2 Woodstock Link
Belfast, BT6 8DD, Northern Ireland, UK
www.ambassadormedia.co.uk

The colophon is a trademark of Ambassador, a Christian publishing company.

"The righteous cry, and the LORD heareth, and delivereth them out of all their troubles."

\- Psalm 34:17

ACT ONE

WALKING THE PATH SET BEFORE THEM

PROLOGUE

Kazil Mikenajolis, carrying a metal box of incalculable importance, ran as fast as she could towards the glowing light in front of her. As an Onchei who had lived eight hundred zohwas, she was in upper middle age, nearly an elder, and had been a well-respected community member in the city of Rofizda in the Southlands. She had married relatively young and held a supervisor position in the technology division of the new Onchei Science Directorate.

And yet, Kazil had been tasked with a responsibility by her father, the same one he had been given by his grandmother, which she had received from her mother from generations before: preserving the ancient metal box and keeping it hidden from the public until it could be sent far away from Algoran.

Kazil had informed her mate after swearing him to secrecy. Their offspring had no knowledge of this. Only her immediate superiors knew of her special purpose, which made achieving her goal possible. Everyone else believed they were merely seeking exploration of other worlds for its own sake.

The receptacle in her grasp was fairly small, about only one ebiin long by eleven doralns wide and six doralns deep. The metallic alloy was hollowed out and not very heavy. Its lid contained an engraving with one of the symbols of their people. Neither Kazil nor her ancestors knew what lay within. The container had been sealed in such a way that no one knew how to open it. However, they had been instructed that it needed to be permanently delivered to another world.

It had been within the last zohwa that the Onchei Science Directorate created stable portal technology for study and ultimately, transportation. Finally, the Onchei had made contact with a habitable world. They discreetly observed its people, determining that world's technological level of advancement. They also deciphered some of the dominant languages. From this, they learned this world was called "Earth" by its people. The Onchei believed this planet and its inhabitants were worth further study.

Kazil had extensive knowledge of the new teleportation machines, since she had been a part of the team that completed and tested them. Presently, she had verified the destination coordinates and steeled herself for the journey she was about to embark on. It saddened her that she would never see her family again; she would spend her remaining zohwas safeguarding the metal container. Kazil tried to comfort herself with the understanding that she had lived hundreds of zohwas with her dearest ones; they would go on without her. She had committed herself and there was no turning back.

She prepared a bag of tools and technology from Algoran to help her survive on Earth. Once she had jumped through the portal, it would shut behind her and no one would follow. This would make it virtually impossible for her—and more importantly, what she took with her—to be found. But perhaps this mission would save her world, as her ancestors had said. That would make this worthwhile, even honorable. Taking a deep breath in that final moment, she pierced the shining light and became the first Onchei to traverse the pathway between her world and any other.

She arrived during the night in the northern hemisphere of Earth, just outside the bustling community of Minsk, Russia. Kazil hid herself and her treasure in the forest. Over the next couple of wiptas, she covertly renovated a small cottage that had been abandoned and was in disrepair, its frame still intact. With a solar-powered cutting tool, she was able to cleave and smooth down wood to make a ladder and replace a small part of the roof. She used a scanner to determine what local plants would make for a good sealant against the elements. Finding some knitting needles left by the former occupants, Kazil did her best to mend the old and tattered curtains.

Kazil was able to drink the water from a nearby river and quickly verified which plants and small animals she could safely consume. The studies her people had performed had been thorough and accurate. She would survive to carry out her mission.

All the while, she observed the townspeople from her cottage using surveillance technology. She continued to learn all she could about them. After determining where she would arrive on Earth, she had mastered their native tongue while still on Algoran. From her research into this new country and culture, Kazil created a new identity for herself and began using their terminologies.

She took the name Jadwiga Bogdana and became known as the eccentric old woman who lived in the forest. Before going into town, she would clothe herself in the style she saw most of the older women wearing. She donned a simple, long double-layered dress with wrist-length sleeves and a long scarf to cover her hair. Determining that the average human lifespan was approximately forty-five years at that time, Kazil more or less looked like a human woman in her early sixties. She mixed a dye from local plants to present a pale version of the human's skin color. When in public, Jadwiga kept her eyes closed and mimicked blindness. She knew her black scleras and lavender-colored irises would alarm anyone who saw them.

Using her machines to scan for precious stones and metals, Jadwiga would later sell or barter with them. What she did sell gave her enough to provide for her initial needs yet was not enough to draw undue attention to herself. She used some of this money to buy crafting tools and furniture. As a profession, Kazil bought clay or gathered mud to create pottery to sell to the townspeople.

She became accustomed to being alone most of the time. Occasionally, some curious young children or teens would venture into the forest and try to mock her or cause trouble outside her home. Simply using a invisible energy field around her house would be enough to spook them if they bumped into it. But for the foolish and undeterred ones, she had another response. She would open the door and approach them with eyes wide open, showing her true appearance while projecting a fierce or angry expression at them. That always sent them running in terror.

A few times, concerned parents came to her door, relaying their children's frenzied stories about magic and a "demon witch" that lived in the woods. But when they saw how friendly and benign "Blind Old Jadwiga" seemed to be, combined with how discernible and spartan her home was, they chalked up the stories to children's overactive imaginations. Kazil would give them fresh fruit as a gift and the parents would apologize for troubling her.

Knowing that she would outlive the humans, Jadwiga would move to a new town or city once every twenty or thirty years. But she always resided away from those communities, preferring the forests. For two hundred years, she maintained that lifestyle, traveling throughout Russia. She took some amusement in hearing that children and their parents had created folk stories about the strange old woman in the woods. Some of the more insistent children who had seen her face even believed her to be the legendary "Baba Yaga."

Eventually, Jadwiga returned to Minsk. Now stricken with age, she feared her time was short. She knew she had to find someone, a human, to carry on the tradition of guarding the metal box she still kept with her.

Jadwiga had developed a friendship with a local baker named Ioann Markov and his wife, Agafya. They had three young sons and lived in a house near the center of town. Jadwiga had a bad back now, and she used a walking stick to keep her balance. She'd lost much of her strength and stamina. But she retained enough to make some pottery and plates for the family in exchange for bread, pastries, and conversation.

"What would you say if I told you I have a box of wonders?" Jadwiga asked with an air of mystery and intrigue. Her voice had become husky with the years but there was no mistaking her warmth and love for this family.

She sat in a wooden chair inside their home, next to the blazing fire. Ioann sat in a chair across the room while his sons sat on a wool rug laid across their wooden floor. Agafya was preparing bowls of hot vegetable stew for them. It smelled surprisingly good to Jadwiga, but perhaps she was just hungry.

"A box of wonders?'" answered Kir, Ioann's oldest son. "Where?"

Kir was nine years old, stout with curly brown hair and piercing blue eyes.

Jadwiga smiled. "I keep it in my house in the forest."

"What wonders does it do? Can it make children fly? Make it rain or stop raining?" asked Lev, Kir's middle brother.

Lev was six, slender and quick. He had blond hair and brown eyes which reflected his growing intellect. His younger brother, Matvey, was three years old, with short and wavy brown hair. His smoky gray eyes were riveted on Jadwiga, but he said nothing.

"Mostly, it protects the contents within the box, which has been in my family for eight generations," Jadwiga replied. "But it can do much more, probably even some of the things you said. I have guarded it my whole life. But I am old and have no children to pass this onto. When I die, I fear men will find the box and open it to sell what lies within. I do not wish for this to happen."

She hoped that indulging the children's imaginations might endear them to the idea of helping her. It didn't take too long to see if it worked.

"Could we help?" Kir wondered, consulting no one.

"I do not wish to impose on your gracious family," Jadwiga insisted. "Forgive my foolish ramblings."

Ioann stared at Jadwiga from his chair with a mixture of curiosity and suspicion. He was a large man in his late thirties with bushy brown hair and beard.

"Come with me, Jadwiga. I wish to speak with you outside."

He motioned for the children to remain quiet as he gently led her by the arm. They walked out of the house, his wife following. He was very patient with Jadwiga's frail condition and slow pace. Once outside, he waited a moment to say what was on his mind.

"What is actually in the box, Jadwiga?" Ioann asked. "It is clear you want us to take this box. I want to know why."

"I was married long ago. My husband was an artist and he made me some small, intricate carvings from metal, wood, and ivory. We stored them in this box. It is locked and I long ago lost the key," she chose to say. "But it has sentimental value to me, so I could never throw it away. I would like your family to have it because I care for you so. Perhaps this is one way you could remember me."

Satisfied, Ioann nodded. "I see. Thank you for telling me."

"If you do not wish to have it, I will understand."

"No, it is all right. We will do this for you. You are a member of our family."

Jadwiga bowed humbly in the direction of the baker's voice. She kept her eyes closed as always. But as poor as her vision had become, she no longer had to feign blindness. Fortunately, she knew nearly every inch of this town.

"Thank you, sir. I feel the same way," she replied.

They went back inside. Ioann viewed his children, who were all looking at him with begging eyes. Then he stared at his wife, who looked at her sons and then to him. She nodded pleasantly. He nodded back at her before turning his attention back to Jadwiga.

"Jadwiga, bring your box of wonders to us tomorrow," Ioann declared. "We will protect it for you. You have my word."

Jadwiga had hoped they would agree but she hadn't been sure until a few minutes ago. Human behavior could be very hard to understand, much less anticipate.

She put her arms in front of her and slowly bowed numerous times where she was. It was worth the pain it caused her aching back, as she had secured her goal.

"Thank you, sir! Thank you! I will be forever grateful. I can die in peace now."

The children had sounded excited at first to know they were helping her. But now, they quieted down.

"Do you have to go away someday, Jadwiga?" Lev asked, his voice trembling.

FIFTEEN YEARS AGO ON EARTH

Kayla Lewis stood at the bottom of the stairs and looked up at her husband, Mark, with concern. He was carrying two stacked and very full moving boxes in his arms as he carefully descended the stairs, obviously straining.

"Mark, put one of those boxes down! You'll throw your back out again," Kayla warned.

"I'm using my legs. I'll be fine," he answered.

Neither impressed nor persuaded, she walked over and grabbed the top box. She angled her lips and blew a long strand of brown hair out of her face as she walked past him towards their minivan. The rest of her hair was pulled back into a long ponytail.

"You are not twenty anymore, Mark, and you do not have to impress me."

"I wasn't trying to impress you, honey. I just thought I could do it."

"My point is you don't have to. I'm right here. I can help."

"Yes, ma'am," he replied with a hint of sarcasm. They'd had this conversation more than once.

Kayla Lewis was forty-eight years old and her husband was a year older than her. They had been married for twenty-eight years and owned a graphic design company called Markayla Designs. She was the artist while he managed the business. It had been profitable enough over the years, allowing them to buy a house, own two vehicles, pay the bills, and provide for three daughters.

But maintaining and growing the business had been very stressful. Kayla had barely kept it together when Mark suffered a mild heart attack at the age of thirty-nine. Her own vision had suffered from her habit of working late into the night with less than ideal lighting. She ate when she remembered to, though it was at irregular intervals. That had been fine when she was a teenager. But time and having children had altered her metabolism, causing her to steadily gain weight.

Still, Kayla was more concerned with her husband's well-being than her own.

The back hatch was already open, and their storage area was half-filled with boxes. The vehicle hovered a foot above the ground using magnetic propulsion technology which hummed quietly. Virtually all transportation had been clean, electric, and wheel-less for over a decade. The van was slightly oval-shaped, large enough to accommodate up to six passengers with room to spare for hauling items.

Kayla put her box on top of one of the others. Mark put his next to hers, but it slipped from his grip. Falling to one side, its lid popped off and she heard him sigh in frustration.

"What's wrong?" Kayla inquired, pushing her glasses back up her sweaty nose. She knew his sigh was about more than a moving box. She was beside him now, one hand resting on his left arm while observing his wistful expression and furrowed brow.

"I just can't believe they're both gone," Mark lamented. "First Mom . . . now Dad. They lived together in this house ever since Mom . . . got back."

"I know," Kayla replied, nodding in understanding. "Your dad was a father to me a lot longer than my own. But they had a long life."

"At least they got back together," Mark added. "That was the best decision they ever made."

"And they got to know their grandkids," Kayla remarked with a sad smile.

Kayla decided to grab the moving box that had fallen to the side and lined it up with the others. Grabbing its lid, she glanced inside the box and something caught her eye: a gray, metallic shoebox-sized object which looked extremely old.

"What's this?" she asked.

"Hm?" Mark turned to look at her.

"This metal, um, container. I think I've seen it before—"

"Oh, that? It was Mom's. She kept it on the mantle above the fireplace with the family pictures."

"What's in it?"

"I don't know. I thought it was just an old jewelry box or something. I've never looked inside it."

"It looks sealed or something."

Mark nodded. "Yeah. Mom and Dad both tried to open it a few times over the years but never managed to. I think I even attempted it once. But there's such a long family history with it, we kept it."

Kayla picked up the old plated box and looked at it with fascination. She smiled.

"Seems such a shame to put an old keepsake like this in storage. I doubt we could sell it if we don't know how to open it," Kayla noted, looking at Mark. "Do you think your mom would mind if I held onto it?"

Mark paused and then made a slight shrug. "Knowing Mom, it would probably make her happy for you to have it. Go ahead, keep it. Where do you want to put it?"

Kayla held the box close to her chest. "For a family heirloom like this? Your mom kept it on the fireplace, so I guess I'll do that, too!"

Mark smiled. "Sounds good. Now, let's go get those last few boxes and take all this to the self-storage facility."

"You go on up and get one of the boxes—and I mean only one!"

She put the family keepsake on the front passenger floorboard of the vehicle. As she exited the passenger seat and stepped onto the driveway, she paused to watch her husband enter the house.

"I'm gonna call Jo and have her meet us to unload this stuff," Kayla stated.

"Won't she be studying for midterms?"

"This is our oldest daughter we're talking about. She'll either be gaming, eating pizza, or writing a new song."

"Right. Then she'll cram the night before and probably ace it."

"Exactly," Kayla answered with a proud chuckle.

Kayla pressed a button on her wristband as Mark went back inside. A holographic interface appeared.

"Call Jo Lewis," Kayla told the device.

While the holo-interface on her wristband was attempting to contact her daughter, Kayla looked towards the front of the van. She found herself surprisingly captivated by the idea of that ancient artifact. Just then, the holo-screen flickered and displayed the words "Connection Established."

Kayla's daughter appeared in the waist-up holo-display. She was twenty-three years old and a junior in college, working on her Bachelor of Arts Degree in History. She was tall and average-sized, wearing a dark blue t-shirt. Her hair was shoulder-length, frizzy, and half of it was covering her eyes. The apartment, which she shared with another female student, was only lit by the small amount of sunlight peeking through the blinds of one window.

"Oh, hey, Mom!" Jo smiled in recognition. "Sorry, I just got up."

"It's two in the afternoon," Kayla replied with measured patience.

"Izzit? Oh, wow. We went to see Eventually Watermelon in concert last night. After we got home, we binge-watched a bunch of sci-fi."

Kayla pushed her glasses back up her nose again. This time, it was more to show her annoyance than to be functional.

"Your Dad and I have been packing up stuff from Grandma and Grandpa's house. We're about to take the boxes to storage. Can you help us unload? I don't want your Dad doing too much."

"Oh! Um, which storage place?"

"The one at Milea and Condor."

Jo looked unenthused, so Kayla gave an insistent stare. After a moment, her daughter gave a surrendering shrug.

"I can be there in twenty minutes. Is that okay?"

"Sure. Thanks, Jo! Love you."

"Love you, too, Mom."

Kayla pressed another button on her bracelet and the holo-interface dispersed. As she walked inside to see if her husband needed any assistance, she couldn't help but reminisce for a moment. She thought about Mark's parents, memories with them in that house. And then suddenly, Mark's older sister came to mind. It had been over thirty years since she'd last seen Jordan. Sometimes, she still wondered how her sister-in-law was doing on that faraway world of Algoran.

1

TRUTH AND DECEPTION

Jordan SnowFire sat in complete silence on the floor of the hut designated to her position as Chieftess of the Mountain Mokta tribe. Alongside her was Bopol, her mate, protector and security advisor. She gave her full attention to Mocheela, a female elder, as she entered. Mocheela had lived eighty-four cycles and was currently the oldest person in the village. She had short, thinning hair, was hunched over and displayed the keenest mind of any Mokta Jordan had known since the late Kitranor. Mocheela used two walking sticks due to her frailty and poor balance. But her vision was still good, and she could project her raspy voice to make it easily heard.

"You called for me, Chieftess?"

"Yes, Mocheela," Jordan responded. "I am in need of your counsel, wisdom, and experience."

"All I possess is yours, Chieftess. How may I counsel you?"

"I want to know more about the Qui Tol from our oral history, even the lesser known tales. Specifically, I want to know anything from very long ago."

Mocheela nodded and sat down next to the Chieftess with some difficulty. Jordan could see her silently searching her memories. After a few moments, she spoke again.

"The stories from the most ancient days are fragmented, incomplete . . . but almost all of them agree about one thing: before the time of SnowFire, Algoran was very different from what we know today," Mocheela recalled. "The world was full of people and there were vast cities, much bigger than villages, with buildings that touched the sky itself. But there was some kind of Great War. In a short time, all life on Algoran nearly perished."

"A Great War," Jordan repeated, remembering that Kitranor had once mentioned this to her. "Do the stories say what caused it?"

That appeared to frustrate the elder, who frowned in response.

"Like most wars, it was probably over land or perhaps one leader offended another. If each king or queen called on all their allies to assist them, it may have spread to the whole world," Mocheela replied. "And there were many kings and queens in those days, if the stories are to be believed."

"I understand. Something similar happened on my world, twice," Jordan acknowledged. "Do you know if any written records still exist—in any language?"

"Chieftess, there were barely any survivors. It is a wonder that there are spoken stories."

Jordan nodded somberly. She looked skyward through the window, systematically pouring through possibilities in her mind, hoping to find something to protect the Mokta from the Onchei threat.

"Why do you want to know about those times, Chieftess?" Mocheela wondered aloud.

"Now that the Onchei have returned from some faraway place, we need to know everything we can about them, including their history,"

Jordan answered. "Maybe if we learn how they behaved in the past, it could help us in the present."

"That is wise, Chieftess."

Jordan kept her gaze fixed on Mocheela but said nothing. The elder looked around uncomfortably.

"Is there something else, Chieftess?"

Jordan relaxed her shoulders, inhaled slowly, and raised an eyebrow at Mocheela as she exhaled.

"You are only fifteen cycles older than me . . . did you know that?" Jordan told her.

"No . . . I did not," the elder replied, displaying some surprise. Then she grinned with a mouth full of crooked teeth. "You look well for a fellow elder!"

Jordan chuckled in response. But she was close to tears.

"What is wrong, Chieftess?"

Jordan opened her mouth to speak but thought better of it. Embarrassed, she tried to cover it with a smile. "I must be more tired than I thought. All is well."

There was some hesitation in Mocheela's expression, but the older woman kept silent.

"I will go now. I—" Mocheela's eyes brightened with inspiration. "Chieftess, I just remembered a story about the Qui Tol! It is old, very old—and strange."

"Tell me, please."

"I heard this from elders when I was almost at my Dawning Time," Mocheela continued. "A Mokta traveling from the Eastern region passed through here and shared the story with one of them. I liked to help the elders with tasks around their huts and they would reward me with tales from long ago.

"They called this story 'The Disgrace of the Qui Tol.' There was a metal box passed down from one generation of Qui Tol to the next, known only to a very few. It dated back to the time of the Great War. No one knows what was within it. But the Qui Tol feared it so much that, according to this legend, they made their doors between the worlds just to get rid of this box."

Jordan was amazed and wondered whether the box contained some ancient weapon.

"Have the Qui Tol visited other worlds besides Earth? Did they ever bring others besides people like me?"

"No, Chieftess. We have only known men and women from Errrth."

"So, if this tale is true, an ancient Qui Tol box may be on Earth? Perhaps I should go look for it?"

"It may be there. But it was sent there over one thousand cycles ago. Would it not be almost impossible to find now?"

Jordan wasn't ready to give up on the idea yet. She needed something, anything to use against the Onchei. And she was willing to figuratively grasp at straws at this point.

"Did that story describe the box, Elder?"

"Yes, Chieftess. They say it was about this long," Mocheela said, holding her hands about one foot apart. Then she shifted her hand position, keeping them at the same distance. "And this wide. It was made of some kind of special metal."

Mocheela was looking at her, seemingly perplexed. Jordan couldn't help but smile. She was amazed that she recognized this description. But she also hesitated, knowing she might be making huge assumptions.

Jordan put her hands over her knees, quelling the anticipation rising within her.

"It was not decorated in any elaborate way but did contain one unusual marking—three separated small circles to represent our three moons, with an arrow pointing leftward below them and a jiyitov facing downward," Mocheela continued, using the Mokta word for triangle. "It was a symbol of the Qui Tol at that time."

Jordan was convinced now. The way the elder had described this artifact from Onchei legend was too similar to what she remembered. *This was amazing.*

Mocheela tilted her head in confusion and waited for the Chieftess to explain. Jordan clasped her hands, looked towards the ground, closing her eyes, and took a deep breath. When she peered at Mocheela again, she was filled with determination.

"I may know where this box is," Jordan responded. "Or . . . at least where it was."

"Where, Chieftess?"

"It would be hard to describe the location, just . . . near where I grew up."

"So, you will be going there?"

Jordan stood up and helped the elder get to her feet as well. They walked outside the hut and Jordan looked up in the dayshine sky, past the clouds. She imagined she could follow a pathway through the stars all the way back to her home world.

"I never thought I would," Jordan replied softly. "But if I am going to save this world, it seems I have to."

Jordan waited until the elder left before she talked with Bopol. She placed her hand tenderly on his shoulder.

"Go ahead and tell me your concerns, my love," she told him. "I know you have them."

Bopol's expression was grim. "The situation with the Onchei is dire, Chieftess, but is it so bad you must return to Errrth?"

"I believe it is, yes."

"Why would the Onchei send something of theirs to another world?"

"I do not know. But somehow, I think it ended up with my family."

Bopol's eyes widened at that. "What? You know this to be true?"

"That is why I asked Mocheela to describe the Onchei box. If I am correct, it belonged to my gemta. And it was passed down to her by her family. I just thought it was an old jewelry box or something . . . but it is far more. If I can find it and decipher its secrets, we may be able to use it as leverage against the Onchei. I think that is worth the risk."

"Yes. But it has been many cycles since you visited your world. Much will have changed."

Jordan nodded with some uncertainty. "True. And my family will be much older, if they are alive at all."

Bopol cleared his throat. "I cannot advise my Chieftess to be away from her tribe in a time of crisis."

"The tribe will have a Chieftess. It just will not be me," she replied, prompting a head-turn from Bopol.

"Jasta?" Bopol asked. "Do you think she is ready?"

Jordan laughed. "Who is ever ready for this kind of responsibility? But she has the knowledge and the heart. She will do well."

Bopol thought over Jordan's words, then he gave her a sly smile.

"I could go with you?" he suggested.

Jordan responded with a half-grin. "Thank you but no. I may be content for Jasta to be Chieftess in my absence, but she needs her torkomm to advise and protect her."

Bopol exhaled through his nostrils. That was his way of grudgingly accepting what she'd said.

"Besides, it would not be safe for you on Earth," Jordan continued. "That world may be toxic to you . . . and even if it is not, the population there would not know how to react to you."

"That may have changed since you left." Bopol replied. Jordan knew he only half-believed it himself.

"I will not take that chance," Jordan insisted. "Even if Jasta did not need your counsel, I could not allow anything bad to happen to you."

"Do you already have a plan in mind?" he asked.

She touched his cheek with her hand and tried to give him a reassuring look.

"I do," she replied.

"Tell me."

A few minutes later, she watched Bopol walk outside the hut and light the Observance Torch. After the Gulstaa War ended and she nearly lost herself in grief, Jordan had ascended the Mokta Mountain searching for answers from God. Half out of her mind, she had been humbled, comforted, and encouraged by the response she had received. And since then, she had created a system to allow her to pray and seek wisdom from Him whenever she needed to without leaving the village. She had maintained this method for forty cycles.

JORDAN'S DELIVERANCE

The Observance Torch was the same as any other torch, but it was adorned with red jula crystals, reinforced with twine, and its top was dipped in animal fat and dusted with crushed dry jikpal leaves which made the flames take on a violet shade. When the Observance Torch was lit, it told the villagers passing by her hut not to enter, since the Chieftess was seeking wisdom and guidance from the Father of Spirits whom she called God.

As a girl, Jordan had seen people pray on television shows, movies, and a few times at school after tragedies occurred. Yet she had never understood the importance of prayer until nearly dying on this world so far from the one where she was born. On the Mokta Mountain, she had felt the presence of the Divine and seen His power firsthand. Over the decades, she had learned to trust in Him.

She lowered herself onto her knees and bowed to the floor, arms stretched before her, and spoke aloud.

"Mightiest of the Mighty, I need your help," she began. "My people need me. As their Chieftess, I am responsible for their survival. The Onchei will be angry when they learn what SnowFire—what my gemta—did to their people on Algoran. They will want revenge on the Mokta. They have weapons and technology I cannot understand nor fight.

"If I try to do this on my own, I will fail. And my people will die. My family will die. Please, do not let that happen! Show me what I need to do, how to handle this.

"I see Your hand in all of this. One thousand cycles ago, this very enemy sent away something to Earth and it ended up in the house I grew up in. And I am the only one with the means to go there and retrieve it. I know that cannot be chance or coincidence.

"Please, help me! I need You. I want Your Will to be done, whatever it is. I only ask that You spare my people . . . please!"

———————

Zeetra had never traveled in space before. In the last two days, she had spent a lot of time alone in her lodging aboard the Onchei spaceship *Kildee*. During that time, she had been given a tour of the sizeable vessel by one of its crew. But the tour had seemed cold and impersonal, much like the ship itself.

Canor Imbador, the vessel's commander, had arranged a meeting with her in an observation lounge. She sat on one side of a small oval table while he sat opposite her.

"I am sorry I have not had time to visit you before now, Zeetra," the commander told her. "My position demands much of me."

She sensed he was being as sincere as he could be. Knowing that he was an Onchei military officer told her plenty about him. She had served in that same service five decades ago under the Science Directive. If his orders, training, or instinct demanded that he kill her, her family, or the entire Mountain Mokta tribe for the good of the Onchei people, he would do so without hesitation.

Zeetra also knew her role in this situation. She had been located by this ship and its crew as the sole remaining Onchei on Algoran. They wanted to know what happened to the rest of their people. She had told the commander of the Algoran Onchei's demise but little else. She had to convince these people, her people—and Imbador in particular—that she was a reliable source of information. And that meant fabricating a believable story. That would buy time for Chieftess

Jordan to devise a way to protect the Mokta. It didn't matter if Zeetra escaped, so long as her tribe—her family—was safe. So, she looked at Imbador with feigned amazement.

"Commander, I am just grateful to be among my people again! I thought I was—I have lived as the last Onchei for so long."

"Please, Zeetra, I know I am this ship's commanding officer but call me Canor," he replied. "It is my name."

"As you wish, Canor."

He leaned back in his chair, lightly stroking his trim goatee.

"Tell me about this colony our people have created," she asked. "I was a girl when this vessel launched."

Canor smiled. "It is called Zarmandos. We left the homeworld with over five thousand Onchei, including crew. It took many zohwas to reach and colonize but we have established two neighboring cities, Zutaz and Kezfan. Between them, their population has now surpassed fifteen thousand. We have made many technological and medical advances as well."

Zeetra was genuinely impressed and let it show through her smile and intent gaze. "That is wonderful!" she praised. "I look forward to seeing everything."

Canor turned his head and looked at her with an analytical eye. After a few seconds, he nodded in satisfaction.

"I have never met an Onchei like you," he continued, "I would have expected to find one of us in hiding, removed from any populated areas, possibly malnourished and distrusting of others. Instead, you were in the midst of the capitol of the Kastadi, wearing their clothes, quite well-fed, and very self-assured. Even though you were raised in the Southlands, you do not act like even the most liberal Onchei

I have encountered, on Algoran or Zarmandos. I admit, I am at a loss to explain this."

Zeetra stood and walked over to an oval-shaped viewport about two feet wide by two feet tall, looking at the stars which were passing at faster-than-light speed. Keeping her direct gaze away from Canor allowed her to consider her words before she spoke. She could still see his reflection on the clear surface, but she tried not to pay attention to it.

As interrogations go, this is probably as good as it's going to get for me. He's trying to trick me into talking about myself. I can't tell him about SnowFire or my own mate and children. But there's no reason I can't use the truth to deflect him. Besides, if I do not reveal something, he'll just get frustrated and hand me over to someone else.

"After I found the bodies of our people, I put them all together and burned their remains," she said somberly.

"That . . . must have taken some time," he noted.

"Yes . . . it did."

She felt cold inside, even though the room temperature was comfortable. Her breathing was shallow, and her throat had constricted from stress. Pressure began building at her temples. It threatened to become a throbbing headache. Beads of sweat dripped down her back.

I knew I would have to tell him about this, but it still rips me to pieces. The nightmares had recently stopped altogether.

"After that, I activated a dampening pulse . . . to destroy our technology so it would not fall into outsiders' hands," she told him.

"Good. That was wise of you," he replied.

"Leaving my home behind, I wandered aimlessly and nearly starved to death. But a group of traveling Kastadi found and rescued me. They did not know what race I belonged to, only that I was someone in trouble. They treated my hunger and sickness, took me back to their capitol and I recovered. They taught me how to become a merchant and that is how I've earned a living since."

She watched the man continue to stroke his goatee, taking long moments to carefully ponder her words. He looked down at the table before making eye contact with her again.

"Had you taken a mate before the tragedy occurred? Any children?" he asked.

"No."

Her appearance was a calm she had practiced many times since boarding this vessel. She tried to convey a sense of quiet loss while remaining stoic.

"And now?" Canor asked.

Zeetra forced a scowling look of disapproval at him but inwardly, she smiled. She had expected this line of questioning and now he had accommodated her. But to reveal that she had a Mokta mate and four mixed-race children had never been an option. That would force a confrontation she was not ready for.

"The Kastadi may have accepted me to live in their community but do you truly think one would take me as a mate?"

"They have shown a surprising openness to outsiders. And you are an attractive young woman."

Is he flirting with me?

"I am too different from them physically," Zeetra insisted. "The Kastadi are a very tall people. They stay with their own."

"A sentiment any Onchei can understand," he nodded. "It . . . must have been lonely."

Zeetra was tiring of these verbal games. Disarming or deflecting the traps Canor was setting for her was relatively easy, but she owed that to the fact that he was not directly accusing. For every simple lure, there were several more subtle ways for her to betray herself, if she wasn't careful. The longer they talked, the more likely she was to make a mistake and it had gotten exhausting. She walked around the table to face him.

"It was," she conceded. "Commander—Canor, I have enjoyed your company, but I am very tired. May I return to my room?"

He stood up and smiled at her. "I will escort you there. It is on my way."

That's a lie. He wants to know where I am at all times and prevent me from exploring the ship. I suppose I would do the same, if I were the one in charge.

"Thank you," she answered with a polite nod.

They exited the commander's small but private lounge and took a right turn. The corridors were narrow, allowing only the width of two people through at any given time. The deck plates and ceiling were a glossy white that sharply contrasted with the dull metal walls. There were no viewports in the hallways.

If all the corridors look like this, it would be easy to get lost on this ship.

A few minutes later, they reached the entrance to Zeetra's room.

"My thanks for your kindness, Canor."

"Dream well," Canor replied with a nod. "Let my crew know if you need anything."

———

Canor smiled as her door closed. Climbing a utility ladder to the next deck, he walked to his personal cabin. Once inside, he pressed a button on his wrist communicator. "What news do you have?"

"We have completed our scans. I am sending the report to your private feed, Commander."

There was a beep on the wrist unit, indicating reception of the signal.

"I have it. Thank you, Specialist."

"Commander," the specialist acknowledged, closing the channel.

Canor pulled up the content of the report and reviewed it over the next few minutes. Then he pressed his communicator and the screen went dark.

"You are skilled in the art of deception, Zeetra of Algoran."

2

DUAL OBJECTIVES

MASKA WAS SITTING ON SOME boulders atop a grassy slope north of the Mokta village on the mountain. She preferred this spot because it gave her a good view of the waterfall and the stars as they descended towards the horizon. The chirping sounds of insects, fluttering of birds' wings, and the steady flow of the cool winds captured her attention and soothed her often-troubled thoughts.

Her eyes flashed to her left peripheral view as she heard footsteps strolling through the tall turquoise-colored meadow. She was annoyed until she saw it was the Chieftess approaching.

Immediately, she got to her feet and quashed any residual aggravation. She was still surprised, though.

"Chieftess! What can I do for you?"

The Chieftess approached wearing a serious expression. "You know of the threat from the Qui Tol—that they have taken Zeetra?"

"Yes, Chieftess."

"I want you to bring her back to us safely, Maska."

Maska pointed to herself. "Me? By myself, Chieftess?"

Chieftess shook her head. "No, not alone. I have chosen someone to go with you."

"Who?"

"My son, Arrow. He will help you."

"Have . . . you spoken to him about this already?" Maska asked.

"No. I came to you first," Chieftess replied.

Maska nodded thoughtfully as she considered the Chieftess' words. "Did the Qui Tol not leave in a ship of some kind?"

"They did," Chieftess replied. "But we can use the portal device to send you both where you need to go."

"When will we be leaving?"

"At sunsrise. Take whatever weapons you feel comfortable with. You may have to use them."

"Yes, Chieftess. Did . . . did you talk with my gemta about this already?"

"I did."

"And what did she say?"

Maska heard a rustling of the grasses behind her.

"I said I thought it was a pretty good idea," Gemta responded, raising her voice against the wind.

"Gemta?" Maska replied.

"You need this, my daughter, even if you do not yet understand. Go . . . and take my love with you."

Maska still seemed unsure as she looked towards Chieftess. "Forgive if this is wrong to ask but why me, Chieftess?"

Chieftess kept a stern face. The expression reminded Maska of Kitranor when she had been Chieftess.

"Why not? You are a full-grown woman. You have speed, strength, skill, cunning, and the blood of SnowFire runs in your veins," Chieftess asserted. "You are the perfect choice for this."

"Many thanks, Chieftess. Your words honor me," Maska responded. "But . . . Arrow and I—?"

"Yes?" Chieftess asked, expectantly.

Maska realized how she was starting to sound and didn't like it. The Chieftess needed her help. Was she going to run away like a child, just because of her feelings towards Chieftess' son? Would she put her pride before Zeetra's life?

"Forgive, Chieftess. It was nothing. I will be ready at sunsrise."

"Very good. At that time, meet me at the village gates. Get rest tonight. You will need it."

"Yes, Chieftess."

———————

As Maska ran back to the village, Zoska made her way over to where Jordan was standing and watching.

"She will not disappoint you," Zoska added.

"I know that, hoszab," Jordan replied, using the Mokta word for sister.

"You really have not told Arrow yet?"

"No."

"Pa-meelah will not be happy."

"No," Jordan said with a sigh. "She will not."

Zoska patted Jordan on the shoulder a few times as she suppressed the urge to laugh. When Jordan looked at her, Zoska tilted her head slightly, smiled, and shrugged.

"Just for that, you are coming with me, old woman," Jordan jested.

"Oh, I would not miss this for anything," Zoska replied.

———————

Pamela had been pacing her hut like a nervous feline for a quarter of an hour. Arrow eventually had enough of it and walked over to her, taking her by the arm.

"What troubles you so?" he asked.

"She is going to send you into danger, I know it," she replied.

"Who is? The Chieftess?"

"Yes, my Heartpath," Pamela responded. "She will send you to return Zeetra to the tribe. You are the one best suited to do that."

Arrow blinked a few times, processing his wife's insight. "Even if this is so, why are you worried?"

"You saw their ship and you know the stories of the Qui Tol. I also know you will do your best and succeed."

"Then why are you worried?"

She kissed him, then revealed the terror in her eyes. "Because I know you. You will complete your mission, even if it means your death. And I do not want to lose you."

Arrow embraced his wife of twenty-nine cycles and held her close. He could feel her pounding heart. After a few moments, it calmed some.

"I understand, Pamela."

Just then, there was a knock at their doorway. When he walked close, he saw the Chieftess and realized his mate may have been correct. He didn't understand why Zoska was with her. It seemed sudden and he wasn't sure how to react.

"Moonslight greetings, Chieftess," said Arrow. "My mate is concerned you will be sending me to retrieve Zeetra from the Qui Tol."

"When did she become a seer?" Zoska whispered to Chieftess.

"Pamela has always been wise, my son. She knows me well," Chieftess ignored Zoska's comment. "Yes, I have come for that reason."

"I see. When will I be leaving and who is coming with me?"

Chieftess' pride in Arrow was evident in the way she looked at him and smiled. She didn't have to lavish him with words of praise; she radiated the sensation. However, Arrow could also see some regret in her eyes. The task she was giving him would be dangerous.

"Meet me at the village gates at sunrise. Maska will accompany you."

Pamela's eyes widened but she held her peace. Arrow inhaled sharply then let it out slowly.

"Yes, Chieftess," he responded.

"You two will have the best chance of success and survival," Chieftess added. "I will brief you on the rest in the morning. Rest up until then."

Both Arrow and Pamela nodded respectfully.

———————

Jordan and Zoska exited the hut.

"She has matured a lot," Zoska said quietly.

"You were hoping she would argue with me?" Jordan wondered aloud.

"Hoping? No. It just would have been fun to watch."

"I could always argue with you," Jordan offered.

Zoska turned in mild irritation mixed with amusement. "You do that anyway!" she snapped.

Jordan raised an eyebrow.

"I just think you should argue with others more," Zoska continued.

"So you can watch?" Jordan asked.

"Of course! If it is a good enough debate, I will even join in and back you up."

"No, you would not. You would argue against me!"

Zoska grinned widely. "You know me well."

———————

Jordan had one last stop this evening. She knocked at the door-frame of her daughter's hut. Twelve-year-old Kalta near-glided across the floor to answer, pleased to see her grandmother and Chieftess. Kalta was short and plump yet growing taller by the day. She wore her long blue-and-white-striped hair braided, and her ice-blue eyes were huge, alert, and happy. She had a grin that greeted Jordan before she did.

"Gemtabana! It is so good to see you!" Kalta gushed, offering a hug which Jordan relished.

"Is your gemta here?" Jordan asked after a few seconds.

"She will be back from the stream soon, Gemtabana. She helped Kaltisa move today."

Jordan nodded. "Of course—to be with her mate, Antam, in their new hut," she said to herself. "Your gemta will be tired then."

"I made some tea to soothe her muscles and help her sleep. Would you like some?"

"Yes, Kalta, thanks. That sounds perfect."

The girl flashed another huge smile and prepared refreshments for Jordan: the tea and a few pieces of sweetbread. The bread looked like she had mixed the light pink irta fruit and juices into the batter before baking it, which made it look and smell delightful. The Chieftess gladly received them and graciously thanked her granddaughter.

"Can you tell me what it is like to be Chieftess?" Kalta asked.

4

"Why do you ask?" Jordan replied after a moment of enjoying her tea.

"I see you speak with so many people and they all love you," Kalta added. "I sometimes wonder if I might be Chieftess someday!"

Jordan reflected on Kalta's words. She hoped her sweet and happy granddaughter would never be encumbered by such responsibilities.

"Well . . . it is more than just meeting people and being liked, child," Jordan stated.

Just then Jasta entered the hut. She looked more than exhausted, as if something were troubling her. Her mostly white hair was still wet, hanging over her shoulders and dripping. Jordan had seen her listening in the doorway for a few seconds. She took in a deep breath before speaking.

"Being Chieftess means you have to keep everyone in the village safe, Kalta," Jasta mildly scolded. "You must meet with many people to find out what is going on. It is not an easy thing to do but someone has to do it, like your gemtabana."

Kalta looked more confused than chastened. "So, it is not fun at all?"

Jordan had to laugh at that. Jasta looked at a loss for words.

"Do not look at her like that, daughter," Jordan grinned. "You said the same thing when you were younger than her."

"I did?" Jasta exclaimed, prompting a nod from Jordan.

"For about a cycle, you wanted to be Chieftess more than anything," Jordan continued. "I had to show you what I actually do for you to believe me . . . and then you understood."

"What else did my gemta do when she was my age?" Kalta interjected.

Jasta quickly held up a hand to silence her daughter. It worked. Then Jasta looked at Jordan.

"You have come as Chieftess, yes?" she said. "What has happened?"

"As you already know, the Onchei are a threat to us all," Jordan replied. "And once they learn that SnowFire killed so many of their people, the Mokta will be in terrible danger."

"But you said it was not hopeless, that you had a way."

"And I do," Jordan answered. "But to make it happen, I must first go to Earth and retrieve something."

"Errrth? You are leaving us?" Her eyes widened in alarm. "Now?"

"If there was another path, I would take it, daughter," Jordan insisted.

Jasta sank into a chair, looking even more burdened. Kalta appeared worried for both her mother and grandmother, looking back and forth between the two. But she stayed silent.

"You want me to act as Chieftess while you are not here," Jasta said, unenthused.

"Yes, I do," Jordan responded.

"With respect, Chieftess, Arrow would be a better leader."

Jordan shook her head.

"I have given your brother another task. He and Maska will go to the Onchei and rescue Zeetra," she answered.

Jasta closed her eyes, defeated. "Arrow will do well in that mission."

"I know you do not want the charge of leadership," Jordan sympathized. "You have seen it weigh heavily on me over the cycles, even with the support of your torkomm."

Jasta opened her eyes again, more confident and accepting of the circumstances. "Yes, but I know you would not ask this of me if there was an alternative. When will you be leaving, Chieftess?"

"At sunsrise. Then, I will only be your gemta. And you will be Chieftess."

"Until you return," Jasta said, giving her a hard look.

"Yes . . . until I return," Jordan confirmed.

Jasta nodded, satisfied. That pleased Jordan. But there was something Jasta wasn't telling her and it was clearly vexing her as much as her pending responsibilities.

"Kalta made some wonderful sweetbread earlier," Jasta said, deliberately changing the subject. "Would you like some?"

"She shared some with me already," Jordan smiled at Kalta. "But I would love some more!"

––––––––––

Not long after Gemta and Zoska had left her hut, Jasta heard a knocking on the doorframe. By the strength of the sound it was her torkomm. Despite her exhaustion, she rallied her spirits and approached with a smile. She was always happy to see him. He had been her hero for as long as she could remember. While she adored Gemta for who she was and how she had nurtured and raised her, it was Torkomm who had taught her the ancient stories, showed her how to operate a boat and fish, taken her on long walks, and reassured her when she was afraid or woke up in a panic from bad dreams. Torkomm had encouraged her to speak her heart to Kabi. Shortly after that, she and Kabi became mates. And when Kabi died, it was Torkomm who helped her raise her daughters. She would always make time for him.

"Torkomm! What brings you by?" Jasta asked. "Kalta is already asleep, but would you like some tea?"

Torkomm smiled but there was concern in his eyes. "I wanted to check on you. I know what your gemta came to tell you earlier. Are you all right?"

Jasta laughed despite herself.

"Am I ready to be Chieftess in Gemta's stead? Is that what you are asking?"

Torkomm inhaled a whiff of air through his nostrils. "That tea does smell good. Yes, I will have some."

Jasta nodded and went to prepare two cups of the beverage in the cooking area of her hut. She returned a moment later and offered one to her torkomm. They went outside the hut to talk further. The breeze was cool but welcome. That and the sight of the three moons in the clear sky helped soothe her jumble of thoughts.

The tea was fruity but slightly bitter. She hoped Torkomm did not mind the taste.

"I am not just asking how you feel about taking on the role of Chieftess, Jasta," he continued, taking a sip from his cup. "I want to know how my daughter is doing. Your oldest just took a mate and moved out. I remember when your brother left home . . . and then you. It is not an easy adjustment."

She tilted her head and snorted through her nose, almost laughing. "I am glad someone else understands."

Jasta leaned against the doorframe and closed her eyes. If she could sleep this way, she would. "I am happy for Altisa and did my best to prepare her for this day. But I fear that she will find wanting a thing is not the same as having it."

"What do you mean?"

"Antam cares for her dearly but he is still more boy than man. And you know how demanding Altisa can be. I wonder if he will be able to handle a SnowFireChild like her."

"I spoke to Antam two moons ago. I had similar concerns as yours. But he is not ignorant of who and what Altisa is. If anything, she has shared her hopes and dreams with him. He knows she can be demanding but he wants to face that challenge. He has a strong heart. I believe he will make a good mate to your daughter."

Jasta drank the rest of her tea before responding. She was relieved and gratified. "My thanks, Torkomm. Watching out for your new grandson then?"

He chuckled at that, a deep sound reverberating in his chest. "Someone has to keep peace in this family, yes?"

Jasta had to laugh at that. "You speak truth, Torkomm. The rest of us are surely mad, the way we behave."

"Not mad," he corrected. "How would your gemta say? You are 'yoo-neek.'"

Jasta playfully wagged a finger at her torkomm. "I thought only Gemta could use the Errrth words."

"I think I would know if she had passed a decree such as that," he jested. "So long as I use the word correctly, I may use it how I wish."

Jasta gave her torkomm a daughterly hug. His visit had lifted her spirits, if not her burdens. It was enough for now.

"Return to Gemta and sleep well, Torkomm. The dayshine will join us soon enough."

"Sleep well, daughter."

———

As Bopol was walking back to his hut, he heard someone running towards him from behind. He turned to see his firstborn son. Arrow did not look troubled, just determined.

"Torkomm, I am glad I found you!"

"What is it, Arrow?"

"You know the mission Chieftess gave to me and Maska?"

Bopol nodded. "Of course."

"I need your advice."

"About the mission?"

"About Maska."

Bopol had given this topic some thought since Jordan suggested her plan to him. He knew very well how strong Maska's feelings were towards Arrow. Bopol had been as perplexed as Jordan that Maska never expressed them to Arrow. He had observed Maska's evident displeasure with Arrow's choice to become Pamela's mate. He had watched her retreat inward and become bitter. He felt badly that he had never been able to properly communicate with the young woman about the matter; she had politely rejected any such attempts. And while Bopol agreed with what the Chieftess was trying to accomplish through this mission, he understood Arrow's trepidation.

He and his son walked the path that led through the center of the village. They stopped by a fire near the gates, one that the sentries used to occasionally warm themselves and light the entryway. The crackling of the flames gave a certain amount of privacy and stretching out their hands, the heat was pleasant in the night breeze.

"Arrow, I know your heart is one with Pamela's. You will not waver in your commitment to her."

"I am glad you know this but that is not my concern. I do not think Maska will listen to me. We have barely spoken at all since I took Pamela to mate. How can we succeed in this mission if we cannot communicate?"

Bopol thought about his son's words. They were wise and well-considered. Then the fire reminded him of something.

"See these flames, Arrow? Why do we use fire as a tool? It is dangerous. If handled foolishly, it could spread and consume the entire mountain and valley. So why use it?"

"Because we have rules for using fire! That way, we reduce the risk and only use it when needed."

Bopol nodded. "Exactly. It is the same with Maska. She is Mokta before all else. She knows the rules of the village and obeys her Chieftess. Regardless of the feelings she has for you, positive or negative, she will accomplish this mission. And since that will require communication with you, she will have to do that. She knows this."

Arrow breathed a sigh of relief. He rubbed his hands together near the fire and then gave Bopol a hearty slap on the back.

"Thank you, Torkomm! You have eased my mind. I am grateful. Sleep well!"

He ran back towards his hut. Bopol allowed himself a satisfied smile. "Sleep well, son."

3

BY THE TWIN STARS' LIGHT

JORDAN WAS ALWAYS CONTENT TO wake up next to Bopol. She had long since accustomed herself to his light snoring and the way he occasionally shifted positions in their kelkono during the night. What she was not used to was her son Teesbin being awake before her.

The teen was placing a pitcher of freshly squeezed irta juice—still her favorite after nearly half a century—on a table. She admired how tall and strong he had grown, having the build of his torkomm when he was younger. And yet, he resembled her in the face and many of his behaviors.

"Dayshine, my son."

"I thought I heard you stirring, Gemta," he replied with a smile. "Dayshine."

Jordan exited the kelkono as unobtrusively as possible, managing to not disturb her mate. She stretched her arms, provoking many little pops from her joints. She did the same with her neck by slowly tilting her head from side to side. Then she walked over to her son and embraced him warmly.

"I overheard you and Torkomm talking last night. I knew you were leaving today," he said. "I did not want to miss you, so I stayed up all night. I wanted to do something for you, and this helped me stay awake."

She was surprised to see him pull away a thin blue cloth that had been covering a wooden tray on the table. The tray held a plate of food next to the pitcher of juice.

"It is not much but I know how you like this juice, sweetbread, and wibb eggs," Teesbin said. "I even made lahna sauce."

Jordan smiled; her heart was warmed by her son's efforts. "I would not have left without speaking to you. But this is wonderful. Thank you!"

Teesbin poured some of the fruit juice into a stone cup for his gemta. She gratefully accepted it and the plate of food he had prepared. It did not escape her notice that their hut was also freshly swept and near-immaculate in appearance.

She scooped up some of the sauce-drenched eggs with sweetbread and took a healthy bite. The eggs were a bit tough from overcooking but Teesbin's lahna more than made up for that. She thought he must have gotten the recipe from Zoska herself for it to be this piquant and delicious. She could see his mood brighten with her visual approval as she inhaled the aroma and another chunk of her breakfast. The juice was a perfect follow-up, diffusing the spiciness of the lahna with its invigorating sugary tang.

"There is still a while before sunrise, Gemta. Will you talk with me?"

"Of course! What do you want to talk about?"

He considered his words before speaking. The way he looked when he did so reminded Jordan of herself. "Will your journey to Errrth be dangerous?"

"The journey there will probably be all right. I just do not know what I will be facing once I arrive," she reflected. "A world can change much in fifty cycles. Everything—or nothing—may be different. I only know that I must succeed."

He furrowed his brow and sighed in frustration. "I wish I could go with you."

"I wish you could also, but I was born there. I am immune to many of the sicknesses and diseases."

"I share your blood. I may be immune as well?"

Jordan nodded. "Perhaps, but I am not willing to risk your life over that chance. You are too precious to me."

"Yes, Gemta," he conceded. She saw him tap the fingers of his left hand nervously against the side of his leg. He still looked frustrated, like he wanted to do something to help.

"Did you make any more breakfast?" Jordan asked him. "I loved it and would not mind more."

Teesbin beamed. "I have more bread, juice, and lahna. If you can wait a few minutes, I will make more eggs for you, Gemta."

"I can wait," she replied, feeling very proud of the young man her son was becoming. "Thank you."

She sat patiently at the table, listening to him cook the eggs in a metal pan over a fire outside. It was enchanting to hear him softly sing a village folk tune to himself. He had a rich tenor voice and a pure heart like his father's. He returned a moment later and added the cooked food to a plate, alongside more sweetbread and juice. Then he poured lahna over the eggs and handed the tray to Jordan. She consumed the remainder over the next few minutes, enjoying every bit while exchanging remarks with Teesbin.

To her, it was worth the slight discomfort of an overly filled stomach to enjoy both meal and time with her youngest child.

"You know, as Chieftess, I hear many things from around the village. Some say you have become very close with Minjo's daughter, Astonji— or are those just tall words?"

Teesbin blushed, his light red cheeks becoming much more crimson. "They . . . are not tall words," he admitted.

Jordan delighted at that. "She is very pretty. And an excellent archer, from what I have seen."

Teesbin nodded. "I was going to talk to you and Torkomm when you got back, but . . . do you approve?"

Jordan sighed but it was lighthearted and joyful. "You are already growing up. What am I to do?" She placed her hands on his shoulders and looked into his eyes. "I cannot speak for your torkomm, but if Astonji will make you happy and accepts your feelings . . . then I approve."

"Your gemta speaks for me as well, Teesbin," Bopol interjected.

Jordan turned, surprised by Bopol being awake and already at her side. He smiled knowingly when their eyes met.

"I have enjoyed listening to your conversation," Bopol added. "I can think of few more pleasant ways to begin a day."

———————

Less than an hour later, Bopol was waiting with Jordan at the village gates. He peered at the distant lights in the vastness of space while she leaned her back against his chest. It would still be half an hour before light pierced the horizon. There was something serene to him about watching the twinkling in the sky, gently cradling his beloved in his arms. He watched her more than the skyscape, taking comfort in the moment. He wanted to preserve this memory to help sustain him during her absence.

"I was only a couple of cycles past the Dawning Time when the Onchei brought me here," Jordan spoke softly.

"You called them 'Abduktorz' then," Bopol added.

As she turned and looked up at him, a bittersweet smile crossed her lips. "You are right, I did. It seems a lifetime ago."

Bopol acknowledged her words with a gentle nod.

"But you and Zoska . . . and Reiban . . . took me into your group of friends. You made me feel welcome, even when I did not know how to share my thanks."

"We knew. Your emotions were easy to read on your face and the way you spoke. This was clear even before you knew our language well."

Jordan leaned against Bopol once more. He could hear her inhale the early morning air through her nostrils and exhale it through her mouth.

"That is the time I learned to rise early like this," Jordan continued. "Our lives were simpler then. Wake up, eat, hunt prey. Then we would relax together, telling stories, singing—"

"You were good at stories," Bopol interjected.

"Not at singing?" Jordan objected, pulling back to give him a surprised look.

"I think I see Arrow and Pa-meelah," Bopol turned to look to the west, deliberately changing the subject.

Jordan laughed. "Nice evade, my love."

Arrow, Pamela, Jasta, and Maska were approaching but were still several minutes away. Jordan grabbed Bopol by the shoulders and pulled him into a brief but passionate kiss.

"Jorr-Don, what—" Bopol said, pleased but confused.

Her expression was stern. "No matter what happens, I will return to you, Bopol."

"I believe you," he replied.

"Jasta and Teesbin will need you very much."

"I will be there for them."

Jordan just smiled. He watched her basking in his presence. Perhaps she was trying to preserve this memory to take with her as well?

———————

Even though Arrow and Pamela arrived first, Jordan waited for the others to reach them before speaking. Jasta was last. Wearing her best golden robes, Jasta looked resolved but walked as if the robes were dragging and slowing her down as the glow of starslight radiated behind her. Jordan sympathized. She remembered the moment Kitranor had informally given her the title of Chieftess.

"It is time," Jordan said. "Arrow and Maska, step forward."

They obeyed immediately. Arrow's face was a mask of calm while Maska kept her eyes riveted on Jordan, not even stealing a glance at Arrow.

Pamela was a dozen feet behind them. Her expression was hard to read, but it was evident this whole mission filled her with worry. Jordan sympathized.

She looked over at Bopol, prompting him to lift the two hideskin bags from the ground and hand one to Arrow and the other to Maska. Then Bopol stepped back and remained close behind his mate.

"These bags have all the essential items you will need for the task I am giving you two," Jordan explained. Then she handed Arrow a small metal box. "We cannot send you to the flying ship where Zeetra is now because it is in motion, but we have located the world where they have an Onchei settlement. This machine is your only way back, so guard it like you would your own lives," Jordan continued. "You will have to wait for that ship to arrive. Hide yourselves in whatever wilderness there is outside their village. You should be able to find food and drink. The Onchei would not have colonized a world too dissimilar from Algoran. However, we do not know what plants are harmful, or what sort of creatures share that world with them."

"Understood, Chieftess," Arrow and Maska replied in unison.

"I will be going to Earth," Jordan added. "So Jasta will be acting as Chieftess in my absence."

"Chiefte—Gemta, why are you going to Errrth?" Arrow's concern etched across his face.

"There is something there I must find and bring back to help us against the Onchei," she replied. "Jasta, step forward."

————————

Jasta walked past Arrow and stood quietly before her gemta, who pulled a necklace from a pocket of her own robe. It was crafted of metal alloys from the mountain and forged into small chain-like links—light and polished smooth. Attached at the bottom was a tear-shaped SnowFire gem pendant. She placed the necklace around Jasta's neck.

"This is your symbol of authority on my behalf, Jasta SnowFire. Until I return, you are Chieftess and will carry out all tasks and responsibilities as you have been taught," Gemta stated. "Your torkomm will advise and assist you as he has me. The village elders will also help you. Use their experience and wisdom to make your own decisions."

"Yes, Gemta," Jasta answered, her voice resolute but inside, she was terrified.

Her gemta smiled compassionately. "You will make mistakes, that is normal. I was very scared when I became Chieftess. But you will learn that you are more ready than you know. And you will do well."

Her gemta stepped back and looked at Jasta, her brother, and all those present. "I feel torn between my own duty and what I want to do. But our people and Algoran need us to do this and be successful. We have fourteen moonturns to complete our missions. If we do not return by then, something has gone wrong."

"What should I do if something does go wrong?" Jasta asked, worried.

"I am confident that at least one of our groups will return safely," Gemta answered. "If the other group does not, you will send the one who did return to bring them back."

"Yes, Gemta," Jasta answered, momentarily satisfied.

"We await your orders, Chieftess," her gemta prompted.

The Chieftess' phrasing caused Jasta some worry. Even understanding how dangerous both of the missions were, she did not consider either her gemta or her brother capable of failure. And yet, it was a possibility her mind had to allow for.

Jasta then looked at her gemta, her brother, and Maska. Then her gaze shifted to Pamela and her torkomm. Her next command could save them all or result in their deaths. It was an intense and sobering moment. She had to resist her rising emotions, her love for all of them, and perform her duty. Feeling the breath fill her lungs, she stepped forward. She forced her hesitation to vanish.

"May the twin stars light your way and bring you back safely," Jasta said with authority. "Now, begin your missions."

Gemta had her own bag. From it, she pulled the original Onchei teleport device. It still contained the coordinates to Earth and Gemta's birthplace, a village called "Chaiz Kuhreek" in a province named "Kollo Rahdo." Gemta pressed a yellow-orange symbol on the device which opened a portal of light in mid-air. Gemta looked at Jasta and the others one last time, smiled, and stepped through. A few seconds later, the gateway closed behind her.

Next, Arrow pressed a similar yellow-orange button on his device and a maelstrom of pulsating light swirled into existence before him and Maska. He turned and looked at Maska.

"Are you ready?" he asked.

"No . . . but that does not matter," Maska replied, still not looking at Arrow.

Arrow stole one more glance at his wife. That pleased Jasta.

"We have to go, now," Maska insisted.

"Agreed," Arrow responded.

Then they ran through the portal before it dissipated.

Pamela did not speak but finally allowed herself to shed the tears she'd been holding back. She did not sob or openly grieve. Jasta knew her well; Pamela's fears were based on uncertainty. Jasta wanted to cry also but she would have to do that in private.

She looked at Pamela and nodded, as if to say, "I understand, and I am here for you." Pamela's relief and gratitude were evident.

Jasta looked at Torkomm. He appeared conflicted, his brow furrowed and his stance rigid. He had experienced Chieftess leaving on dangerous missions many times over the decades, but this was different. Jasta could relate. Gemta was going to Errrth, another world. Gemta would do everything in her power to accomplish her mission and come back to them. But there were so many things that were still outside of anyone's control. Those were the elements that worried both her and Torkomm.

4
THE ROOTS OF ANIMOSITY

AFTER A TUMBLE THROUGH THE realm inside the portal, Arrow and Maska were unceremoniously hurled into a field of tall deep blue grass with white and red flowers. Rolling a few times from their momentum, Arrow ended up on his back and Maska on her stomach.

It took several seconds for Arrow to recover his senses. When he did, he noticed it was warmer than the hottest day on Algoran. The breeze blowing over the field was soft but feverish. The skies were a shade of mauve with white clouds stretched thin by wind currents. He had to shield his eyes from a single searing blue star.

Turning over and getting to his knees, he searched for the transport device. Frantically, he rustled through the grass until his hand brushed against it. As he inspected it, verifying it was undamaged, he heard Maska moan as she regained consciousness.

"Maska, are you all right?"

"Yes," she replied with a slightly strained tone. "Why is it so hot here?"

"We are on another world. No one ever said it would be the same as ours."

"That is not good. It will take us time to adapt to this place."

Arrow stood up and looked around. There were jagged black mountains a dozen kilometers in the distance. Surrounding the field were blue-leafed trees with pale, ashy bark, and faded blue bushes with small white berries. About two kilometers away, a tinted lake reflected the sky. There seemed to be no avian life in sight, but he did hear the buzzing of insects.

Beyond the pond, he saw two Onchei settlements, each rivaling the size of Mekit on Algoran. Unlike the capitol city in the Kastadi lands, these settlements were far more advanced, with multi-story buildings of various shapes and heights. There could possibly be hundreds or thousands of people living there.

"I suspect we will have enough time to adapt, so long as we do not draw attention to ourselves," Arrow said.

"Then we need to get somewhere safe and out of the way," Maska replied. "We are too in the open here."

"Agreed," Arrow pointed to the left. "Do you see that particular group of trees at the base of that hill?"

Maska followed with her eyes and located them. "Yes. We should go right away."

She grabbed her bag from the ground with one hand and wiped sweat from her brow with the other.

Half an hour later, they reached the forest-like area. The ashen bark of one of the trees had deep grooves, enough for them to grab hold of. These trees easily averaged one hundred feet tall. Arrow leapt a dozen feet straight up, a benefit of his SnowFire heritage. He clasped onto the trunk, beginning his ascent. Maska closely followed. It did not take them long to find shelter within the leaf-and branch-covered interior of the giant timber. Arrow scanned the area for predators but found none. He pulled himself up onto a wide limb while Maska did the same facing him.

They were both drenched in sweat.

"At least we made it," Arrow said.

Maska looked around nervously, breathing a bit hard.

"What is it?" Arrow asked.

"At least there are no akasvas in this tree," Maska replied.

"No, I have not seen any animals on this world."

"Perhaps they all died from this heat."

"You will get used to it. It will take more than a bad warm season to kill us."

Maska exhaled her skepticism through her nose. "Hopefully the vegetation here is edible, since the Onchei chose this world to live on. We should not have to worry about food and water," Maska wiped the perspiration from her forehead. "Just melting."

Arrow couldn't help but chuckle at that. And he couldn't stop. Maska stared at him with irritation.

"I am so glad my discomfort amuses you," she said through gritted teeth.

"That is not why I am laughing," Arrow replied, still entertained.

"Then what is it?"

"Do you realize that it took the Onchei returning and leaving our own world for the two of us to say more than a handful of words to each other?"

"That is . . . not so unusual," she mumbled.

"In thirty cycles?" he added.

Maska's semi-scowl settled into a straight line. Arrow watched as it slowly curled into the faintest hint of a smile.

"Okay, maybe that is a long time," she admitted. "And . . . kind of unusual."

"Kind of? How many times did I try to reach out to you? We used to be friends, good friends."

"Best friends."

"So, what changed?"

Maska caught a side glance at Arrow and their eyes met. She turned her head away quickly. "I am not ready to talk about this yet."

"How long do you need? Another thirty cycles? One hundred? We could live longer than that!"

Maska kept her head turned and said nothing further.

"How are we supposed to succeed in our mission if we do not trust each other?" Arrow exclaimed, throwing one hand up in frustration, holding onto the tree with the other.

Maska loosely wrapped her arms around one of the branches near her, resting her head against it. Sadness radiated from her.

"I . . . trusted you once," she said slowly. "That is the problem."

"What?"

"When we were children and you saved my life with your blood, I told you we were bonded, remember?"

"Yes, I remember."

"I knew we were too young to be mates. But I told you we were promised to one another and you agreed."

"I remember."

"I trusted you then. I believed that you would honor our bond when we reached the Dawning Time . . . but you did not."

Decades of rage seemed to simmer inside Maska.

"I will do my part in this mission," she growled. "I shall help find and retrieve Zeetra. I would risk my life to save both of yours."

She suddenly got within an inch of his face, so close that he could hear how she was trying to control her breathing through her nose.

"But do not think, Arrow, just because we have time to talk, that I will give you my trust so easily!"

Arrow lowered his gaze, sensing the cycles of bitterness behind her words, unable to deny them. Her feeling of betrayal was rooted in such a simple thing—that he would become her mate. And he had not. It was something he could not change.

When they were still children, her reasonings made a strange kind of sense. But Arrow was too young then to know what it meant for a girl to pledge her heart to a boy. He had never fully accepted her hopes as his own. And as time went on, he let himself forget about it.

When Pamela declared her feelings for him, he was ready to receive them, getting immediately caught up in their personal adventure. He devoted himself entirely to Pamela while Maska apparently watched everything.

Maska refused to be there when Arrow and Pamela publicly acknowledged their relationship and became mates. Since SnowFire had declared that blood from her descendants could no longer be shared, Arrow and Pamela simply held hands and spoke their vows. Within a short time, Pamela became pregnant with their first child, a daughter they named Meespa. Over the next ten cycles, Pamela and Arrow had four more children.

Whenever they saw one another, Arrow and Maska would be civil but they were no longer friends, not even acquaintances.

He had broken her heart and destroyed her dreams and their future.

Maska had started to move away, tearing Arrow from his memories. "Maska—"

She stopped when he spoke, but she did not turn around. He chose not to say anything more. She began to look into the distance, scouting for their enemies. He did the same.

Zeetra had not been able to sleep all night. From her bed, she had a clear view of the ship's electronic chronometer. It displayed the Onchei date and time in a glowing red hologram, using their native symbols, on the metal space above the doorway. The hours passed slowly, almost painfully.

I know I'm tired. Despite the circumstances, I should have fallen asleep already.

She sat up suddenly, having a disturbing epiphany.

The food—they added a stimulant to it!

Zeetra lifted her hands, they were slightly trembling. Then she heard a shuddering vibration throughout the ship. She watched out her small porthole as the stars ceased streaking by and the ship returned to space-normal speed.

Nothing appears to be wrong with the vessel and we have not changed course. Why would they slow down—unless . . .

The door chime to her room sounded, startling her.

"Come in," Zeetra said.

The sliding metal door revealed Commander Imbador. His dark gray uniform looked even more crisp and unwrinkled than the last time she had seen it. His expression was pleasant but guarded.

"Yes, Commander?"

"I apologize if I am disturbing you."

"You were not. I was having trouble sleeping anyway."

"Perhaps some conversation will relax you. I was hoping we could talk some more."

"Perhaps," she replied, equally guarded. "May I ask why we have slowed down?"

The commander nodded. "A routine check of all systems. We have not taken the colony ship outside the atmosphere of our new world in a long time. The Engineering Officer is very thorough. I am afraid this will delay our arrival at Zarmandos."

"By how much?"

Imbador shrugged. "We should be there in seven dayturns."

He could keep me awake for that long! I am already feeling physical fatigue. By the time we reached his world, I would not be able to resist. They could drug me in order to tell them whatever they want. What should I do?

"Tell me about your children, Zeetra."

Her breathing froze in her chest and she narrowed her gaze. "What?"

"While we normally respect the privacy of our citizens, you are a special case," Imbador continued as she watched his satisfied glint. "Since I felt you were being . . . evasive, I had the Medical Officer run a few detailed scans."

Zeetra didn't have to feign offense. She remained silent but showed her outrage through her grimace. Imbador seemed to make a mental note of it.

"Earlier, you claimed to have no mate or children," he continued calmly. "But our scans revealed that you have been pregnant four times. Was this before or after the disaster that befell your countrymen?"

"I'm surprised your scans didn't tell you that also."

"Lying to a military officer is a serious offense, Zeetra. Do not add belligerence to that."

"I am sorry. I get irritable when I can't sleep."

Imbador smiled briefly at that. He sat down in a chair facing Zeetra, his back ramrod straight. She decided to lie back down, but her eyes stayed focused on him like laser light.

"Do your children still live?" he asked.

"If I tell you 'no,' you will claim I am lying to you again," she responded. "But if I tell you 'yes,' you will ask why I did not reveal this to you earlier and you will catch me in another lie. So, either way, I am caught in a lie and will face punishment. Why should I tell you anything?"

The commander leaned back in the chair and looked up towards the ceiling for a moment. He sighed.

"I am prepared to offer you full immunity for any infractions you may have committed, Zeetra of Algoran, in exchange for whatever information you can offer me. What do you say to that?"

"I say prove it."

"Excuse me? What do you mean?"

"You are the Commander. On your ship, you can say or do anything."

"Within reason, yes, that is true. So?"

She sat up on the bed and radiated no small amount of contempt. She twirled a long strand of her hair for a few seconds then looked at the commander.

"So, you could make me an offer and rescind it once you get what you want. That's a good deal for you . . . not me."

"What do you want instead?"

"A full pardon, in writing, signed by the ruling council from your planetary government," Zeetra said flatly. She looked at him with disgust. "Until I see that, I am not talking. And you may as well give me a counteragent to your stimulant and send me some untainted food."

"You are taking a big risk acting this way," Commander Imbador warned. "Getting that pardon will take even longer."

"I am the only one who has the information you need. I think that justifies the risk," Zeetra countered, her frown transforming to a smile. She put her hands behind her head, locking her fingers as she leaned back against the bed confidently. "And right now, I have nothing but time."

5

PLANETFALL

JO CARSTENS DIDN'T MIND THAT her magped was a ten-year-old model with fading blue and yellow colors. She had named it Mabel. It was surprisingly plush, sturdy, and dependable. She had installed new magnetic shock absorbers and recently replaced the failing core module. That allowed for smoother travel or idling in place. Mabel wasn't the fastest model, but she didn't have to be. Jo only lived three miles from her job as a history professor at Chintawka University in Chase Creek, Colorado. The cool afternoon wind was picking up and the clouds were threatening rain. A few drops bounced off the windscreen and her helmet.

She smiled as she passed the slower-moving 305 bus, which was currently empty. During her time as a student, she had ridden the 305 at all hours of the day and night. All mass transit had become remote controlled and thus driverless about fifteen years ago. Behind her, she heard the bus release its magnetic seal with a loud whir and it began moving forward again.

She should get home before it stormed. Ethan would become spooked by thunder and lightning. It wouldn't help if she got in an accident, either.

A block ahead of Jo, there was a flash of bright light. Instinctively, she made a wide swerve to avoid whatever it was, then eased into the brakes, pulling over to stop. A multi-colored portal appeared and began swirling in mid-air. Her eyes widened as she saw a blue-haired woman in some kind of long robe stumble out of the phenomenon.

The woman stood, apparently uninjured. But she was in the bus's path. The woman appeared disoriented.

"Lady, get out of the way!"

The vehicle automatically blared its piercing horn at the living object in its path. The woman had triggered its proximity sensors and its brakes screamed to life. Horrified, Jo watched the other woman plant her feet to the ground and extend her arms forward, her head down.

"Are you insane? Jump! It'll—"

Before she could cover her eyes, Jo witnessed the impossible. The front of the bus's metal frame came to an abrupt halt and crumpled, smashing against the blue-haired woman's grip. Glass from the windshield and windows shattered into thousands of tiny pieces. Tilting from the impact, the bus fell on its left side. And instead of a bloody pulp, the woman was almost unscathed, aside from some scratches caused by tiny, razor-like shrapnel. More startling to Jo, the woman's feet had dug into the pavement where she had been pushed backwards by the transport vehicle, creating twin trails in the concrete.

Jo was frozen in place, stunned, her mouth hanging open. She blinked several times.

That . . . couldn't be real!

———

Jordan hadn't felt the rush of the vortex in decades. It had grabbed her like a thing alive and thrashed her about in its clutches, shifting violently in a torrent of motion as lights flashed all around her. When it finally released her, she was barely coherent enough to land on her feet and run to a stop. Then she heard something approaching. Whatever it was, it was big and so close, it was almost on top of her.

I cannot get out of the way in time!

Instinctively, she dug her feet in place and reached out to protect herself. A heartbeat later, it felt like a wall of metal rammed into her. She held onto it and rode out the shockwave. She could feel her feet burning as they ripped up the ground. She screamed, determined to survive, though the noise from the collision's aftermath drowned her out. Jordan heard whatever had hit her topple onto the ground. For an instant, she feared it might fall on her.

Seconds later, it was over. Jordan's adrenaline was fading fast and she felt herself sliding down towards the ground. Now on all fours, she was trying to catch her breath, but the air had a chemical tang to it that was offensive; she coughed, almost gagging at one point. She leaned forward, covering her mouth and nose with her hand as her hair covered her eyes. It took an effort not to lose consciousness or vomit.

"How are you even alive?" a female voice reached through to her.

As she lifted her head, she saw the blurry silhouette of a woman walking towards her.

Is that—English? It has been so long; I had forgotten how it sounded!

Jordan had not used English since she and Erica were initially reunited on Algoran forty cycles ago. Yet her gems should translate for her until she could remember.

A few drops of rain were falling. People down the street pointed at her and held up small devices. Were they recording her? There was so much she had left behind when she'd returned to Algoran. Unsure of what to do, she returned her attention to the woman in front of her.

"You . . . might not believe me if I told you," Jordan answered slowly in English.

The other woman offered Jordan her hand. "Are you able to stand?"

The other woman gasped as she saw Jordan's icy blue eyes, but she didn't pull back. She stared at them briefly before casting her eyes to the ground. Taking in a nervous breath, she let the woman help her up.

"Yes."

She turned from the woman who had aided her and looked at the damaged vehicle. She tried to locate the teleportation device and was disheartened to see it dashed into many pieces, broken on the ground not far from the other wreckage.

Then Jordan heard piercing, high-pitched wailing noises in the distance and vaguely remembered what that meant; emergency vehicles would be there soon. That meant she might be taken in for questioning about the accident by the authorities, and that could derail her entire mission.

"I have to get away from here," Jordan insisted. "The police must not know about me!"

"Are the police looking for you?"

"No. But they will question me about this. Please . . . will you help me leave this place?"

Noticing the other people moving in with mobile devices, Jo hid her own face as best she could and took the blue-haired woman by the hand.

"Come with me, I'll get you away from here and we'll talk," she said. "You can explain things later."

The strange-looking woman nodded. They ran across the street to where Mabel was. Jo took off her jacket and draped it over the back of the hovering transport to cover her license plate.

"I wasn't expecting company, so I don't have a spare helmet," Jo said. "You can use mine."

Jo stepped behind her temporary companion. She quickly placed the helmet onto her head, lowering the eye shield.

Jo mounted the vehicle, with the other woman following suit. The hovering craft sped them away just before people got too close and the police arrived.

———————

Jordan had never ridden on a hovering moped before. It was strange and disorienting that all the moving vehicles around them floated from one location to another. The torrential rain did not help, with either the traffic or her perceptions. The sensation of such rapid motion without feeling wheels turning made Jordan feel even more nauseous. Even riding an animal would be less of a challenge.

I wonder how close Earth technology is to the Onchei's? There have been many advances.

After about five minutes, she started to acclimate to the situation. She'd had her arms around the other woman's waist the entire time. She also realized something.

"Where are we going?" Jordan asked, talking over the wind.

"We might have people following us," Jo answered. "I'm going to make sure we're clear. That way, we can have a proper discussion."

Jordan was impressed with the other woman's caution and said nothing further.

———

Several miles down the road, Jo pulled into a parking garage and drove to the fourth floor. There, she shut off Mabel, since there were hardly any vehicles on this level. After dismounting, the two women faced each other.

"Thank you for helping me," the blue-haired woman said.

"Can you at least tell me your name?" Jo asked impatiently.

"My name is Jordan Lewis."

Jo's eyes widen in surprise. "Really? That's my name, too. Are you supposed to be me from an alternate dystopian reality or something? I mean the blue hair is sling. And whatever you used to get here is very tomorrow but—"

"I am sorry, but I do not understand you," Jordan interrupted. "You say we have the same name?"

Jo's eyes narrowed. "Lewis is my maiden name. I go by Jo, but my full name is Jordan Kay Lewis Carstens."

Comprehension seemed to dawn on Jordan's face. "You are Mark Lewis' daughter?"

Jo put her hands in her pockets nervously. "You knew my father?"

"He is my brother."

"Are you saying you're my Aunt Jordan?"

Jordan looked equally surprised. "Apparently, I am."

Jo recalled an old holophoto of her mother, father—and this woman! But it was from a time when her parents were teenagers. "How could you look the same?"

"What? I do not understand."

"I've seen you in my mom's old pictures. But why haven't you aged? Weren't you older than my dad?"

Jordan nodded and sighed. "That is a long story."

Jo hugged herself, tapping her index finger a few times on her arm, looking downward. This would be totally unbelievable if she weren't actually experiencing it.

"C'mon, let's get back on the bike," Jo suggested. "I need to get back home anyway. My son will worry about me if I take too long."

———

Ethan Carstens felt another pang of anxiety as thunder roared outside. He had decided to begin preparing supper after he heard the first sheets of rain splash against the window of his room. The precision of slicing vegetables and seasoning meat kept his mind off the weather. But as the storm intensified, that became increasingly difficult.

"Where is Mom?"

Mom always knew what to do to calm him down, whether through soft and reassuring words, hugs or just redirecting his attention by watching a movie or listening to music with him. Dad had been inconsistent with him and now, he hardly saw him at all. But Ethan had one certainty in his life: Mom loved him.

She had told him how, when she and Dad were first married, they tried to have a child and couldn't. It was Mom's idea to adopt. She and Dad went all the way to China to bring an infant into their lives. Now he was fourteen. Mom and Dad had divorced and she had been granted full custody of him.

The lights flickered momentarily, and he feared the power might go out.

"C'mon, Mom! This is driving me crazy. If we lose power—"

He put his hand on his chest, like Mom had taught him.

"Easy, Ethan. It's just some weather. Deep breaths. You can hang on 'til Mom gets home."

Just then, he heard the electronic beeps of someone punching the entry code to the front door. There was a click and Mom entered. But who was that with her?

———————

MINUTES EARLIER . . .

The magped came to a stop in the driveway of a small one-story house. Jo dismounted from the vehicle first and Jordan followed. They hurried to the doorway. Jordan waited patiently as Jo keyed in a code to unlock the door.

"I'll need to get you a wig and sunglasses before you step outside again," Jo mentioned to Jordan. "And we'll have to hope some of my clothes fit you. You can't wear that robe."

"Why not?" Jordan asked.

"Too many people have seen you appear out of nowhere and break a bus," Jo looked at Jordan, her brow furrowed with concern. She then moved some wet strands of hair out of her own eyes with her hand. "They took pictures and videos. The holo-vids will probably go viral. With your appearance, you are the definition of conspicuous. We need to hide you."

Jordan took a few seconds to recall what conspicuous meant. Then she sighed.

I did not like it when I had to hide my appearance on Algoran after I was first changed by SnowFire's blood. But it was needed. If hiding myself will let me complete my mission to Earth, I will have to endure it again.

The keypad beeped and Jordan heard the door unlock. She followed Jo inside. She kept a respectful distance as Jo rushed forward to embrace a young man. He was a couple of inches shorter than Jordan and had a semi-athletic build. His shiny black hair was just past shoulder-length and when he peered at her, Jordan could see his inquisitive, deep brown eyes. Jo turned, her mood considerably lifted, and faced Jordan.

"This should make for an interesting introduction," she said. "Aunt Jordan, this is my son, Ethan. Ethan, this is your Great Aunt Jordan."

"Great Aunt what? I don't understand."

"That's okay, I don't really get it, either. But I'm sure she's going to explain . . . right?"

Jordan opened her mouth, hoping she could find the right words to convince them who she was. "I already know how this is going to sound," she said slowly. "I know what I need to say but I do not know how to make you believe it."

The smells of roasted meat and vegetables wafted from the kitchen to the living room. It was making her hungry. She looked at the floor, unsure how to continue.

"Are you sure you don't need to see a doctor?" Jo asked. "You have some serious cuts and that impact could have given you a concussion or something."

Jordan shook her head. "No ambulance. They would not be able to treat me. Do not worry, I heal fast. In fact, I have not been sick in over forty cy—" Jordan started to say, then corrected herself. "In over forty years."

Jo raised an eyebrow. "You don't even look forty. Why wouldn't medical personnel be able to treat you?"

Jordan half-sighed and half-laughed at that. She decided to sit down on the living room couch. "I know how to treat myself. Do not worry, I will be fine," Jordan said. "Do you have any bandaging cloths to cover my cuts?"

Jo gave her a more-than-disbelieving stare but did not openly challenge her. "Sure. Give me a minute to go get a few bandages."

Jo returned a few minutes later with the bandages. She sat down on the couch next to Jordan and handed her a few. Once Jordan covered her worst cuts, she returned her attention to Jo. Ethan sat attentively beside his mother.

"Okay, I want to know what's going on," Jo insisted.

"I cannot be treated at the hospital because my blood is not entirely human anymore," Jordan replied.

Jo wasn't very shocked at that. But when she looked at Ethan, he was wide-eyed. He looked more curious than afraid. She put her hand on his reassuringly.

"Your Great Aunt ran out of a hole in the sky and survived a bus crash," she told him. "She really is my father's sister, even though she doesn't look anywhere near your grandmother's age."

"Despite my appearance, I have lived for sixty-nine years," Jordan confirmed.

She then explained her circumstances to Jo and Ethan, including the changes brought on by SnowFire. It took each of them a few moments to process this information. Jo wasn't skeptical anymore; she looked almost overwhelmed. Ethan seemed fascinated.

"So . . . when I saw you run out of that light, was that—some kind of gateway to another world?" Jo wondered aloud.

"Yes."

"And obviously, your mother—my grandmother—was able to return to Earth," Jo continued. "Why didn't you?"

"I did, very briefly," Jordan replied. "But I had already taken a mate on Algoran. I chose to return—and live—there."

Jo let out a very long sigh.

"You hungry? I have some cheeseburger mac in the fridge," she offered.

6

THE PATH TO HAPPINESS

ARROW AWOKE THE NEXT MORNING to the aroma of kati spices and grains, bubbling together in liquid over a cooking fire. It was early and he spied the blue shining lone star peeking over the horizon through the open flaps in his small tent. The night had lowered the temperatures some, but it was still very warm compared to anywhere on Algoran. When he exited his tent, he saw Maska attending to their breakfast. Or at least he hoped it was for them both.

"Dayshine, Maska."

"I was wondering when you would wake up," she said without turning. "Dayshine, Arrow. The porridge will be ready soon."

"My thanks."

"The wood here burns easily. I took water from a pond over that hill," she pointed westward. "It looked and smelled fine and did not make me sick when I tested it."

"That was a big risk. I am glad you are okay."

He stood by as Maska took the small pot from over the fire, set it on the ground to cool, and extinguished the flames as she had been trained long ago. She sat down next to the pot, poured its contents into two small bowls, and put one down next to him. He then sat down, facing slightly away from her. He was grateful the insects were not out in force yet.

"Neither of us gets sick very easily," she said. "SnowFire must not have ever gotten sick."

"Probably not," Arrow acknowledged.

When they made eye contact, he could see she was still upset. But there was something else as well.

"I am not happy with the way I spoke to you before," she said. "You were right. It has been many cycles since those days. And we were both children then. I tell myself now that the oath of a child does not mean the same as the oath of an adult."

Arrow nodded. "I am glad you see that."

Maska tilted her head a bit and sighed, a slight smile tugging at her lips. "I said I tell myself that. Believing it is another matter."

"Oh," Arrow replied.

He lifted the bowl to his mouth and took a sip. It was steaming hot, but the taste was a pleasing mixture of sweet and spicy. He smiled and nodded at Maska. He was surprised when her eyes smiled back.

"We should probably scout ahead today, take a closer look at the Onchei village," Arrow said.

Maska shook her head. "No. Chieftess said we should hide ourselves until the colony ship arrives."

Arrow tensed in frustration. "I know that is what she said. But should they not have gotten here already?"

"They could have been delayed. We do not know. That is why we should wait."

Arrow huffed. "I know you are right. I just do not like waiting. What are we supposed to do?"

Arrow continued consuming his breakfast. When he looked up from his bowl, Maska was gazing at him.

"Why do you think Chieftess sent you on this mission instead of making you Chief in her place?" she asked.

"Why? She knew I was better suited for something like this," Arrow replied. "I may have learned the ways of a Chief when I was young, as did my sister, but it was never my goal to be one. Yet I am surprised that she asked my sister."

"She was leaving Algoran for a time," Maska interjected, somewhat defensively. "Someone had to act in her place."

"It could not have been me. I serve the Chieftess with all my heart. I will follow whoever is in that role, whether Gemta or my sister, and I would give my life for them. But I am not someone who could manage all the matters of the tribe, solve disputes or perform joining ceremonies . . . burial ceremonies."

Maska crossed her arms disapprovingly.

"What would you have done if she had asked you to act as Chief?" she wondered aloud.

"There was almost no chance of that happening."

"You seem very certain of that."

"Gemta will live longer than me," he refuted. "She may even be immortal. Whatever this mission is that she has undertaken, she will succeed and return home shortly."

"I am sure she appreciates your confidence in her, Arrow, but that is not always how this life works."

He chuckled before sipping some more of the porridge. Maska exhaled through her nose with irritation and then began eating her own breakfast.

Moments passed and she finished her meal.

"How is your family?" she asked nonchalantly.

"You want to know how my mate and children are doing?" he replied, his disbelief evident in his voice. "Now? Really?"

Maska shrugged. "It will pass the time."

"I know it will pass the time. But do you care?"

"I know your mate and children are important to you," Maska replied, her eyes looking at the grass.

"They would be important to anyone!" Arrow rebutted.

"I would not know," Maska said.

"Yes, you do," Arrow insisted. "You may not have a mate or children, but I know how much you loved your torkomm. No one could have taken better care of him than you."

"Thanks," she replied, somewhat defensively.

"You love your gemta and your brothers."

"What is your point, Arrow?"

"They are your family."

He was surprised when she lifted one eyebrow and looked at him as if that was the stupidest thing he could have said.

"I know that," she said coldly. "I was just trying to give us something to talk about. If you do not want to talk about your family, that is fine. We will talk about something else or sit in silence. I really do not care."

Arrow crossed his arms. "I would love to talk with you about Pamela and our children, if I did not think you would resent every moment of it."

"Why should I resent it?"

"That is a very good question, Maska. Can we talk about that?"

When she next looked at him, it was with a certain level of respect.

"That is fine with me," she replied.

Long seconds passed with no words between them.

"I am waiting," Arrow insisted.

"You want the answer that badly? You think you are ready?"

"I do," he said confidently while not entirely believing his words.

"All right, I will tell you: Your children should be mine," she said with no hint of regret. "And so should you."

Even though he suspected she might say something like this, the reality was almost more than he could bear. He saw her conviction, her absolute belief that what she was saying was correct. It was astonishingly pure. And completely wrong.

"I see. Thanks for finally saying it." Arrow sighed, contemplating how he might respond further. The wind blew, spreading around the smell of the baked porridge. But after what had just transpired, he was no longer hungry.

"There is one aspect to this you may not have considered," Arrow stated.

"Oh? And what is that?" Maska said.

Arrow allowed himself a nervous smile and shook his head in disbelief. Then he calmed himself before he returned his attention to Maska.

"You have never had a problem telling me what you felt, but did my feelings ever matter to you?"

He saw her start to open her mouth in response, but no words emerged. Arrow knew she couldn't answer because the answer was "not really."

"When we were little, you insisted that we were bonded to one another, once I shared my blood to save you," Arrow continued. "You did ask how I felt then. Do you remember what my answer was?"

Maska shook her head. Arrow nodded, appreciating her honesty.

"I told you I did not know what to think," he added. "I was just glad you were alive."

Maska's eyes registered comprehension. "I remember that now."

Arrow nodded again. "You were my best friend, as you said before. I have always loved your friendship. I just never felt 'in love' with you. I am truly sorry that has caused you pain. I never wanted to hurt you."

Arrow sympathized with Maska as she closed her eyes and lowered her head. She did not cry, but her eyes did brim with tears.

"It does hurt to know your feelings, that you never loved me like a mate," she admitted. "But you did feel that way towards Pameelah. She is in your heart . . . in a place I will never be."

"My heart will always have a place of friendship for you, Maska. It never went away."

Her smile to him seemed very bittersweet. "I know you mean that, Arrow. But you will need to forgive a woman's pride."

He nodded. "I think I understand."

Arrow decided to watch some mountains in the distance to pass the time while respecting Maska's wishes.

"You have a lot of children," she said suddenly.

"What?"

"Five, right? Four daughters and a son?"

"Yes."

Maska nodded. Arrow was at a loss how to respond to this.

"You and Chieftess took mates from the village, knowing you would live longer than they do," Maska continued. "What is that like?"

"I guess it is no different than you watching your parents see the passage of time while you have not."

"Yes," Maska answered, taking a sip of her porridge. "Parents will grow older and eventually die. But I think it must be different when it is a mate."

"You and I—Chieftess and her sister, Ereeka—we are the unusual ones," Arrow said. "Most mates grow old together. It is natural and something to be cherished. It honors the cycles those mates have shared."

Maska put her bowl down on the ground and focused on Arrow. She seemed genuinely curious now.

"Have you and Pameelah talked about this?"

Arrow smiled. "Many times over the cycles, yes."

Maska looked down contemplatively. "It must be hard for her," she said.

"Sometimes it is."

"And I think it is hard for you, too," she replied, sympathy softening her eyes.

Arrow nodded. "I tell myself to cherish each day with her."

Maska stood up and stretched her arms and legs.

"That is wise." She sighed.

7

IN REMEMBRANCE

JORDAN HAD SPENT THE LAST thirty minutes waiting for Jo's mother to arrive. The small, narrow room she occupied was illuminated by yellow-tinted lamp light on a desk that hugged the wall next to the window. There was a small black glass square embedded on the right side of the tabletop. Jordan sat in front of the desk and thought the room looked like some kind of office. There was a closet along one side and framed art hanging on the other wall.

Simple conveniences like electricity, running water, and indoor heating had become unfamiliar. It wasn't that she didn't remember them, but she could no longer relate any more than she could to wheelless transportation. Algoran was open and free; signs of life were everywhere. In comparison, Earth seemed to be carved into tiny closed boxes of unliving mechanical devices, wiring and other ways to escape direct interaction with others. She hoped she could accomplish her mission quickly and return home.

She could hear the shower running. She reasoned that Jo was probably taking this time to try and make sense of the information Jordan had shared with her. She knew Ethan was intrigued with her. She could hear him setting utensils on the dining room table down the hall.

Her mind wandered to the past. It took her back to the worst night of her life, atop the Mokta Mountain in the midst of a terrible storm.

She had been desperately grief-stricken over causing the Gulstaa annihilation. She had sought God for answers atop that precipice. And for a while, her only response had been worsening weather. But then the hurricane-force winds abated, and Jordan found herself in a zone of perfect calm. Her hair had returned to the brown color she was born with and the gems in her palms were dark and powerless.

There was someone else there, one who was shining so brightly she couldn't look on him. His presence was so powerful, it made her lose all strength. And close by was an angel. She could not see the angel, but he spoke:

Shadrach, Meshach, and Abednego, answered and said to the king, "O Nebuchadnezzar, we are not careful to answer thee in this matter. If it be so, our God whom we serve is able to deliver us from the burning fiery furnace, and he will deliver us out of thine hand, O king. But if not, be it known unto thee, O king, that we will not serve thy gods, nor worship the golden image which thou hast set up."

Then was Nebuchadnezzar full of fury, and the form of his visage was changed against Shadrach, Meshach, and Abednego: therefore he spake, and commanded that they should heat the furnace one seven times more than it was wont to be heated. And he commanded the most mighty men that were in his army to bind Shadrach, Meshach, and Abednego, and to cast them into the burning fiery furnace. Then these men were bound in their coats, their hosen, and their hats, and their other garments, and were cast into the midst of the burning fiery furnace.

Therefore because the king's commandment was urgent, and the furnace exceeding hot, the flames of the fire slew those men that took up Shadrach, Meshach, and Abednego. And these three men,

Shadrach, Meshach, and Abednego, fell down bound into the midst of the burning fiery furnace. Then Nebuchadnezzar the king was astonied, and rose up in haste, and spake, and said unto his counsellors, "Did not we cast three men bound into the midst of the fire?" They answered and said unto the king, "True, O king."

He answered and said, "Lo, I see four men loose, walking in the midst of the fire, and they have no hurt; and the form of the fourth is like the Son of God." Then Nebuchadnezzar came near to the mouth of the burning fiery furnace, and spake, and said, "Shadrach, Meshach, and Abednego, ye servants of the most high God, come forth, and come hither." Then Shadrach, Meshach, and Abednego, came forth of the midst of the fire.[1]

When the voice had stopped speaking, the brightness was gone. Everything remained peaceful around her.

"That is—that was from the Bible, right?" Jordan had asked.

"Yes," the voice had answered. "One day, you will understand."

Jordan looked around for the angel but still could not see anyone.

"Am I like those three men . . . the ones who were put into the furnace?" she had continued.

"They refused their king's order to worship other gods," the angel had replied. "That is why he punished them. But the Holy One would not let them perish in the flames. He was with them and He protected them."

Jordan felt exposed and ashamed.

"Is He here for me now?" she had asked. "I have done terrible things. I am a terrible thing!"

"Are you? Look at yourself. Are you a child of SnowFire at this moment?"

---

1 Daniel 3:16-26

Jordan took in the sight of her long brown hair flowing over her shoulders. At that moment, she was as human as the day she was born.

The doorbell chime brought Jordan's thoughts back to the present. She heard Ethan rush over to answer it. There was a flurry of whispering that Jordan couldn't understand. Soon, someone entered the room. The woman was quite a bit heavier and older than Jordan recalled. Her long brown hair was peppered with silver strands now, but Jordan knew her immediately.

"Kayla!" Jordan declared brightly, standing up.

"Well, this is a surprise, I'm glad you remember me," Kayla replied with a smile, looking over her glasses. "Didn't I used to be younger than you? You look almost exactly the same as the last time I saw you! Must be nice."

Jordan stared pleasantly at the woman whom she had known for only a few days, Mark's girlfriend at that time. Then she walked over and embraced her.

"You and Mark got married, had a daughter . . . and now have a grandson."

Jordan motioned to the desk chair, offering for Kayla to use it. The older woman looked grateful to get off her feet and sat down with some effort.

She nodded in response to Jordan's words. "We married two years after you left. We had three daughters. Jo was our firstborn. And between all the kids, we have four grandchildren."

Jordan grinned, delighted. Mark's family had flourished. "I told Mom that Mark would have a family one day, when we were still on Algoran."

Kayla nodded again slowly in response to her words, but Jordan saw the bittersweet look in her eyes. It sent a sinking feeling into her stomach. She found herself stepping back a few paces.

"Mom is . . . gone?" Jordan asked.

"Yes," Kayla confirmed. "Your father, too. About fifteen years ago, within six months of each other."

Jordan had tried to prepare herself for this possibility. Before this trip, she'd reminded herself how much time had passed. Even so, she couldn't help but feel the loss. Decades of acting as Chieftess had given her a tough exterior towards all kinds of situations, but this was different. She felt her mouth tug downward on either side and tears well up in her eyes. She barely noticed Kayla standing up and hugging her, offering solace for the next few minutes. Then a thought suddenly struck her.

"Wait," Jordan said, alarmed. "Where is Mark?"

Jordan watched as Kayla let go of her and sat back down. Her sister-in-law took in a breath and sadly shook her head as she exhaled.

"No," Jordan sobbed, stung more by this death than her parents'. She leaned against a wall for support. "W-When? How?"

"Six years ago. A heart attack. There was nothing we could do. He was fifty-eight. I'm sorry, Jordan, I know how close you two were."

Jordan looked over at Kayla, deeply wounded from her sorrow. She could feel the tears streaming down her cheeks.

Jordan shook her head vigorously in desperation. "I had hoped, out of everyone, that at least he—would still be alive. You, too, Kayla."

She was grateful when Kayla pulled some tissues from her purse and handed them to her. Jordan wiped her eyes.

She made a concentrated effort to put aside her grieving for the moment.

"Maybe we should talk about something else," Jordan suggested.

"All right. Tell me about your life after you went back to that other world, Jordan. You were married when I met you. Did you have any children?"

Jordan remained leaning against the wall. But some of her sadness was briefly replaced by familial pride.

"Yes," Jordan answered. "I have three children as well. Two sons and a daughter. Seven grandchildren. And one of them is expecting her first child."

Kayla's eyebrows raised in amazement.

"Wow! You're a great-grandmother!"

Jordan smiled slightly, almost blushing. "That is what I said when I learned about it—wow."

"Mark would be happy for you, too. I know I am," Kayla added. "But Jordan, why have you come back? When I last saw you, you said you were never returning."

Jordan felt her mood shift darker, followed by a slight twinge of anxiety. Her duty awakened within her once more.

She nodded at Kayla. "You are correct. But I had to."

"Why?"

"The same people who abducted me and Mom are now a threat to my tribe, my village. But there is something here that may be able to stop them. Would you help me find it . . . please?"

8

BOX OF SECRETS

JORDAN IMAGINED THAT SHE AND Kayla must have been an odd sight together. The shoulder-length blonde wig Jo had attached to her head, combined with the gray short-sleeved dress that was a few sizes too large, and the sunglasses were a stark contrast to the crisp and sunny yellow dress and golden vest Kayla wore. Jordan wasn't sure this disguise made her any less conspicuous than her blue hair and ice-colored eyes.

As they walked into the Lacey's clothing store at Chase Creek Plaza, a nearby shopping mall, Jordan was aware she looked young enough to be Kayla's daughter.

She noted that mainly older adults and young parents with their children were out browsing for deals this morning. The same wheelless technology which propelled automobiles had also been adapted for infant strollers. For a moment, Jordan wondered they had against wheels.

"You know, this is oddly familiar," Kayla mused, distracting Jordan. "Didn't I take you shopping the last time you visited?"

"Yes," Jordan admitted. "I was wearing huntress clothes then."

"And you about scared me to death as I recall. I'm glad I've gotten to know you again," Kayla continued, turning her head to look at Jordan. "Knowing that you're some kind of leader and a fellow grandmother makes you less frightening."

Jordan chuckled at that. "I am glad to get to know you better, too."

A saleswoman with short black hair, who was perhaps in her mid-twenties, spotted Kayla and Jordan. She briskly walked straight over to Kayla with a practiced smile and helpful demeanor. Her name tag read "Lisa."

"Is there anything I can help you find, ma'am?" Lisa asked cheerily.

"Yes. My relative is in town for a little while," Kayla said, looking towards Jordan. "And we need to find her a few things. You know, something nice."

Lisa startled at first when she got a good look at Jordan, who sensed the woman's snobbish judgment of her appearance. A second later, the saleswoman recovered her pleasantries.

"Of course. Is there anything in particular you're looking for?" Lisa asked.

Jordan shrugged, deliberately putting on a nonchalant air.

"I like comfortable clothes," Jordan responded. "And the color blue."

Lisa blinked several times, looking dumbfounded. Jordan eyed Kayla repressing the urge to giggle.

"Right this way," Lisa said, turning away from Jordan and heading further into the store.

Jordan left the store wearing a silky dark blue blouse, black slacks, and low-heel midnight blue shoes. She was also carrying a couple of shopping bags full of more apparel. As she turned her head, she saw Kayla sporting a satisfied smile.

"It makes you this happy to buy me clothes?" Jordan asked.

"I enjoy shopping, especially with someone else," Kayla replied. "Normally, I ask one of my daughters, so it's a treat to go with you. And now, we need to do something with your hair."

Jordan stopped and slightly tilted her head, confused.

"My hair?" she repeated.

"That look may cut it on 'Algorr' or whatever that world is called, but not here," Kayla added.

Jordan put one hand to her hair. Underneath the wig, she knew her mane felt like it could use some taming but wasn't completely unruly.

"Would you believe it looked better before I got hit by a bus?" she said with a self-deprecating smile.

Kayla did not look convinced. "Well, it needs help now. You can't wear a wig the whole time you're here."

"My hair does not respond to dyes."

"Look, the blue won't stand out that much these days; it's the style that matters most. You're kind of like a queen in that village, right? Well, let me give you the 'royal' treatment here."

It made sense to Jordan that Kayla had mellowed and become more adaptable over the cycles. She had also developed a better sense of humor.

"Please, lead the way," Jordan answered, pointing towards Kayla's vehicle.

———

Three hours later, Kayla pressed her palm against the biometric reader at the front entrance to her house. There was a hum for a couple of seconds as the device scanned her, and then a click from the door unlocking.

Kayla looked over her shoulder to see Jordan's amused and impressed expression. Jordan's hair had been washed and conditioned, slightly trimmed and styled in a way that framed her face in a complementary way.

"That is pretty fancy," Jordan offered.

"I'm old. I kept losing my keys, so I had one of these installed about five years ago," Kayla answered. "As far as I know, I can't lose my fingerprints."

Jordan grinned. "Smart idea. And you are not that old."

"Says the seventy-year-old who looks twenty-five," Kayla quipped as she entered the house.

"Sixty-nine!" Jordan corrected.

"Like that distinction really matters?" Kayla chuckled.

Kayla watched Jordan consider that a moment.

"I suppose it does not," Jordan added.

Kayla walked towards the living room and Jordan followed her. The lights turned on automatically, sensing their body heat. The cream-colored walls of the living room had quite a few pictures of Kayla, Mark, their kids and grandkids. There was a plush white couch, a few comfortable chairs the same color, a stereo system and a fireplace with a mantel above it. They both sat down.

"You have a nice house," Jordan remarked.

"Thank you," Kayla replied. "It's not as lively as it used to be but it's a roof over my head, I suppose."

Jordan wondered what her sister-in-law meant by that. Was Kayla lonely?

Kayla slapped her hands onto her knees and forced herself to stand back up. She started walking towards the fireplace.

"I almost forgot!" Kayla chided herself. "The reason we're here—"

She reached to the mantel and grabbed the ancient box. Turning to face Jordan, she held it out in front of her.

"It's this, isn't it?" Kayla asked. "The thing you're looking for, the reason you travelled here?"

Jordan stood up and took the offered box. It felt solid but wasn't heavy. She tried to open it, but the lid wouldn't budge. Even putting her considerable strength into it, the box would not open.

"I do not understand—" Jordan grunted.

"Yeah, it's sealed tight," Kayla noted. "Mark and I tried to open it several times over the years. It won't budge."

Jordan held it close to her face as she inspected it visually and frowned.

"Then we have a problem." Jordan sighed.

ACT TWO

THE CALM BEFORE

INTERLUDE

BOPOL HAD NEVER SEEN HIS daughter so nervous before. Though she wore the ceremonial robes of Chieftess and the SnowFire gem necklace he had crafted for her, she paced inside her hut like a cornered zala beast. Bopol espied his granddaughter, Kalta, brewing some tea in the cooking area, no doubt to soothe her gemta's frayed nerves.

"What are you so afraid of, Chieftess?" he asked.

Jasta stopped pacing and looked at him, her eyes wide and filled with terror.

"Being Chieftess, Torkomm!" she replied defensively. It made him wonder if there was more to it. "What else could it be? I do not feel ready!"

"You have been trained for this for many cycles," he reassured.

Her gaze continued to plead with him. "That is not the same as going to stand in the center of the entire village. I will be telling everyone that Gemta has gone to Errrth, that I am now Chieftess in her place! What if they do not accept or respect me? What if they do not believe me? What if they . . . laugh at me?"

Knowing his daughter well, he had prepared himself for this. Bopol stood tall and looked at her. Jasta responded instinctively, matching his posture and facial expression.

"You are Chieftess. The SnowFire gem you wear is the symbol of your authority. The tribe will respect that," he stated. "You must wear your authority the same way you wear the gem. It is a part of you. It is who you are."

"Only until Gemta returns," she insisted.

Bopol snorted in frustration and stomped towards Jasta.

"No, you cannot think that way!" he demanded. "If you are always looking for an escape, you will only be pretending to be Chieftess. And when you need to make the hard choices, you will fall apart! If that happens, people will die. Do you want that?"

His next move was purely as her torkomm. He grabbed her by the wrist and held it. His was a tight grip but not enough to be painful. He exhaled.

"Your gemta trusts you with this position. She believes in you and so do I," he said warmly. "I know you lost a part of yourself when Kabi died, that you only wanted to raise your daughters in peace."

Jasta nodded, fighting back the urge to cry.

"If Kabi were here right now, I think he would be very proud of you, as I am," Bopol continued. "He would want you to put your whole heart into being Chieftess. What was that saying he had that he used to tell us all the time?"

Jasta smiled slightly at the memory and blushed. "'Do not build only half a hut. Finish what you start.'"

Bopol nodded. "You accepted this position, Jasta. Do our people deserve 'half a Chieftess?' Do your daughters?"

He saw her eyes flash a warning towards him but after a moment, she relented. He released her arm.

"You are already Chieftess, Jasta, whether you like it or not. Become the one you want your people to see. Remember how you felt when you sent your brother and gemta on their missions this morning. You had no hesitation, no fear."

He could tell by her contemplative expression that she was mentally replaying those moments.

"That is who you are now," he added. "That is who you will be from now on. And that is who the Mokta need you to be."

Bopol saw his daughter clench her fist so tightly that it began to pale. She breathed in quickly and harshly through her nose, and the look in her eyes hardened. When she walked forward, she released her fist. And the fear was banished from her countenance.

"I am ready, Torkomm."

Kalta walked up to her gemta proudly. She was smiling as she held a cup of steaming hot liquid.

"And so is your tea, Chieftess!"

9

RISING TO CHALLENGES

JASTA WALKED OUT FROM HER hut, followed by her torkomm and youngest daughter. Her hair was flowing freely behind her, almost glistening in the sunslight and cool breeze. Her stride was measured and confident. Inwardly, she was trying to channel her gemta as best she could. From the eldest villagers to the youngest, there were hushed gasps and confused stares, but no one was openly disrespectful to her. A minute later, she reached the middle of the village.

"Everyone, gather and listen! I have something to tell you," she boomed.

It took a few minutes, but the tribe did as she commanded. There was a silent dread among the villagers, a fear that Jasta might be about to announce her gemta's demise. The unspoken question of why she was dressed as Chieftess loomed in the air. She stood by silently as her people approached.

"You all know me. I am Jasta SnowFire, daughter of Jorr-Don SnowFire. Since the Qui Tol have returned, taking our dear Zeetra with them, my gemta devised a plan. First, she sent my brother, Arrow, and Maska to bring Zeetra back to us!"

She saw more than a few smiles and could sense the hope growing among the people as well as some relief from this news. She could also detect concern for Arrow and Maska's safety on such a mission. Fear of the Qui Tol had resurged with their recent return.

"My gemta has also used the Qui Tol machine to go to Errrth. I cannot say why but it is vitally important. And she will return within fourteen moonturns," Jasta continued. Then she took off her necklace and held up its SnowFire gem pendant for all to see. "As you can see, she has made me Chieftess in her absence!"

Jasta could tell that no one would speak against her, but she saw apprehension in their eyes. Her gemta, Jordan SnowFire, had been their leader for over forty cycles and done many wondrous feats on behalf of the Mountain Mokta. She knew that some feared her gemta might not return from Earth and resume her leadership.

Her torkomm started to speak but she lifted a hand to stop him. As she attempted to find the right words to address the villagers' concerns, she felt a growing tenseness within her chest. That feeling expanded, taking over her and suddenly she could sense not only the SnowFire gem within her necklace but all the nearby gems as well. She felt a connection to them, like they were hers to command. Instinctively, she stretched out her fingers. From the mountain itself, dozens of small SnowFire gems flew towards her from above. Before reaching her palm, the jewels converged into a javelin and began to glow. She tried not to show her own astonishment. Instead, she took in a deep breath and was grateful something had actually happened. She grabbed the sapphire-hued javelin with both hands, pulling it close to her chest. A new fire burned in her gaze.

"I am the granddaughter of Snow and Fire! I will protect you and look after your needs," she declared. "Give me your trust and I shall not disappoint you. I will also consult with my torkomm and the village elders. All will be well."

There was a dazed silence for several seconds, even from Torkomm, whose face displayed a mixture of pride and fear. All eyes were on Jasta. She waited for any response, wondering if she had made a terrible mistake. But deep down, she knew she hadn't; this was in fact the best possible outcome. She heard one person clearing their throat. Another shook their head in stunned disbelief. Some people spoke among themselves in hushed whispers. There was a general sense of astonishment that bordered on fear, but it quickly faded when she lowered the javelin and handed it respectfully to her torkomm. Then she saw some parents explaining things to their children. There were nods of acceptance and respect. His face calm and dispassionate, Torkomm clasped his hands together loudly twice and then spread his arms to each side, signaling to everyone that the village gathering had concluded. Jasta walked towards the village gates and heard her torkomm following behind her. She stopped just short of the gates and turned her head to make eye contact with him.

"That was not exactly the enthusiastic show of support I was hoping for," Jasta said softly. "But I suppose it will do."

She relaxed a bit when she saw her torkomm's smile, but her hands were trembling.

"You had no idea that was going to happen, did you?" he asked. She shook her head in response.

Something felt unusual to her. She looked down and saw the links of her necklace lying on the ground. She frantically viewed the area around her feet looking for the pendant. Then she placed her hand just below her neck but above her bosom and gasped. In response to her touch, the SnowFire gem began glowing through her robe. It was now embedded in her chest.

Erica SnowFire had heard the call to meet at the village center and promptly ignored it. Like most mornings, she stayed in her kelkono as long as possible, the light kept dim by the curtains she had created for the windows. She kept a wooden table near it, containing a cup of water and a bowl of half-eaten egisban for snacking. It also contained a tear-shaped crimson jula crystal her daughter Izikaa had shaped and smoothed out for Erica many cycles ago. Next to it was the bone carving Vakar had made of Kavnor's head when their son was five. Now Kavnor had a mate and children of his own, as did all Erica's offspring. Looking at the crystal and the bust brought back comforting memories of her deepest loves. She had lost the motivation to interact with others. It wasn't that she had anything against anyone, she just didn't care anymore. Knowing she was depressed did nothing to stem the symptoms.

So, when there was a knocking at the entrance to her hut, Erica paid no attention to it. She was facing away, uninterested in seeing who it was. When she heard footsteps inside the hut, Erica fumed and clenched her fist.

"Get out!" she barked, still not looking over her shoulder.

"Dayshine to you also, Eree-Kah Gloomshade," Zoska needled. "I see you are your usual warm and friendly self."

Erica stepped out onto the floor in a defensive stance. "What do you want?" she snapped.

"Well, I had news to share with you. But then I got worried about your hearing since you did not invite me in," Zoska continued, unfazed by Erica's mood. She smiled and raised an eyebrow knowingly. "The ears can go bad once you get to be old like us."

Erica stared at her in contempt for several seconds, not bothering to move her unkempt hair out of her face.

"Are you this annoying to Jordan?" Erica asked.

"Actually, I am worse to her," Zoska replied truthfully.

"I believe you. How have you and she remained such close friends for so long?"

"She finds me funny."

Erica curled her mouth down into a frown and her teeth clenched together. "I do not find you funny."

"That is because you lost your sense of humor eight cycles ago."

Erica angrily slammed her hand down on the dinner table. "That is it! Get out, Zoska!"

Zoska held her hands up to chest-level in a placating gesture.

"I only meant that Stone Face made you laugh and smile," Zoska said.

"Stone Face? Is that a reference to my mate, Vakar?"

"That was my name for him. He always had this one expression," Zoska continued, half-lowering her eyelids, closing her lips and peering at Erica with mild irritation. Zoska's overall body language was stiff but it did remind Erica of her mate, which made her half-smile for a second.

Zoska resumed her normal demeanor and made eye contact with Erica.

"I never did understand how he did it, with as little as he said," Zoska added. "But you were obviously very happy with him."

Erica appreciated the compliment and realized that she was smiling and starting to cry at the same time. She turned around and wiped a tear from her eye.

"I could read Vakar so well," Erica answered, looking out the window of her hut. "Every subtle movement, every type of breath, every unspoken phrase—I knew what they all meant. Over a matter of cycles, we became each other's worlds."

"And now that he is dead, your world is gone," Zoska replied.

There was pain, wonder, and joy in hearing those bluntly honest words. Agony at the forever-absence of Vakar, amazement that such an irritating person could have this kind of insight and yet, happiness at being understood. Erica recalled that Zoska was still mourning her own mate's passing.

"I am sorry for your loss, Zoska. I should not have lashed out at you, especially not now."

Zoska smiled. "I wanted you to vent to me. It was the only way to get you to talk to me. I had to lure you away from your own caged mind."

Erica turned and stared at Zoska.

"My own daughter has had to do the same with me," Zoska continued. "Fortunately, I taught her well."

Erica remembered Zoska's earlier words. "You said you came here to tell me something?"

"Yes," Zoska nodded.

"Would you like to tell me now?"

"Make me some tea first."

"What?"

"I put on a big show for you," Zoska explained. "The least you can do is get me something to drink. I am thirsty now."

Erica blinked several times. "I only have irta leaf tea. Is that all right?"

———

Zoska lifted the cup to her lips and inhaled the rich aroma of the irta leaves rising on the tea's steam. Then she took a quick sip. The liquid had an initial bite to it, followed by the natural sweetness of the fruit. She smiled, and then surprised Erica by making a thumbs-up gesture. They were both sitting in chairs around Erica's dining table.

"I guess Jordan taught you that?" Erica assumed.

"Who else? None of the Mokta would have any idea what that means," Zoska replied. "But I have asked Jorr-Don to tell me things about the world you two were born into."

"A world we will never see again. And that is probably best."

Zoska's smile faded.

"Jorr-Don is there now," Zoska added.

"What? Jordan went to Earth?"

Zoska nodded in response.

"Why?" Erica wondered as she stood up.

"She said something important is there and she has to retrieve it. She believes it could save the Mokta from the Onchei who have returned."

Erica paced for a moment.

"It would have to be important for her to risk going there," Erica continued. "It has been fifty cycles! Earth will not be the same anymore. Hardly anyone we knew would even be alive. How does she expect to find whatever it is she is looking for?"

Zoska cleared her throat.

"If it makes you feel any better, I asked her all of those same questions," Zoska added. "But you know that could not stop her."

Erica shook her head. "No. Once she makes a plan, she sticks to it, no matter how crazy it is."

"Was she that way as a child, too?"

Erica chuckled. "She was much more impulsive when we were kids." She sat back down, looking contemplative, and took a sip of her own tea.

"You cannot go after her," Zoska anticipated. "She and Arrow have the only teleporting machines."

"Arrow? Why does her son have one?"

"She sent him and my daughter to rescue Zeetra."

Erica drank the rest of her tea in one big gulp. "Can we not just build another machine?"

Zoska scrunched her nose and bit her lip before answering. "And who is going to build it? Which Mokta understands the Onchei machines well enough to craft something like that? Will they recite the instructions from memory?"

"I thought her mate could—"

"He understands machines, but he cannot make one from nothing."

Erica leaned back in her chair, quiet and sullen.

"What would you do if you could go after Jorr-Don?" Zoska prompted. "Errrth would be no less different for you."

"I know that," Erica admitted. "But at least she would not be alone."

Zoska eyed Erica knowingly for a moment. "You do not have to be alone either, Eree-Kah."

"What are you talking about?"

"I am on the Council of Elders now. We received an interesting report this afternoon from villagers returning from trading in Mekit, the Kastadi capital. I would like to share that information with you."

Erica sat up; her interest was piqued. "Why me?"

"Datonn and his mate, Meeshi, told the Council they saw three Ullvarr in Mekit. Two males and a female."

The teacup dropped from Erica's hand as pure astonishment consumed her. "Are—were they certain?" Erica whispered.

"Pink skin, green hair, shaved on one side? Yes, Eree-Kah, they were sure."

"How? No one else escaped the village when the Gulstaa attacked!"

"Maybe they are from somewhere else," Zoska alluded. "I guess there is only one way to find out, yes?"

A smile crossed Erica's lips. "You are a sly one, Zoska. This is why you came to visit me?"

"I think I said that earlier," Zoska confirmed. "And now I will leave. You have plans to make."

Erica loosely gripped her arms and looked out the window. She heard Zoska shuffle towards the doorway.

"You have my thanks, Zoska."

Zoska stopped and turned her head towards Erica. "Find your people, Eree-Kah. And live again."

10

MAKING CONTACT

"YOU WANT ME TO COME with you, Kacheela?" Pamela asked in Ullvarr, still astonished.

"Perhaps you should sit down before you answer that," Kacheela replied in Ullvarr. "You look like you're about to faint."

Pamela allowed her adoptive mother to guide her to a sitting position at the dining table a few feet away. Her green hair was flowing over her shoulders and she was surprised to see her tears falling onto her blouse.

"It is a lot to consider," Kacheela added.

She sat down beside Pamela. It was comforting to feel Kacheela's strong hand on her back steadying her.

"I feel like I am in a dream," Pamela continued. "We have lived for so many cycles thinking we were the only Ullvarr left . . . but there may be many of us somewhere else in the world?"

"That's right. I will leave for Mekit tomorrow at starsrise. I admit, I would feel better about the trip if you accompanied me."

Kacheela stood up and went to pour them both some water.

"Izikaa has a young son and your brother is away hunting," Kacheela continued, handing one of the cups to her. "Your children are all past the Dawning Time. And you are my eldest child."

Pamela accepted the cup and drank some water immediately. "Today is a day of proclamation and change, Kacheela. I have learned that Jasta is now Chieftess, our people still live, and I am to become a grandmother."

"What?"

Pamela looked at her kacheela and smiled. "Meespa is pregnant. She and Karfaz visited me before you arrived. So, joy to us both?"

Kacheela put down her cup and warmly hugged her daughter. "That is wonderful news, Pamela! I am so happy for you all!"

"I am happy, too. I needed some good news."

"You have been worrying about Arrow?"

"How could I not? He is on a dangerous mission. You did not see the Onchei space vessel, but I did."

Kacheela nodded and became more serious. "That is true. But you and I both know how capable your mate is," she related. "And he has Maska with him. She is equally proficient."

Pamela nodded. "Yes, I know. But it is Maska. He is alone with the woman who loved him before I did."

Kacheela raised an eyebrow. "Perhaps. But I know your mate well. His love for you could outshine the twin stars. He will never betray you."

Pamela chuckled. "I am not worried about him betraying me."

"Then do not worry about Maska. She has her honor."

"I hope you are right, Kacheela."

———

Pamela and her kacheela arrived by foot in Mekit twelve days later. Kacheela had taken the precaution of tying her blue hair back in a ponytail and wearing a hooded gray cloak to divert attention from her unique appearance. Pamela had no such concerns. She had told Kacheela that she wanted to be seen as an Ullvarr in the midst of the Kastadi. And in the bustling city of mostly ten-foot tall, muscular people with gray-hued skin, a woman almost half that height with long green hair and pink skin certainly stood out.

She walked up to one of the merchants, an adult weaponsmith. He had his back to her and was pounding his hammer on a red-hot sword blade.

"Excuse me!" Pamela shouted in Mokta, which most Kastadi understood.

He stopped and looked over his shoulder at the two women.

"Do you want to buy something?" he grunted.

Pamela looked at his collection of swords, axes, and spears. She was impressed with the handiwork. "Maybe," she replied with a confident nod. "Do you make daggers?"

"You want a dagger?" Kacheela whispered, surprised.

Pamela quickly hushed her kacheela. Then she placed her hands on her hips and made eye contact with the Kastadi.

"Can you make me two daggers to match the sword with the green gemstone?" Pamela inquired.

The hulking merchant put his hammer down and looked at the weapon she was pointing at. His eyes narrowed and he nodded at the sword appraisingly for a few seconds. Turning, he faced Pamela and attempted to turn his grimace into something resembling a smile.

"I am Haazor. You have a good eye," he remarked. "For one hundred kootyrs, I can make both daggers. You will find no better price in Mekit!"

Pamela reached into her travel bag and grabbed a handful of coins. She placed the requested amount in Haazor's hand. "Then we have a deal, Haazor of Mekit!"

"Come back in three stars-rising and they will be ready. I will make the sheathes at no extra cost since you paid in full."

"My thanks."

Kacheela peered at one of the smaller and more intricately designed swords in the merchant's display area. She reached forward to touch the smooth metal of the blade, but Haazor grabbed her hand angrily.

"Thief! I have kept an eye on you since you arrived," Haazor roared. "You hide your appearance, so you can sell my fine work and make a nice profit! I should slice off your fingers for—"

Kacheela slowly removed her hood with her other hand and focused her angry, ice-colored gaze at Haazor. She closed her fingers around his and began to squeeze, causing him to squint in discomfort. She easily pulled Haazor towards herself. Pamela saw Kacheela's eyes glow slightly and her hair began to flicker with blue flames. Haazor's gray skin paled and his eyes widened in terror.

"I am Erica SnowFire," Kacheela spoke Mokta in a low, menacing voice. "I am no thief. I was admiring your work, since you will be making daggers for my daughter. You should not make assumptions about people. It could be the death of you."

"Um, Kacheela?" Pamela added sheepishly in Ullvarr. "Can you just forgive him? You are causing a scene."

Pamela's warning caused Kacheela to take a glance at the area surrounding them. The entire block's inhabitants had stopped moving. Everyone's attention was on them, specifically on Kacheela.

Kacheela exhaled slowly and reigned in her temper. Her appearance returned to normal, but Pamela knew it was too late.

Pamela facepalmed and muttered under her breath. "So much for us slipping in and just asking the locals for a little information."

Haazor fumbled through his drawer and nervously handed Pamela back her money.

"I am sorry to have offended such a being!" he offered, sweat pooling at his brow. "I will do the work in two stars-risings for no money. Just spare me!"

Pamela actually felt sorry for the man. Then she gave her mother an "I can't take you anywhere" stare for a few seconds and sighed.

"Kacheela, make peace with the man before his heart gives out from fear," she insisted in Ullvarr.

Kacheela still had a fierce demeanor, even though she wasn't upset anymore.

"No harm will come to you or yours, Haazor of Mekit," Kacheela assured him calmly in Mokta. "I know now that you were just protecting your work and meant no disrespect."

"Oh, many thanks to you! Many thanks!" he exclaimed, his extreme relief evident as he relaxed his shoulders and licked his lips eagerly. "You will see—I will give your daughter my best work!"

Pamela had not felt this embarrassed in some time. She grabbed her kacheela with one hand, pulled the hood over Kacheela's head with the other, and started dragging her away from all the commotion. Once they had made their way through to another part of the crowd, the people began to nervously return to normal business again.

Pamela and Kacheela sat down on the grass by a large tree, slightly away from the merchants. Pamela leaned back against the trunk, closed her eyes in frustration, and lightly bumped her head a few times against it.

"Why did you have to do that, Kacheela?" she fretted. "Everything was going so well!"

"That Kastadi insinuated that I was a criminal!"

"Perhaps that is because you were dressed suspiciously."

Kacheela sighed loudly. "I can't win for losing, it seems."

Pamela heard several people approaching and quieted herself. When she opened her eyes, she saw two young men and a woman her age. They were all Ullvarr.

"We saw what happened back there and just now," the woman said, looking directly at Kacheela. "We heard you speak our language. Who are you and where do you come from?"

"I could ask you three the same question," Pamela chimed in.

Kacheela held up a hand and silenced them all with her intense stare. She appeared to be showing at least some restraint.

"I have lived almost seventy cycles," Kacheela interjected. "So, I am the eldest here, am I not?"

After a moment's hesitation, everyone else nodded at Kacheela.

"Then according to Ullvarr custom, grant me the respect I deserve as eldest. Introduce yourselves first," Kacheela said, an edge laying beneath her words.

"I am Evtaz," the woman said, giving the traditional bow with a circular hand gesture as she rose back up. "These are my sons, Holzak and Kizam. It is an honor to meet you both."

Kacheela nodded respectfully. "I am Erica SnowFire. And this is my daughter, Pamela."

Evtaz looked confused. "These are not Ullvarr names?"

Pamela stood up, followed by Kacheela.

"I was born Makazi, daughter of Daraz and Kalami. I became 'Pamela' when this woman became my kacheela."

Evtaz pondered Pamela's words. Her sons stayed silent but never left her side.

"Where were you raised, Pamela Makazi?" the woman asked.

"In a village less than six moonturns from here," Pamela replied. "But that place was destroyed by the Gulstaa more than forty cycles ago. I was one of two Ullvarr survivors of that massacre. Kacheela saved us both back then."

Evtaz nodded, fascinated by Pamela's words. She turned to face Kacheela and made what appeared to be a sincere half-bow to her.

"For your kindness and bravery, saving two of our people and raising one as your child, I thank you, one-called-Eree-Kah SnowFire."

Kacheela looked pleased by the esteem being given to her. She smiled and returned the half-bow.

"We are staying in an inn close by," Evtaz added. "Will you join us for dinner?"

11

VOICES OF THE ULLVARR

THE KASTADI TAVERN'S WALLS WERE made of crafted stone but the floors and ceiling were made of hearty wood. There were tall windows with excellent views of the surrounding streets and venues. Many candles lit the tavern in the evening. Inside, there was a large fireplace which kept the building warm during these cold times, accommodating on average two hundred patrons. The smells of grilled meat and vegetables blended with the spices that made for savory soups and gravies. Many conversations made for a loud yet inviting atmosphere.

The establishment had a section for tourists with smaller tables, chairs and dinnerware. Kacheela, Pamela, and their new Ullvarr companions sat in a corner of that section.

"Where are you three from?" Kacheela asked.

"A set of islands about eight moonturns south of Mekit, one moonturn off the Kastadi coast," Evtaz responded.

"How many Ullvarr live there?" Pamela wondered.

"Many thousands," Evtaz answered with a smile. "You would both be very welcome there."

Pamela felt her jaw drop when she heard the word thousands. "Even in the village, when I was young, I never saw more than a few hundred Ullvarr," Pamela began, looking amazed. "We—would love to visit and learn about this place. But we live with the Mokta and have family there."

"Family? Would you tell us about them?" Evtaz encouraged.

"Vakar—the other Ullvarr survivor—asked me to be his mate," Kacheela replied. "He became Pamela's asta. Vakar and I gave her a brother and sister as well."

"You had two children with an Ullvarr?" Holzak said to Kacheela. He was tall and slender. His green hair was shaved on one side but unusually long on the other side.

"Do not be rude!" Evtaz hissed at him.

"I meant no disrespect," Holzak told Evtaz and Kacheela nervously. He spread his hands out and lowered his gaze. Even so, Pamela could sense his intrigue with her and especially Kacheela. "But I do not know what you are or how an outsider could have offspring with one of us."

Kacheela was not offended. In fact, she laughed. "Of course," she replied. "You have never met one of my kind before."

"Where are you from, Eree-Kah SnowFire?" Evtaz asked, attempting to be diplomatic.

"I was born on a world called Earth. My best friend and her kacheela were brought here by the Onchei."

"The Onchei?" Evtaz repeated. "Who is that?"

"The Mokta call them the Qui Tol," Kacheela explained.

Evtaz's eyes widened. "The Heelos?"

"That's right! I heard First Asta speak of them once," Pamela recalled. "He called them that—the Heelos!"

Kacheela nodded in understanding. She remembered Daraz, Pamela's biological father. It did not surprise her that he had knowledge of the Onchei/Heelos.

"It . . . is a long story," Kacheela alluded.

"Since it led to you being here, saving Ullvarr, and making you a SnowFire, I must ask that you share this story with us!" Evtaz responded.

Two hours later, Erica concluded the story of her experiences on Algoran, living among the Ullvarr and the Mokta. She did not explain that Daraz and Kalami had drugged her for six years in a failed plot to attack the Mokta. Those were complicated details best left to history, she decided. They knew enough. Evtaz and her sons were completely silent; only their eyes broadcast their astonishment.

Erica thought her daughter looked uncomfortable. Pamela picked up her dinner knife and stabbed a fresh serving of the sliced, roasted zala beast meat and placed it on her plate. Then she poured some water into her cup.

"Does anyone else want more meat or vegetables?" she asked. "We shouldn't let them go to waste. Kacheela? Evtaz?"

Evtaz shook her head.

"Sure, Pamela, I'll take a little more," Erica responded.

"You are like no other person I ever encountered," Evtaz began. "You were of one world but now you live on this one. You speak and live as Ullvarr, raised children with an Ullvarr. And you are the child of a legend . . . almost a celestial being."

"SnowFire was not a 'celestial being,'" Erica insisted. "There are no beings like that."

Clearly attempting to shift the attention from Erica's behavior, Pamela tenderly placed some more meat, then some kishtah, a yellow-orange vegetable grown by the Kastadi, and chopped muznal stalks on Erica's plate.

"My thanks, Pamela," Erica replied with a warm smile.

"Can I refill your drink also?" Pamela asked.

"Yes, please."

After completing that task, Pamela made eye contact with Evtaz.

"The subjects of SnowFire and celestial beings are . . . sensitive to my kacheela," Pamela shared. "Be aware of that."

Evtaz nodded. "I meant no disrespect, Eree-Kah."

"I understand," Erica replied.

"My sons and I will be returning home tomorrow. We only came here to see if Mekit would be a good place for trade, which it certainly is."

"We sold all we brought with us at better prices than we imagined," Kizam added, prompting a nod of agreement from his brother. "Would you two like to come back with us?"

Kacheela leaned forward in her chair and placed her hands on her knees.

"Tell us again, where is your home?" Erica asked. Then she looked up at Evtaz eagerly.

Evtaz sat back in her chair, appearing cautious. After a few seconds, she managed a pleasant smile.

"Why is this so important to you?" she asked Erica. "You seem to have a good life and family. You are even welcome among the Mokta and you are the sister of their Chieftess. You are . . . quite an extraordinary individual yourself. Why do you want to know the location of our home?"

"Kacheela, what are you doing?" Kizam whispered, looking at his mother in near-dismay.

Erica chuckled and nodded in understanding.

"You and your people have nothing to fear from me and my family," Erica stated confidently. "As I said before, when I arrived on Algoran, the Ullvarr welcomed me. In time, my mate and I made sure that our children and their children knew the Ullvarr language and culture. Now that my mate has passed away, we thought our family members were the only Ullvarr left in this world. To learn that there are others has given me and my daughter a new joy in our hearts. If we seem overly eager, it is because we are excited."

Evtaz scrutinized all of Erica's words like a gatekeeper but eventually relaxed.

"I cannot imagine what it must have been like, to see your entire village slaughtered, thinking you were the last," Evtaz pondered aloud. "And then to not see any of us in so many cycles. I imagine I would feel much the same as you in coming across more Ullvarr. Pardon my suspicion, Eree-Kah SnowFire."

"You were trying to safeguard your people, even your sons," Erica replied. "I understand."

Evtaz took a drink from her cup and put some more food on her plate.

"We live on a set of lush islands to the east of here that I think will impress you. They are about one dayturn from the Kastadi coast."

"How long have the Ullvarr been there?" Pamela interjected, fascinated.

"As far as I know, all the generations of my family were born there," Evtaz replied. "There are tales of our people settling on the islands after a Great War, many thousands of cycles ago. But those may only be stories, I don't know."

Kacheela looked at Pamela, her eyes enthusiastic. Pamela gave a slight dip of her head to signal her agreement.

"We would be honored to go with you and meet our fellow Ullvarr," Erica announced.

"Then meet us in front of this inn at sunrise, Eree-Kah."

———

They rented a room that night, but neither Pamela nor Erica were able to sleep right away. Erica paced the room nervously while Pamela was at least attempting to relax on the bed.

"She said there were thousands of Ullvarr, Pamela! Can you imagine?"

"I want to, but it is difficult," Pamela admitted. "I want to see these Ullvarr as much as you, but—"

Erica stopped and turned her head. A realization dawned on her.

"When is Arrow supposed to return?" she asked.

"It could be any time," Pamela answered. "He and Maska were supposed to return within fourteen moonturns, the same as Chiefte—the same as your sister, Jordan."

Erica nodded. "I'm sorry, Pamela. I got too excited about our countrymen. I should not have committed us to—"

"It is all right, Kacheela. Arrow would understand, if he knew it was for the Ullvarr."

Erica studied Pamela's expression for a moment. "Then why do you still look like that, Pamela? What troubles you?"

"I am worried about the Heelos and their ship, what they could do to my mate and children. Part of me wishes I was there, although I don't know what I could do."

Erica sighed and then smiled. "If there is one thing I know, it is this: Jordan SnowFire and her children will not let anything happen to the Mokta," she assured. "They will be fine."

12

EASING THE BURDENS

BOPOL WAS BECOMING CONCERNED ABOUT his daughter. She had not moved from where she stood, at the edge of the Mokta village staring at the sky and the rest of the mountain, for more than an hour.

"What troubles you so, Chieftess?"

"We have not heard from my brother, Maska, or Gemta in thirteen moonturns. What am I supposed to do if they do not return soon?"

She pivoted to face him. Tears welled in her eyes.

"I was taught so much about what it means to be Chieftess, Torkomm, but—there is nothing I can do for them! They are on different worlds and I have no way to help them."

"Do not give up on them," Bopol insisted. "Your gemta is one of the most resourceful people I have ever known. She will find a way, even when there seems to be no way. And your brother is the same."

Jasta began to walk back into the village. Bopol followed.

"I feel unsure of what to do while I wait for their return, Torkomm," Jasta said, wringing her hands at waist level as she ambled forward. "What would Chieftess—what would Gemta do in times she had to wait on others, especially when it was so important like this?"

"Your gemta has told me many times over the cycles that there is some great God who watches over us all. When she is troubled, she talks to Him. Perhaps you should, too."

She stopped and looked at her torkomm, narrowing her gaze in confusion. He halted when she did.

"What is a god?" she asked.

"As I understand it, there is only one God. He is a being Whose power and presence far surpasses SnowFire's."

She looked amazed by his words. "That is hard to imagine, Torkomm. Have you ever seen this being?"

"No, but your gemta has encountered Him, more than once."

Jasta looked down, pondering that. "How do I talk to this God?" she asked.

"Your gemta always goes some place private and quiet. That is why she made the Observance Torch."

"But what should I say?"

Bopol lightly put his hand on her shoulder. "I have listened a few times. Your gemta says what she is feeling and thinking. I think if you speak from your heart, that will be enough. You will know what to say. And maybe He will hear you."

"Very well, Torkomm. Let us return to the Chieftess Hut and you can light the Observance Torch."

"Yes, Chieftess."

———

Jasta felt awkward entering the Chieftess Hut as Chieftess for the first time. This was now her hut, for however long she fulfilled this role. She had been visiting with her gemta since before she could walk, and as recently as four moonturns ago. But now, when she looked at the mud-reinforced walls, she almost envisioned them reaching out to embrace her and offer solace, as if they understood the burdens she now carried. Even the dirt beneath her feet somehow felt different, as if she were on another part of the mountain, somewhere higher and more remote.

The larger-than-average dwelling had been designed for two purposes: for the Chieftess to meet with tribal elders, villagers or visitors to the region; or for the Chieftess to be alone to contemplate and reflect. Therefore, it was sparsely decorated and had only one window, which could be covered. There were metal forged candle holders inside and the Observance Torch outside.

Torkomm had lit the Observance Torch and stood a respectful distance from the doorway. Jasta walked to the center of the hut on unsteady feet. She slowly lowered herself to a crouch, and then put her hands and knees on the ground. She closed her eyes and felt the cool breeze from the open window wash over her skin.

"I will speak my heart to you, God of my gemta. I will believe You can hear me, and I thank You for showing kindness to Gemta these many cycles. I need help in being Chieftess. I know how to act like Chieftess did. I have seen how she governed this village and region of the land. I have been taught our stories and I know I can talk to Torkomm and the village elders. But I do not know how to be Chieftess. How can I judge the matters of the tribe like Gemta? I am not her and I will never be her. Please . . . God of my gemta . . . show me what to do."

For several seconds, Jasta remained silent, not knowing what to expect. She fought the urge to be embarrassed. She had done nothing wrong. And though she had never met her gemtabana SnowFire, she had seen Gemta use the power of SnowFire many times. And yet, according to Gemta and Torkomm, this God was so much more. If He had a far greater power, such that even Gemta respected it and sought Him for guidance and help, then the least she could do was be pure and earnest.

"God of my gemta, I seek You! I believe You exist, and I want to know You! Please visit me here and show me what I need to know, what I need to do. Please help me and I will serve You as my gemta has served You!"

Jasta could hear the wind pick up outside and the trees swayed in the breeze. Yet inside the hut, all was calm. A quiet soothing presence fell all around her and for a moment, she did not feel the ground beneath her hands, knees, and feet. With eyes still closed, she felt as though she was floating serenely. She heard no words, but she didn't need to. She could sense that this was the answer to her plea, and she was pleasantly astonished.

This was God. He would guide her, if she was would do as she said. He would do the same for her as He had for Gemta. More than anything, she felt His love and peace.

The sensation lasted for a couple of moments and then she felt the ground beneath her once more. When she opened her eyes, she found that she was crying, yet they were tears of relief and satisfaction.

As she walked out of the Chieftess Hut, her torkomm appeared concerned as he approached. She was surprised that the stars were on the verge of setting. How long had she been inside the hut?

"Did you find what you were looking for?" he asked.

"Yes," Jasta replied. "And much more."

"Will you tell me about it?"

"I will try." She smiled.

ACT THREE
PIECES IN MOTION

INTERLUDE II

ON EARTH, SIX DAYS HAD passed since her arrival and Jordan was no closer to opening the ancient Onchei container. She had alternated between using tools and her own considerable raw strength to pry it open. Nothing had worked.

All the while, Kayla and Jo had done their best to make Jordan feel welcome and part of their family. Jordan had resided in Kayla's guest room. They had taken her on a tour of the city, and she had been amazed at how much it had changed, even since her last visit. Aside from the surrounding hills and mountains, almost everything else was different: alternately colored buildings, missing businesses, new neighborhoods, and roads.

After a light evening supper with Kayla, Jordan returned to her primary task with the box. She had set up a workbench in the unused half of Kayla's garage. Jordan grabbed a large flathead screwdriver to use it like an ice pick. She slammed its head down against the center of the impenetrable seal, which lined the side of the small chest. Jabbing at it over and over, the screwdriver slipped and sliced upward into Jordan's forearm, taking a line of her skin along with it. She yelped in pain as a one-inch streak of her blood splattered against the seal. The screwdriver clattered to the ground as Jordan grabbed her injured arm.

Kayla heard the commotion and ran to the garage. "Jordan, are you all right?"

"I am . . . all right," Jordan answered, squinting in mild discomfort. "But this thing does not want to—"

"Jordan, look!" Kayla pointed at the box.

Where Jordan's blood had stained the lining, it was starting to hiss, and light blue smoke began to rise. There was a momentary flash of blue flame and a loud cracking noise. As the smoke cleared, Jordan saw that the rock-like seal had been burned all the way through.

Kayla put a hand on Jordan's shoulder and looked on in amazement. "You—you did it, Jordan!"

Jordan was genuinely confused. "All of that effort and all I had to do was bleed on it? That is strange!"

"Aren't you going to open it?" Kayla asked.

Jordan looked at her arm first. It was already almost healed.

She pulled the lid back. A gasp of sealed air pushed out of the container, along with some dust. The box contained long, thin metallic tablets with elaborate carvings of Onchei art, symbols, and letters. Jordan took one of the tablets and stood back, wanting to get a better view of it in the light.

"Can you read it?" Kayla stretched to peer over Jordan's shoulder and view the tablet.

"I do not know. It is the Onchei language . . . clearly a very old version of it."

"'Awn-chai?' What is that?" Kayla asked. "You've said that word a few times since you got back."

"They are the people who abducted me and Mom," Jordan answered. "And the ones threatening my tribe now."

"What?" Kayla shrieked, looking terrified.

Jordan looked at the tablet closely, but one part of the carving made her gasp. She almost dropped it but continued holding on with one hand.

"What's wrong?" Kayla inquired.

"This," Jordan pointed to the right-hand side of the carving. "You see this part, where the man is grabbing another man by the neck?"

Kayla pushed her glasses up on her nose and looked closely. "Yes. What are those four lines going down his neck supposed to be?"

"That man's blood," Jordan said angrily.

"How—how do you know that?"

"Because this happened to me on Algoran. An Onchei woman attacked me. She grabbed me by the throat and dug her nails into my neck, causing it to bleed . . . a lot."

Kayla's eyes widened at that, stunned silent. Jordan put the tablet down on the workbench and clenched one of her fists.

"Her name was Amstar. She was half-Onchei and half-Mokta," Jordan continued. "The Onchei are a very long-lived people, but the Mokta have normal lifespans. She told me her father had researched forbidden ways of their people to extend her life. It involved drinking blood from someone who was young."

"She was a vampire?"

Jordan half-smiled at Kayla's imagery but it was too bitter of a memory to find amusing. She supposed that, to anyone else from Earth, Amstar would have seemed like a vampire.

"No, there was nothing supernatural about her or what she was doing," Jordan continued, her voice filled with disgust. "It was just a form of alchemy that even the Onchei found too repulsive to allow."

Jordan, cold inside from the terrible memories, sat down at the workbench and looked at the metal tablet. She tried to keep from scowling, but it was hard.

"I will have to read all of the tablets to find out why they sent this to Earth, Kayla." Jordan sighed and peered up at her. "The Onchei are very thorough, from what I have seen. They may have had good reason to do what they did."

"You can understand the 'Awn-chai' language?"

Jordan held up her palms facing Kayla. The SnowFire gems had a faint blue glow around them.

"These let me understand spoken languages and speak them to other people," Jordan explained. "Perhaps they will let me read and understand written words as well."

13

IN GOD'S HANDS

TEN MORE DAYS PASSED, AND Jordan was becoming restless. She sat on Kayla's couch and was watching the news on the holographic television screen that spanned most of the opposite wall.

"—President Cravalho is currently attending the V14 Political Summit in Switzerland. His presence is a clear show of support for the proposed agenda," the young anchorwoman reported. She had short brown hair and a dark green blouse which complimented her almond-shaped emerald eyes.

"Anastasia," Jordan addressed the house's Artificial Intelligence computer system. "Change the channel. Show me local news."

"Very well. Switching to KCCK News 2," Anastasia's saccharine voice answered through the speakers. The screen flickered between channels.

Suddenly, Jordan saw a video of the portal and her arrival through it. The video shook from side to side, as if the person taking it had been running towards what was happening. Seconds later, Jordan observed her collision with the bus from the video taker's perspective. It was breathtaking to watch. If she were not a SnowFireChild, she would not have survived that impact.

The view switched to a handsome thirty-something male news anchor with tan skin, well-groomed black hair, and brown eyes.

"City Officials have begun a probe into the incident involving what the public has called the Colorado Wonder Woman, but they have not given an official statement on the matter. An anonymous source with the city has confirmed that there were no injuries or fatalities and they have not determined the identities of the woman in the video or the person who helped her leave the scene."

"Jo will be pleased to know that," Jordan said, relieved.

The anchorman continued. "Anyone with information pertaining to their identities can contact the Chase Creek Police Department at—"

"Anastasia, change the channel again. Play some soft music."

"Very well. Switching to the Burt Bacharach Channel." The screen flickered between channels.

Kayla walked into the room smiling at her. She tried to smile back but couldn't force herself. It felt awkward. She enjoyed being around Kayla and it certainly seemed like Kayla felt the same. She was doing everything she could to make Jordan feel at home. But this wasn't home. This wasn't even Jordan's world anymore.

"I see you're adjusting to the new technology," Kayla observed.

"This AI of yours is incredible," Jordan confessed. She tried to find some humor in the situation. "But how can so much time pass on this world and the entertainment be no better than when I left?"

Kayla tilted her head back and laughed at that. Then she joined Jordan on the couch.

"You're bored, aren't you?" Kayla said, turning to look at her.

"A little, but I am mostly anxious and frustrated," Jordan began. "I do not wish to seem ungrateful, Kayla. You and Jo have been wonderful to me. I just . . . do not know what to do with myself right now."

Sympathy showed on Kayla's face. "Tell me more about these 'Awn-chai,' Jordan. Why did they pick you and your mother? And why did they send her back? Why are these tablets such a danger to them? Do you think they'll come after you here?"

"I only know what I have learned from my Onchei friend, Zeetra," Jordan answered. "Her people lived on the other side of Algoran. They abducted random people from Earth and sent them to live with the Mokta. Even Zeetra did not know why they did that or why they eventually wanted to send me and Mom home. I am . . . not concerned about any coming after me to this world."

Kayla tapped on the couch's armrest with the fingers of her right hand as she listened. Then she rested both hands across her abdomen. "Thank you for explaining that. But there's still something I don't understand. You translated the 'Awn-chai' tablets. Don't you have what you need now? Shouldn't that be enough to satisfy you until your people come for you?"

Jordan sank back into the couch, leaned her head back, and looked towards the ceiling.

"Normally, that would be enough, yes. I do have what I need. But it is useless if I cannot get back to Algoran," Jordan grumbled. "I should have held onto the teleport device better. I should be home already!"

Kayla reached over to comfort her, lightly cupping her hand on Jordan's upper arm. It was only then that Jordan realized her own arm was trembling. She didn't know whether it was from adrenaline or anxiety.

"You're—you're worried, aren't you?" Kayla asked.

Jordan sighed and looked down.

"You are worried!" Kayla continued. "You said your son would come for you . . . and yet he hasn't. Is there something you haven't told me?"

Jordan put her hand on Kayla's and nodded. "I sent him and my best friend's daughter on a dangerous mission."

Now Kayla looked worried. "What . . . kind of mission?"

"We thought all of the Onchei but Zeetra had been killed," Jordan stated, prompting a gasp from Kayla. There was silence between them for a minute or so.

"However, we learned that twenty years before Mom and I were brought to Algoran, several thousand Onchei took a spaceship and apparently colonized another world," Jordan resumed. "They returned to Algoran recently and took Zeetra captive. I sent Arrow and Maska to bring her back from that colony."

Kayla looked surprised and shifted to face Jordan on the couch. "You sent your child and one of the villagers to another planet, against a hostile race with advanced technology like theirs? How could you do that?"

Jordan bridled a bit at Kayla's tone and words. "My child is nearly fifty years old. He is stealthy and has combat skills," Jordan retorted. "Also, he and Maska both have SnowFire blood running through their veins. Together, they make a formidable team."

Kayla absorbed Jordan's response and relaxed some. "Even so," she continued. "Sending them into enemy territory like that—"

Jordan slumped forward and put her head in her hands, no longer hiding her apprehension or guilt. "I would have gone myself . . . but only I could come here and do what I did. Arrow and Maska had—have the best chance of succeeding."

Kayla put her hand on Jordan's back and slowly rubbed it in an up-and-down motion. "You've been through far more than I could have imagined, Jordan. I wish I could tell you something more reassuring. But it sounds like they're in God's hands now."

"I . . . I suppose you are right," Jordan agreed.

Kayla patted Jordan's back lightly a few times. "I think it'll be fine. You're in His hands, too, and you're okay!"

———————

Thirty minutes later, Jo was sitting in front of her desk at home and its holoscreen verified that she had completed grading the last of her undergraduate students' papers for the evening. She was fairly comfortable in her light blue pajamas and dark blue robe, but she felt unsettled, like she'd forgotten something. She went to check on Ethan to remind him to go to bed, but he was already fast asleep.

As she exited his room, she left the door slightly ajar. Then she heard three quick knocks at the front door, followed by another three. She walked quickly to the entrance and confirmed who her visitor was with the monitor next to the doorframe. With a smile, she opened the door.

"Mom, what are you doing out this late?" Jo said. "You didn't call, either."

"I'm sorry, kiddo, I don't mean to bother you like this. I just couldn't sleep and you're the only one I can talk to about . . . your aunt."

Jo nodded and helped her mother step up and into her home. "Your timing's good. I wasn't ready to sleep yet, either. You want tea or coffee?"

"Tea sounds wonderful, Jo. Whatever you've got is fine."

Jo walked towards the kitchen then turned around. "Ethan's asleep, but I'll put on some light music and he'll never hear us talking. You can stay over, Mom. I don't like the idea of you driving at night."

Her mom pulled a chair out from the dining room table and sat down, not caring how snug the space was between the table and her belly. She took off her glasses and laid them down on the table.

"I know I'm half-blind in the day and even worse at night, but I can't leave your Aunt Jordan alone," she said, sounding exhausted. "She's really been through a lot. I think the Lord's brought her back to us so we can help her."

"Us? Help her?" Jo replied. "She's strong enough to break a bus. She has some kind of alien blood and hasn't aged in fifty years."

"I know. You're barely getting by with Ethan and I'm doing good to get out of bed in the morning. But we're her family. And we're Christians. If we can help her, we should."

Jo put teabags into mugs filled with steaming hot water and brought them to the table, where she sat down next to her mother. "I know you're right, Mom. It's just hard to comprehend."

Her mom lifted the string attached to the teabag and moved it up and down to hasten the steeping process. "Is that enough to prevent you from praying for the woman? She may have been changed on that other world and given abilities that are strange to us. But when I look past those things, I see a woman who's a mother and grandmother like me. She worries about her children and her tribe. She misses them and wants to go home but she can't. She has to wait for her son to come get her."

Jo put her elbows on the table as she leaned forward a little. "I guess if I lived in another country and I traveled here, I'd really be missing Ethan and home by now."

"Exactly," Mom replied. "And you'd have a much greater sense of urgency if you knew they were in danger and you couldn't do anything about it."

Jo lifted her head in alarm. "What do you mean? Who's in danger?"

"Your Aunt Jordan's whole tribe, including her family. The aliens who abducted her and your grandmother were gone for a long time. But they've returned and they have very advanced technology. They may destroy them."

"Why?"

"I don't understand it all, Jo. But a lot of the aliens who abducted Jordan and your grandmother were wiped out somehow and Jordan thinks the remaining aliens may want revenge. She thinks they'll blame her tribe."

Jo felt her heart starting to beat faster and she stood up nervously, still holding her teacup. She took a sip from it and started pacing. Now things were starting to make sense—Aunt Jordan's urgency, her fears, and apparent desperation. It sparked a new question in her mind.

"Why did she come here in the first place, Mom?"

Jo's mother told her what she knew, what she'd learned from Aunt Jordan. Then Jo had to sit back down.

"That's—astonishing!" Jo gasped. "The same aliens who took her and grandma sent a box containing something like that . . . and it ended up with our family? With grandma . . . and then you?"

"I don't believe in coincidences, Jo. This all happened for a reason, even if we don't know what it is."

Jo took another sip of her tea and contemplated what she'd heard. "I remember when you got that box, Mom. It was the day we moved out grandma and grandpa's things. You're saying that old metal box had ancient carvings from the same world Aunt Jordan lives on now?"

"Is that any harder to believe than seeing your Aunt Jordan exit a spinning portal of light?"

"How did you know it was a spinning portal of light?"

Her mom looked at Jo and pointed at herself. "Because these eyes saw the same thing fifty years ago, the first time she returned to Earth."

Jo nodded thoughtfully. Then she leaned forward and put her elbows on the table again. "Why would those aliens send the box to Earth?" Jo asked.

"Jordan said those tablets contain some kind of forbidden knowledge. Something so terrible these 'Awn-chai' people erased all record of it. They created their world-hopping machines just to get rid of it from their planet."

"Did Aunt Jordan tell you why that knowledge was forbidden, Mom? Or how long ago it was sent here?"

Her mom shifted in her seat, looking uncomfortable. Then she took a sip of her own tea.

"It was about a thousand years ago when they brought it to Earth. And it was some grisly instructions that made those Awn-chai sound like vampires to me."

"Vampires?"

"They used to grab their victims by the neck and make them bleed by digging in their fingernails," She lifted up her arm and tightened her hand into a "c" shape. "Then they'd drink the blood and it helped them stay young. Your Aunt Jordan was attacked by one of them. She was badly hurt, maybe dying. But that 'SnowFire' chose to save her. She gave Jordan some of her blood."

Jo sat up straight again, confused.

"Wait a second, Mom. If the 'Awn-chai' sent that knowledge away to Earth and erased all knowledge on their planet, how could someone use that technique on Aunt Jordan only fifty years ago?"

"Your aunt said these Awn-chai live a very long time anyway. The ones Jordan ran into still had that knowledge."

"And they wanted to extend their lives even further? How does that fit in with banning the knowledge? I don't get it!"

"Oh, I don't think it's so hard to understand, Jo. There must have been two factions: those who wanted to get rid of the knowledge and those who wanted to hang onto it."

"And there were more of the ones who wanted to wipe out the knowledge?"

"That's what it sounds like to me, kiddo."

Jo stroked her chin, fascinated. "So, the Awn-chai sent the forbidden knowledge away to Earth and our—our ancestors were entrusted with the secrets from another world," she added.

"They wouldn't have been able to open the box," her mom replied. "So, they wouldn't have known its true nature."

"Right," Jo considered. "If whoever brought the box convinced our relatives from that time to help, then it was passed down from one generation of our family to the next . . . until now? That's . . . incredible!"

"And now, after hundreds of years, Jordan is planning to take this information back to her world. She thinks it's enough to stop them from destroying her tribe, the Mokta."

"How?"

Her mom shrugged. "This is only a guess, but Jordan seems like she's going to try and convince these Awn-chai that the Mokta aren't to blame for what happened. Beyond that, I've told you all I understand. But your aunt seems pretty confident in what she knows. I believe her."

"A thousand-year-old mystery spanning two worlds, determining what happens to two races of people," Jo said in awe.

"And we're a part of it. We've been a part of it since the beginning, just like Jordan," Mom added. "That's how, no matter what ends up happening, I know this is God working. It will be seen through to its perfect completion."

For a very long moment, Jo found herself running her hand down the side of her own face. Then she sighed.

"I guess I'll be driving you home in your car then," Jo suggested. "I'll have to drive it back here tonight, so Ethan won't worry when he gets up. But I can return it to you in the morning and take a PayMeRide back."

"No rush, kiddo. I appreciate your help."

———

Having lost track of time after Kayla left to run some errand, Jordan found herself pacing outside her sister-in-law's house. The moonlight filtered through the scattered clouds, illuminating the neighborhood. This Colorado evening was cold by local standards, but Jordan did not even need a jacket or long sleeves. At any other time, this would be comforting weather.

Her thoughts were troubled by images of her son and Maska being apprehended, injured or killed by the Onchei. Or Zeetra being tortured by her captors. Then her mind considered her beloved village being destroyed by weapons' fire from the huge Onchei ship.

She gripped her arms and tried to shake off the troubling mental specters. A sensation like panic built deep within her and pushed its way to the surface. She fought it with all her mental resolve, but it felt like she was losing that struggle as the minutes passed.

Then a memory of Kayla's voice cut through the impending dread. "It sounds like they're in God's hands now."

Jordan let herself fall to her knees right there in the front yard. She didn't care how she looked to anyone passing by. She put her hands on the grass in front of her and bowed her head towards the ground, praying aloud in Mokta.

"Please hear me! I know you are the God of this universe. You have watched over me, my family and my people for all of these cycles. Your angel told me to acknowledge You in all my ways and that You would bless me and my people. I have done my best to do that and You have blessed us."

Tightening her arm muscles, Jordan gripped the grass in her hands and let her head touch the ground. "I am going to trust You now, as I have before. I am asking You for a sign because I believe that You will show me one. I need to know that my son and my people are all right, that You are going to help us."

Jordan heard two people walk by, their footsteps evident on the sidewalk several feet from her. They were talking in hushed whispers. She tried to ignore them but couldn't help hearing a small dog's panting breath. It faded as the three seemed to hurry past her.

"I ask You to do something, anything that no one else in creation can do," she continued. "I cannot do any more to resolve this. I will wait as long as You want me to wait."

With that, she released the grass from her grip. She could feel her arms trembling, not from physical but emotional exertion. She felt a tingling from adrenaline all over her, but she was not finished yet.

"I thank You, God of this universe! I thank You for all You have done for me and my people! Thank You for hearing me now."

Jordan breathed deeply, waiting to see if she would sense or see any sign. She let her eyes open but remained on all fours. She chose not to be disappointed that nothing had happened yet. She had said she would wait as long as God wanted. After a few minutes, she stood up, feeling a little lightheaded. Thinking she might have gone too long without eating, she went inside to eat something light before laying down. She heard Kayla enter through the front door and go to her bedroom. Soon, Jordan drifted off to sleep.

14

SISTER TO SISTER

DURING THE NIGHT, JORDAN'S DREAM resurfaced once again. She was on the Mokta Mountain near its peak in the midst of frigid blustering winds, rain, hail, and lightning. Screaming from the pain of guilt at causing untold thousands of deaths in a war she never wanted, she beat the damp and muddy ground with her fists. Then without warning, there was calm all around her, along with a blinding light and the voice of an angel.

Once again, she heard the angel's Biblical words that she had come to memorize.

The moment the scripture ended in her thoughts, Jordan opened her eyes and was surprised to see sunlight shining through the blinds of the guest room in Kayla's house. From the looks of it, she had slept till mid-morning. That in itself was unusual; she was normally an early riser. She sat up, still groggy, and put her feet on the floor. Standing up, she attempted to stretch her arms upward but could only lift them halfway before unexpected tension and soreness forced her to stop.

That is strange. That has not happened to me before.

Cautiously, she slowly tilted her head from side to side and felt both surprise and frustration at how stiff her neck was. Then she noticed something strange about several strands of hair dangling in front of her eyes and nose; they were lighter in color than normal. Maybe it was just the daylight making them seem that way. But when she looked at the hair draped over her shoulders—it had the same lack of pigment.

She lurched forward to run over to the mirror in the adjoining bathroom but stopped suddenly. Her entire body was sluggish, stiff, and sore. She had to walk in measured steps as she tried to remain calm.

What is wrong with me this morning?

She reached the bathroom and felt around for a switch but couldn't find one. Then she remembered what to do.

"Anastasia, bathroom lights."

There was something different about her voice. In that brief instant, she wondered if being on Earth had caused her to catch a cold somehow. But that shouldn't have been possible.

As the room brightened, Jordan saw her reflection in the large mirror. Her eyes widened and she cried out hoarsely. She almost didn't recognize herself. Her hair was no longer blue but a blend of smoky gray and silver. Her eyes were now brown, the color she'd been born with, although she could also see a faint blue outline around each pupil. However, what had alarmed her the most and caused her whole body to tense up were all the lines and wrinkles on her face and entire body. She was her actual age now—sixty-nine years old.

Seconds later, Kayla rushed into the room. Jordan could see her from the mirror.

"Jordan, are you all right? I heard you cry out . . . " Kayla stopped short when she saw Jordan. She blinked several times, momentarily speechless.

Jordan looked at her hands. They were still strong-looking but clearly weathered by the passage of time. When she turned them over to look at her palms, she saw only skin. She looked back towards the bed where she'd slept the night before and saw her two SnowFire gemstones lying on the carpet. A feeling welled within her and made its way up to her throat.

"Kayla . . . I am human again!"

She felt Kayla pull her into a gentle warm hug. "I'm happy for you, Jordan!"

"I am human," Jordan pondered.

"I think you should sit down," Kayla added.

She was still holding onto Jordan as she led her out of the bathroom back towards the bed. Jordan felt numb inside, even as she sat down.

"Do you have any idea how this happened?" Kayla asked.

Jordan shook her head. "No. I just woke up like this."

Jordan's thoughts raced back to the evening before. "Is this the sign?" Jordan softly asked herself.

"Say again, Jordan? I'm sorry, I couldn't hear you."

"I—I was pretty upset last night, so I—I prayed to God."

Kayla sat down on the bed next to Jordan, clasping her hands in front of her. Looking at Jordan, her eyebrows were raised in amazement, but a smile tugged at her lips as well.

"I want to hear all about this. What did you pray for last night?"

Jordan focused, trying to remember her exact words from the prayer. "I asked Him for a sign to let me know that my son and people are all right. I said I believed He would provide that sign, so I asked for a sign that . . . no one else in creation could do."

Kayla's eyes widened at that. "You have a lot of faith, Jordan! God answered your prayer!"

Jordan thought about Kayla's words. God had indeed answered her prayer. In making her human again, God had done something even

SnowFire hadn't been able to do. And within herself, she understood that He had done this because she had sincerely asked God in faith.

Kayla ran her hand through Jordan's hair. "Has anything like this ever happened before?"

"God did this once before. But it was only for a few minutes." Jordan turned her head to look at Kayla's smiling face.

"You have led an incredible life, Jordan. I think this is wonderful!"

Jordan felt herself smile. This was still overwhelming, but she knew Kayla was right. She was human again, mortal again. But more importantly, she had her answer. Arrow and the rest of the Mokta were still alive. She hadn't failed.

Forty-five minutes, a shower and change of clothes later, Jordan was sitting down and facing Kayla at the dining room table. She poked at the scrambled eggs she'd barely tasted, lost in thought.

"You want something else?" Kayla wondered. "I can whip up some pancakes or—"

"No, thank you," Jordan interrupted. "I do not seem to be hungry."

"Are you okay?"

Jordan just looked at Kayla and tilted her head slightly.

"What am I saying? Of course, you're not okay," Kayla answered her own question.

"It is strange. I have been a SnowFireChild for so long," Jordan considered, her voice sounding slightly deeper and carrying a warmer tone than she was used to. "Almost everyone I have known has grown older, but I remained young. I used to think it was horrible, a curse. But somewhere along the way, I became used to it."

Jordan looked at her hands as if they belonged to someone else. Then she ran her hands down her cheeks to newly-formed jowls which were equally unfamiliar to her. She sat back and placed her hands in her lap.

"Now, in one night, I have gone from young to old," she continued. "I feel weaker than I am used to."

Kayla nodded. "Welcome back to the human race, sister. You are perfectly normal for a woman your age."

The doorbell rang.

"That's probably Jo. She drove me home last night but needed my car to get home," Kayla said, wincing as she pushed her chair back with her legs and stood up. "She said she'd return it this morning."

"Are you okay?" Jordan asked.

"Just normal aches and pains, Jordan. I'll be fine." Kayla walked over to the front door and invited her daughter in.

"I really can't stay, Mom. I may not have a class today, but my students' papers won't grade themselves."

"Oh, I think you'll make an exception today," Kayla insisted. "Your Aunt Jordan had a miracle happen overnight."

"A miracle," Jo repeated in confusion.

Kayla turned and pointed at Jordan, who suddenly felt strangely exposed. Jo's eyes narrowed and she involuntarily began to dip her head to the left. Then her jaw dropped, her eyes widened, and she gasped loudly, putting a hand to her mouth.

"Aunt Jordan? Is that you?"

Now Jordan felt more than a bit self-conscious. She turned away, not knowing what to say.

Jordan could hear Kayla lightly swat Jo somewhere on her body. Jordan looked over at them, curious.

"Now I know I taught you better manners than that, Jo!" Kayla wagged a finger at her daughter, who now looked abashed.

"I—uh—I'm sorry! This is just—I wasn't prepared for anything like this," Jo replied, still dazed.

"Neither was she, kiddo."

"Oh! Oh, wow. You mean, it just happened on its own?" Jo asked, splitting her attention between the two other women.

Kayla nodded.

Jo walked towards Jordan, viewing her with a combination of intrigue and compassion.

"A—Are you all right, Aunt Jordan?"

"I am . . . okay." Jordan shrugged. Then Jo watched Jordan as she ran her hand through the hair that flowed over her right shoulder. "But it will take some time to . . . get used to this."

Jo surprised Jordan by giving her a gentle and sincere hug. When Jo pulled back, she kept her hands on Jordan's shoulders and looked at her tenderly.

"If there's anything I can do to help you, just ask, Aunt Jordan."

"Thank you, Jo."

Jo cocked an eyebrow. "There is one good thing about this: you won't have to wear any more wigs or sunglasses."

That made Jordan smile briefly. "You are right. That is good."

It took about twenty minutes for Jordan and Kayla to relay everything that had happened since the evening. Jo made some fresh coffee and offered some to her mother and aunt. Then a troubling thought occurred to Jordan and she frowned as she pondered it.

"What's wrong, Aunt Jordan?"

"I was just wondering . . . when my son finally comes, will he even recognize me?" Jordan replied. "I look so different now."

"He'll know you," Kayla said with a smile.

"Hey, I recognized you and I've only known you a couple of weeks," Jo added. "He's known you his whole life."

Jordan relaxed some in her chair. "Of course. You are right. I am starting to understand how my becoming human again is going to change things . . . for me and everyone else I know."

———————

Three hours later, Kayla was sitting across the living room from Jordan. Jo had gone back home some time ago. Now, Jordan was admiring a wall-mounted painting of the Rocky Mountains which Kayla had made in her twenties. Kayla had insisted on a wooden frame and not a holographic electronic representation. Even to her failing vision, the artwork lost something that way.

Kayla was still adjusting to Jordan's changes. It had been somewhat rattling to see her again after so long, seemingly unaffected by the years. But just like then, it only took a few days to get used to being around Jordan again. Gazing at her sister-in-law, she was both relieved and troubled. Jordan looked so vulnerable and unsure in her own body. It made Kayla want to protect her.

"What is it you need, Jordan?"

Jordan snorted, looking both frustrated and amused.

"I could really use the company of my mate or one of my children right now," she answered. "I have not been away from them so long before. In the village, we see everyone almost every day."

"That sounds really nice," Kayla interjected. "My daughters have busy lives, especially now that they have children. And I don't get out as often as I used to. I miss when they were little, and I had them all to myself most of the time."

"Since I returned here, you have taken me many places."

Kayla smiled and lightly patted Jordan's leg. "You're my sister! I haven't seen you in so long, it's been worth it. Besides, you gave me a good reason. Honestly, I've . . . I've been less motivated to get around since Mark passed. And maybe the Lord is using you to show me that I need to move on with my life."

Jordan's expression softened and she put an arm around Kayla to hug her. "If so, that makes me happy. And I think Mark would agree, you need to be active . . . and happy."

Kayla felt her heart beat a little faster and a new spark of joy rose up within her.

"I had to say something similar to Erica not long ago," Jordan shared with a thoughtful look.

"My cousin Erica?"

Jordan nodded.

"She's alive! What a relief!" Kayla exclaimed. "I want to know all about her! We saw her run into the portal after you but then—nothing. What happened to her?"

"She is well . . . and living in the Mokta village with us."

Kayla waited as patiently as she could while Jordan considered her next words.

"Did—did she find the peace she was looking for?"

Jordan's smile was bittersweet. "Yes and no."

"What do you mean?"

"When we got to Algoran, we were separated. After several years, we were reunited. She had been taken in by another tribe called the Ullvarr. She lived with them, learning their language and ways. But their village was viciously attacked by another. She and two others were the only survivors."

Kayla gasped in shock.

"The other two who made it out alive were a warrior and a young girl," Jordan explained. "She nursed the warrior back to health and they raised the girl as their own daughter. Erica eventually married the warrior and they had two more children together."

"You've both led incredible lives!"

Jordan waited a moment before continuing. "Erica and her mate Vakar were together for more than thirty years. But he died eight years ago, and it has been difficult for her."

"Oh! I'm so sorry to hear that."

"I have done what I can to comfort and help her," Jordan added. "These days, she finds the most joy in her children and grandchildren."

"She's a grandmother, too? I suppose I shouldn't be surprised."

Jordan gave a wan smile. Erica's grandchildren through Pamela were Jordan's grandchildren, too. That made Jordan think of her own parents, her children's grandparents. She missed them. It had been so very long.

"I would like to go somewhere, Kayla."

"You would? Where?"

"Please take me to see where my parents and brother are buried."

Kayla looked briefly taken aback. She humbly lowered her gaze. "Of course. I'm sorry I didn't think of offering that—and long before now."

"It is all right, Kayla."

There was an awkward silence for a moment.

"After that, do you think I could meet the rest of your family?" Jordan asked.

That brightened Kayla's expression immediately. "I'll have to call my other daughters and see if they're available. They don't live in Chase Creek, but they're still in Colorado. I told them you're here, though I haven't told them your circumstances yet."

Kayla stood up next to Jordan and patted her on the back.

"No time like the present, eh?" she said with a grin. "You'll like Karla. She's a lot like me."

Then she tapped her bracelet to activate its holographic interface and initiated the call.

15

THE HEART OF MASKA

Arrow had been on the run for twelve days. The Onchei had started sending patrols to the area from their city within twenty-four hours of his and Maska's arrival on this world. They had split up to increase their chances of evading their enemy until the spaceship containing Zeetra arrived. There were only two problems with that plan: the Onchei had scanning equipment that could detect non-Onchei lifesigns; and the Onchei knew the planet better than them. It had been a harrowing span of time filled with close calls, careful strategizing, and outright guile.

Still, Arrow was considerably faster, stronger, and more agile than the armored soldiers. He had quickly determined that something in this world's mud could temporarily mask him from their sensors. The caves and ravine near the mountain had also been kind to him. That is, until today. A rifle barrel poked into his back while a soldier barked a command in a language he didn't understand. Even so, Arrow knew enough to freeze in place.

He felt the soldier slowly turn him around with one of their hands until Arrow saw the weapon pointed right at his face. The soldier was male with a strong build. The Onchei's long white hair was tied into a bun at the nape of his neck. All Onchei were tall compared to Mokta.

"Do you speak Mokta?" the soldier said in Mokta.

"Yes," Arrow answered.

"How did you get here from Algoran?"

Arrow said nothing. The soldier studied Arrow's appearance.

"You have Mokta features, but you do not look like any Mokta I studied at the academy."

"I am special," Arrow replied with a hint of sarcasm.

"What do you mean special? And how did you get here from Algoran? What is your objective?"

Arrow smiled at the irony of the situation. If he cooperated, the soldier would be satisfied with the information, kill him, and eventually track down Maska. If he didn't cooperate, the soldier would likely still kill him. Arrow needed to buy himself some time.

"My gemta is from Errrth and my torkomm is Mokta," he admitted.

"Humans from Earth do not have blue hair like yours," the soldier insisted.

"Generally, that is true. But my gemta is also special. She—"

The soldier grimaced, his patience exhausted by Arrow's obfuscations. "Enough!" the Onchei interrupted. "How did you get here from Algoran? What is your objective?"

There was a loud thumping noise to the rear of the soldier. His eyes rolled back, and he fell forward unconscious. Maska was standing behind him with her fist close to her chest. She was looking down to make sure the soldier was truly knocked out. Then she peered at Arrow with a mixture of annoyance and amusement.

"You would have talked him in circles for hours if you could, yes?" she asked.

"Only if necessary," Arrow replied. "Thank you for saving me."

"You are welcome. I used to do this quite often, you know," Maska added.

"I imagine you will never let me forget that."

Suddenly, Maska stomped on the soldier's right leg. Arrow heard a squint-inducing crunch.

"There was a saying Chieftess taught us: 'That is what friends are for.'"

"Are we friends now?" Arrow asked sincerely.

She snorted and looked away. "Leave it to you to not see the obvious. Like the fact that this Qui Tol will not be able to follow us if his leg is broken. You should have done that before I had to."

"That is true. I suppose I was distracted by . . . memories," Arrow deflected. "He may still be able to call for help with some of the machines in his armor."

"You could be right. We should remove his armor and dump it in the river."

"We will have to be quick. We do not know how often they report back to their superiors."

Once they accomplished that task, Arrow led Maska to a nearby cave.

"It will be night soon," Arrow noticed. "I have stayed here before. This cave's walls seem to deflect the Onchei's scans like the mud."

"Good," Maska replied. "I gathered some edible plants while we were separated. It will be enough to sustain us until morning." She patted a bag at her side hanging from her.

Arrow nodded. "Then we will not have to start a fire for cooking meat. Good."

"A fire would also make it too hot," Maska complained with a sigh. "And this world is like a stove as it is."

Arrow sat down against one of the walls and chuckled to himself.

"What?" Maska wondered.

"You gripe like an elder, Maska!"

Maska looked at him incredulously for a moment. Then she sat down beside him and leaned her head back.

"I have spent too much time around my parents. I talk like them now," she admitted.

"They bickered that much?"

"When Gemta is not heckling her friends, she is a never-ending source of grumbling and disapproval."

Arrow almost burst out laughing but hushed himself. Maska cracked a grin.

"You are not your gemta," Arrow suggested. "And there is too much in this life to be happy with."

"Perhaps if one has an adoring wife and children," Maska half-chided.

"You have much to offer," he said, gesturing towards her. "You just have to let someone into your heart, and they will love you, too."

"You make that sound as easy as catching rainwater in a bucket."

Arrow raised an eyebrow at that and nodded.

"Like catching rainwater, it takes effort. You have to get the right kind of container and place it in a good spot."

Maska looked unimpressed and sighed. "You know I was not being serious," she added.

"But it was a good example, Maska," Arrow replied in a coaching manner. "My point is it takes effort even to catch rainwater."

"Do you talk like this to your mate?"

"Of course."

"Does she agree with your thinking?"

"Not usually, no."

Maska laughed quietly. "She is as smart as she seems then."

Arrow kept an eye on the cave entrance. He and Maska would go quiet occasionally to listen for approaching footsteps, spot any movement or activity outside. At the moment, they were still alone in this area. The clouds were darkening, and the humidity was rising. It would rain soon.

"All these cycles . . . did you hate Pamela?" he asked.

"Hate? No," she replied. "I was jealous. So jealous I could have caused her harm. So, I stayed away."

Arrow's eyes widened at her revelation, but he did his best to remain calm. He considered several things before continuing. "Why—why did you not approach me with your feelings before Pamela did? Or even after she did but before we became mates?"

Maska's gaze narrowed. She hesitated a moment before looking towards the cave entrance. "Why ask this? You did not share my feelings . . . then or now."

"I want to understand. I also wish I could have prevented hurting your pride."

She turned her head and glanced at him, as if gauging his sincerity. "I had many feelings and they all conflicted with one another," she admitted. "I wanted to be your mate, but I was afraid at the time. I was also . . . intimidated by Pamela."

He noted that she pronounced his mate's name perfectly.

"She was confident . . . in herself, in her feelings for you," Maska continued. "I became fearful you would reject me if I did approach you."

"You never had problems with confidence when we were children. What changed?" he wondered aloud.

"I changed, without and within," she answered. "My thoughts and feelings became complicated."

Arrow's eyes had adjusted within the cave to the dimming light while this world's star descended outside. He saw Maska close her eyes and grip her own arms nervously. He heard her breath quicken as she bore more of her past to him.

"It hurt so much to see you and Pamela together, to see her bearing your children," she continued. "I became numb inside. I know I worried Gemta and Torkomm as well as my brothers. They knew what it all meant to me, so they could not comfort me. I was alone . . . and I blamed myself. That made it worse.

"As the cycles passed and your family grew, I made myself useful where I could. And when Torkomm became sick with the Shilvaba, I welcomed the chance to help him," Maska shared. "It felt good to have—"

Lightning flashed and split across the sky, startling them both. They positioned themselves on either side of the entrance, instinctively guarding against the possibility of an Onchei machine or some other threat. A few seconds later, distant thunder echoed across the land and they allowed themselves to relax once more. Maska cleared her throat.

"It felt good to be needed by someone," she resumed. "I cared for him as long as I could. But now he is gone . . . and suddenly Chieftess needed me to help Zeetra. And you. So, I am here."

Arrow's heart ached in sympathy for his former best friend. One last question burned in his mind. "Maska, why did you never choose another to be your mate? You could have been loved and had your own family."

Her pained eyes threatened tears. After a moment, she swallowed and cleared her throat again. "I will take first watch, Arrow. I will wake you in four hours."

He nodded his acknowledgment. Then he laid down on the ground and rested his head on one of his bags. It took a while, but sleep eventually found him.

———————

Maska was relieved when Arrow began lightly snoring. The winds picked up outside, and rain pecked the trees and ground. She walked near the entrance and listened again for any Onchei movement. Aside from insects, she detected nothing. Another burst of lightning danced across the thickened clouds in the sky. Believing it safe, she walked outside the cave and raised her hands upwards, enjoying the sensation of the waterdrops bouncing off her skin. It was not a full downpour yet. And even if it were, she would have remained where she stood.

"Arrow, I know you mean well," she said softly to herself. "You have always been kind to me, since we first met."

She lowered her arms.

"I have made many mistakes. I am not smart like Pamela or my parents. I only follow my heart. I knew you saw me as a great friend . . . but only a friend."

As more precipitation fell, Maska began to dance to memories of music only she could hear. It felt good to lift one foot and spin around, arms extended on either side or raised briefly in response to her movements. She wanted to sing but knew that would alert others to her presence and wake Arrow. This brief frolicking was enough.

Finally, she sat on a large rock near the entrance to the cave. The rain had cooled her skin against these sweltering temperatures she so despised. She wanted to complete this mission and return to the soothing crisp air of Algoran. She spied Arrow inside the cavern, still unconscious.

"I have tried, Arrow, but I will never love anyone else but you," she admitted to herself. "Because of our blood, we will live a long, long time. I will wait one hundred or more cycles for you, if you will have me. Or I will die alone if you will not. This is who I am."

She looked at the ground sadly.

"This is who I am."

16

THE PAST MEETS
THE PRESENT

THE SPACESHIP KILDEE
TWENTY-ONE DAYS SINCE LEAVING ALGORAN

When Commander Imbador found himself facing Meylor Oztan, high official from the Zarmandos colony with the title of Zhizhal, he issued a sharp salute, gripping his hand tightly at his chest and bowing his head. On either side of the commander, several officers and security personnel also showed their respect to the head of their government. Accompanying the Zhizhal were his lieutenant and several aides who stood behind them.

"Zhizhal, we are honored by your presence," Imbador said, head still lowered. "How may we serve you?"

Oztan was tall and stocky, a well-spoken, intelligent middle-aged man elected by the people during the voyage to the new colony. Unlike most Onchei, he kept his white hair close-cropped except for a narrow six-inch ponytail. His off-white skin was relatively smooth for his age. His customary dark gray public servant's uniform was immaculate, and his boots polished to perfection. To Imbador, the Zhizhal appeared somewhat unsettled, not as confident as he usually did in his public broadcasts. The fact that he had travelled to meet the Kildee more than a day out from the colony spoke volumes to the commander.

"Where is she?" Oztan demanded angrily in his deep baritone voice.

"Do you mean Zeetra, sir?" the commander replied.

"Who else? I wish to see her."

"She is in her quarters three decks down. She has been treated well."

Oztan nodded. He clasped his hands behind his back and lifted on the balls of his feet nervously.

"I knew the Onchei we left behind would bring calamity on themselves one day, Imbador. Visiting other worlds to capture aliens and bring them there? Then leaving their captives with those brutes, the Mokta? Utter madness. We turned our backs on them to forge this new society, considering them lost to us forever. But now, to learn they were actually slaughtered? I am stunned."

"So, you've come to issue the pardon she requested?"

"Of course," Oztan replied. He leaned forward slightly towards the commander, who did the same. "We have to know what happened."

Imbador stiffened and held up a hand in caution. "With respect, Zhizhal, I do not fully trust her. She has lied to me about several important facts already."

"I read your report, Commander. But I'm prepared to give her some leeway. If she thought she was the only Onchei left in the world, she would have no reason left to enforce our traditions. I can accept that she found a mate somewhere and had offspring."

"But, sir, that is our highest law!"

Oztan scoffed derisively. "You have seen what, two hundred zohwas, Commander?" Oztan asked, using the Onchei word for "years."

"Two hundred and thirty-seven, Zhizhal," Imbador replied curtly.

Oztan nodded slowly. "I have seen six hundred and ninety-seven. With experience comes some understanding. That includes perceiving the perspective of others. What good is the law if there is only one person left? There is no one to remind and no one to enforce. There are no penalties anymore. There is only survival."

Imbador tightened his jaw, unable to hide his outrage. He chose to resist the Zhizhal's words by not responding with any of his own.

"Is it the fact that she lied to you and broke our law? Or is it her faction?" Oztan asked. "Which is more important to you?"

"Her faction, sir. That is indisputable. She was one of those who remained on Algoran."

Looking amused, the Zhizhal began to pace around the commander. "And tell me, Commander, how old is this woman?"

"Approximately seventy-five zohwas, Zhizhal."

The commander remained perfectly still but he followed the Zhizhal with his eyes, looking uncomfortable. "And how many zohwas have passed since we left the homeworld?"

"Sixty-seven zohwas, Zhizhal."

Oztan stopped, narrowed his eyes and stared at Imbador as if he were a fool. "That would have made this Zeetra a childling of six, Commander. Can a childling make a decision to join a faction?"

"No, sir."

"Correct. And can a childling make a decision to leave her parents and join an expedition?"

"No, sir."

"Also correct. She would have been in her parents' care and the decision was theirs. If this tragedy to our people occurred when she said it did, she would have barely been more than a cadet in the Science Directive. I believe she deserves some consideration for that fact. Or had you realized these things?"

Imbador felt a rush of embarrassment and knew his cheeks were probably turning gray. He stiffened his shoulders as he forced down the urge to correct the leader. He took a couple of deep breaths. When he felt in control once more—several seconds later—he responded.

"I . . . had not realized them, Zhizhal."

Imbador remained upset with the Zhizhal challenging and humiliating him so directly in front of his crew. However, the leader was wise and had the full authority to conduct himself in this manner. The commander had shown ignorance, forcing Oztan to make him see another point of view. It did not alter Imbador's belief that their supreme law should be enforced, but it did soften some of his resentment towards Zeetra. She might not be the enemy after all. Unlike Imbador's own father.

———

Zeetra squinted at the electronic data pad in her hands. She put it on the table next to her bed and rubbed her bleary eyes.

"Either I've been reading too long or I need to design some optic lenses for myself," she mumbled in Onchei.

She stood and stretched her back slowly in either direction. Then she walked across her newer, more spacious quarters to the porthole window. It was still distant, but she could see the planet her people had named Zarmandos. It was a hazy, puce-hued world to her poor vision, but it still was more interesting than the vast black nothingness of the cosmos she had coped with for the last three weeks.

A harsh door chime—the electronic tone reminding her of the shrill of a tisa bird near the Mokta Mountain, high-pitched and loud but mercifully brief—snatched her attention. She turned her head toward the door.

"Open."

The door clicked and opened. She recognized the commander and security guards, but she did not recognize the man with them. He was wearing some kind of government uniform. She turned to face them respectfully.

"Zeetra, this is Meylor Oztan, the Zhizhal of Zarmandos colony," Imbador announced.

"I am honored," Zeetra bowed her head.

"Leave us," Oztan ordered to Imbador.

"Sir, let me leave a guard," Imbador requested.

"Unless you expect her to assassinate me with a data pad, I think I can handle myself, Commander."

The commander looked like his patience was running out, but he mastered his emotions almost immediately. "Yes, Zhizhal."

Zeetra had to restrain her amusement until the commander and security personnel left the room. Then she allowed herself a satisfied smile.

"He is a good commander but not the best diplomat," Oztan said. "It is a pleasure to meet you, Zeetra Ketranos. You already know who I am."

She appreciated his respect to her. It might be deception, but it was a nice change from everyone else. She relaxed her shoulders and offered as genuine a smile as she could under the circumstances.

"What can I do for you, Zhizhal?"

"Young woman, despite my office, I dislike formalities. Call me Meylor."

Zeetra nodded. "Of course."

"I knew your grandfather, Mizho Ketranos. We trained together in the Political Directive and worked on several campaigns. He was a good man. I tried to talk him into joining us on this expedition but by then, he was committed to the Science Directive."

Zeetra was impressed. The Zhizhal had researched her and prepared well for this encounter. But unlike the commander, she sensed no hostility or deception from this man. Even so, she became even more cautious. Either he was being honest, or she was in great danger.

"Grandfather was passionate about the Science Directive," she said somewhat reminiscently. "He is probably the main reason I chose it myself."

"He had that effect on people," Oztan agreed with a slight smile. "How far did you advance?"

"I was a fresh weztuk, barely a month past cadet graduation," Zeetra admitted. "I had just completed several scouting missions when the Directive sent me to return one of the humans to Earth. I went to the Mokta lands looking for one more. When I returned home . . . everyone . . . was dead."

Every time she recalled that terrible moment, it threatened to overwhelm her. No matter how much time passed, it never lessened the pain of having seen everyone she'd ever known brutally slaughtered. She suddenly became lightheaded and had to grab the wall to steady herself. Oztan surprised her with how quickly he moved behind her and gently grabbed her upper arms to keep her upright.

"I've got you," he said. "Szotran! You're trembling, child!"

He helped her sit down on her bed.

"All these zohwas have passed, but the memory still does this to me," Zeetra said softly. "Thank you for helping me."

"You are Onchei. I swore to help every one of us," he replied. "Unlike the commander, I do not distinguish between our people on the colony and those who remained on the homeworld."

She looked up and noticed that the Zhizhal looked at her with concern for several seconds but respectfully kept his silence. She nodded at him when she was ready to continue.

"Do you know who killed our people on the homeworld?" he asked.

She looked at him, communicating her hesitation through her eyes. Zeetra felt like she could trust him, but she wanted the reassurance of the pardon. Realization flashed in his eyes. He reached into his pocket, pulled out a small data pad, and handed it to her.

"This has been signed by me and my council of advisors," Oztan said. "It is a full pardon for any laws you may have broken, knowingly or unknowingly, at any time during your life. You can speak freely without any fear of retribution. We only want the truth."

Zeetra sighed. It was relieving to hear this, but it was also a burden of its own. She had asked for the pardon to put off telling them the truth, and now, they had called her bluff by giving her what she wanted. She was now obligated to deliver her part of the agreement.

"Thank you," she replied. "I will tell you what you want to know."

"Good," he said. "Let's start with who killed our people on Algoran."

She looked at him and almost felt pity for the Zhizhal. She could imagine how he might react to what she was about to say. She inhaled through her nose and closed her eyes as she exhaled through her mouth. Then she looked right at Oztan.

"It was SnowFire."

The Zhizhal frowned, looking perplexed. "I thought SnowFire was a fable, like the snow fairies of our childling tales?"

Zeetra shook her head. "No. She's real."

Oztan put his hands on his hips and narrowed his gaze. She figured he was trying to determine whether she was lying to him or not.

"You have seen her, met her?" he asked.

"No. But I have met her daughter. What I am about to tell you may be even more difficult to believe."

"Go on," he answered, motioning with his hand for her to continue. "I have seen many things in my time. I will try to keep an open mind."

The Zhizhal remained where he was, his hands clasped behind his back. Zeetra stood up and began to look out the porthole.

"The Mokta call SnowFire the Spirit of the Mountain but she has taken female form," she began. "She is said to have mated with the Mokta's first chief and had ten offspring. She is their ancestor from thousands of zohwas ago."

She heard Oztan stifle a derisive snort. "That still sounds like folklore to me."

Zeetra nodded. "I felt the same. And the Mokta did, too . . . until something changed their minds."

"Really? Please tell me, Zeetra."

She turned to face him and walked a little closer. "As you know, our people were in the practice of taking some humans from Earth and leaving them with the Mountain Mokta tribe. One of those humans, a female named Jordan, set out to find the Onchei. She travelled to the Southlands to find out why we brought her and her mother to Algoran."

"It has been tried before. I have never heard of anyone who succeeded."

Zeetra leaned against one of her walls, crossed her arms, and closed her eyes. "Jordan almost perished more than once. But she continued on, almost by sheer force of will, along with her small group."

"Impressive."

"Along the way, she met some of us—Onchei."

That made Oztan do a double-take. "What? Outside the Southlands?" he asked.

"Yes," she replied.

"Did this Jordan tell you who they were?"

"Yes, she did. It was Queen Amstar, King Yami, and their entourage."

Oztan gasped. He looked down then back at Zeetra in disbelief.

"How? I was there when they were deposed!" Oztan declared. "I was told they were executed."

"Apparently, everyone was told that. But they were sent into exile to a castle in a land with very harsh weather. Jordan and her hunting pack were introduced to her . . . and then the queen tried to kill them."

"What? Why?"

"Amstar was quite insane, according to Jordan. She grabbed Jordan by the throat and was going to consume her blood to stay young."

"That cannot be! Even I have heard of such things happening long ago, but that knowledge was destroyed. No one should know of it; much less be able to perform such unspeakable things!"

"King Yami learned of it and taught it to his daughter to extend her life."

Oztan nodded. "He would be one of the few who could do so." Oztan sat down and paused a moment. Then he sighed. "Please continue, Zeetra. What ended up happening? One of us could easily slay a human."

Zeetra remembered when she first met Jordan in the Southlands, how savage she had initially been towards her. The blue-haired woman with ice-like eyes held her dual-bladed javelin so close that it nicked Zeetra's throat. Had this been what the Onchei had seen before they died at SnowFire's hands?

"Jordan told me that SnowFire herself appeared in the castle and confronted Amstar," Zeetra added. "According to her, SnowFire impaled Amstar with a two-handed broadsword and killed all the other Onchei in the castle."

"This Jordan, she saw SnowFire?" Oztan asked.

"She didn't just see her. SnowFire gave Jordan an infusion of blood to save her life. It turned Jordan into a daughter of SnowFire."

"What do you mean, it turned her into SnowFire's daughter?"

"Jordan took on SnowFire's appearance, her eyes and hair changed. She has blue SnowFire gems embedded in her palms. She also gained incredible strength, can instantly translate any language, commands the Deathwings, and has barely aged at all since she was transformed. I have witnessed these things myself. She is the current Chieftess of the Mountain Mokta."

Oztan was clearly amazed. He closed his eyes. He chuckled mirthlessly. "Those fools—"

"What?"

"The Onchei who stayed behind on Algoran, some of them had hoped to increase the Onchei lifespan. Most of them believed SnowFire was real. They had been taking the humans to see if interbreeding with Mokta would increase how long the humans lived, since the Mokta claim to be the descendants of SnowFire. The ones who stayed hoped to emulate SnowFire's power without directly attempting to contact her," Oztan explained. "It sounds like they finally achieved some success but not the way they hoped. This—this SnowFire was real. They angered her somehow and she killed them all."

Zeetra nodded hauntedly. "At that time, Jordan had become the mate of the Chieftess' son. Attacking Jordan was like attacking SnowFire personally."

Oztan's eyes widened briefly but he said nothing. He stood and began pacing around the room. "The scientists meddled with something they didn't understand," he said. "It would be like a childling trying to play with a zala beast."

"More like a Sasstonn," Zeetra added.

"You said Jordan became Chieftess. Is this because she became SnowFire's daughter? Do Jordan and SnowFire rule together somehow? I need to know what we are facing."

Zeetra shook her head. "You are only partly correct. SnowFire determined that Jordan would be the next Mokta Chieftess, but they do not rule together. In fact, SnowFire has been gone from our world for over forty zohwas."

Oztan sat back down in a different chair by the bed. "This is bad."

"I don't understand," Zeetra responded, perplexed.

"I may be the Zhizhal on Zarmandos but I am only one voice on the Ruling Council. Even if I relay all this information myself, exactly as you told me, there is only one response my people can have."

"What will that be?" Her pulse quickened in anticipation.

"You said it yourself: SnowFire attacked the Onchei; she was defending the Mokta. When the Ruling Council learns that SnowFire actually exists and that she slew our people without mercy or exception, they will order the destruction of the Mountain Mokta."

"They can't! The Mokta didn't do this!"

"Do you think that makes any difference? It will be a matter of honor and pride. I cannot stop it."

Zeetra was horrified. Any pretense of secrecy and self-protection vanished with this news. "But I have a mate, childlings, and grand-childlings there!" she exclaimed, walking up and grabbing him by the arms, her face pleading. "I can't let them die!"

Oztan appeared sad and sympathetic. "If there were time, I would suggest you take them and leave," he sighed.

"If there were time? What are you saying?" she demanded.

"A sister ship, the *Amzatar*, is already heading back to Algoran. It was sent to gather information on how the planet has changed since we left. But once the Ruling Council deliberates my findings, they will contact the ship and have them attack."

"No! Can—can you just not tell them?"

Oztan took Zeetra by the hands and gave her a bittersweet smile.

"I have been a politician much longer than you have been alive. I have no illusions about this. I am duty-bound to tell them the truth. And after I tell them why SnowFire killed our people, the Ruling Council will break into two camps of thought: half will believe it and blame the Mokta for SnowFire's actions. The other half will not believe and will still blame the Mokta for the slaughter. They will immediately call for a vote and overwhelmingly decide to wipe out the Mokta."

Zeetra slumped against the wall feeling helpless and at a loss for words.

"I must leave for home after we're done here. It will take a day to return to Zarmandos at our best speed. The meeting of the Ruling

Council will be convened as soon as I arrive. The order will be sent to the *Amzatar* the same day. Within two days, the Mountain Mokta will be gone. I am . . . truly sorry."

Just then, there was a flash of light on the other side of the room. Zeetra was shocked to see Arrow and Maska appear.

"Well, this device is good for something besides opening holes in space after all!" Arrow said, grinning widely.

"Who are these people?" Oztan demanded.

"Forgive for interrupting your conversation," Maska interjected, calling to Zeetra. "But we thought you might like to go home?"

Zeetra rushed to hug them both.

"I do not know how you found me but thank you!" Zeetra almost shouted. "We have to get to the village! There is danger!"

"There is always danger, Zeetra," Maska remarked. "Why do you think Chieftess sent us after you?"

"Please—let us go home. Now!" Zeetra pleaded.

"All you had to do was ask, friend Zeetra!" Arrow replied.

Arrow pressed a button and a new portal formed. The three rushed through and then it closed.

———

Meylor Oztan was not easily impressed. But what had just occurred in front of him was noteworthy. Two strange-looking Mokta had just used Onchei technology to locate Zeetra over forty light-zohwas from their homeworld and effect an escape. How had Zeetra living among the Mokta made such a large difference, that they could undermine the security of one of their spaceships and make off with a prisoner with no difficulty at all? At that instant, the ship's alarm began to drone, making a clanging sound. Ship personnel ran down the hallways in response.

"Perhaps our self-imposed isolation for all these zohwas has actually been hurting us?" Oztan wondered aloud. "If just one of us living among the Mokta for a short while can make this kind of change, what would happen if we embraced them openly? What could we learn?"

He would have to return to this idea another day. Oztan walked to one of the wall panels and called for the commander. A few minutes later, Imbador joined him in Zeetra's room.

"Zhizhal, where is she?" Imbador asked, unnerved.

"Probably back on Algoran by now," Oztan replied feigning disappointment.

"What? How is that possible?"

"Two Mokta appeared using one of our teleport devices. She left with them willingly."

"Mokta? Using one of our teleport devices?"

"She has been living with the Mokta. She obviously taught them how to use the technology."

The commander looked very troubled at the implications of that. "I see, Zhizhal. Well, did you get any useful information from her before she left?"

"Yes. She told me what happened to our people on Algoran."

"And you believe her, Zhizhal?"

"Yes, I do. And now, I need your ship to take me back to Zarmandos. I need to report to the Ruling Council as soon as possible."

Imbador crisply saluted the Zhizhal without question.

"At once, Zhizhal! We will have you there within a rotation!"

The commander swung around curtly and walked briskly out of the room while giving orders to his subordinates via his wrist communicator. The door closed behind him and Oztan looked out the porthole, not towards Zarmandos but his homeworld.

"At least you will be with your offspring when the end comes. I wish you well, Zeetra Ketranos."

ACT FOUR
CROSSROADS

INTERLUDE III

SEVENTEEN DAYS HAD PASSED SINCE her arrival on Earth. Jordan stood in front of her parents' graves under a bright afternoon sky. A few birds flew overhead beneath the scant clouds. Wisps of a breeze were surprisingly cold, reminding her of Algoran and making her miss her dear ones. Kayla waited in the car, giving her this time to do whatever she needed to. Kayla had been there when the whole family had last been together. Had it really been so many decades ago? She looked at the time-etched lines on her hands and received her answer.

She carefully placed the flowers she had brought into the permanent vase in front of the granite gravestones and knelt; the sunflowers and white roses glistened in the sunlight. She thought her mother would have appreciated their lovely scent. Her father would have been happy that Jordan was home on Earth again. She tried to imagine her father's proud face, but it was hazy in her memory, dreamlike and beginning to fade. Her mother's visage was easier to recall; they had spent so much time together on Algoran. They had bonded in a new way after their abduction and relocation. Tribe was family but not like blood, Zoska had once told her. She and Mom were tribe and blood for several cycles.

Jordan then remembered the burial ceremony for Kitranor, former Chieftess and her beloved "other gemta." It had been so hard to let her go. Kitranor, Reiban, Vakar, Kobu . . . there had been so many, too many. They were gone but not forgotten.

She truly felt like a woman who had lived sixty-nine cycles now. She felt the burden of lost opportunities, the consequences of a choice her younger self made to build her life on Algoran instead of Earth. She missed the parents and brother she had grown up with, knowing she would never see them again. She did not regret her decision but now she was a woman who walked between two worlds.

"I do not know if you can hear me . . . Mom, Dad. I am sorry that I am so late in doing this," Jordan said. "I did not think I would ever be returning here. Maybe that was wrong of me."

Her eyes followed the lines and grooves of the gravestones, including the numbers depicting the dates of their births and deaths. It reminded her how long they had been gone. And it made her realize she was not so far from the ages they had been when they had passed away.

"Maybe I should have visited before now. I could have, I had the device that let me come back the first time," she continued. "But I would have wanted to bring Bopol or our children . . . and that might have been harmful to them. I could not risk that. I think you accepted that. You let me go back then. You freed me to pursue my life on Algoran . . . and I have."

She closed her eyes and breathed in the cold air, letting it fill her lungs. Then she let it out slowly, listening to the trees sway in the wind, their leaves rustling along the way.

"I have missed you. I do think of you both," she continued. "Things have not always been easy. There have been conflicts, even a war. I did terrible things . . . "

She lowered her head, squinted her eyes, and then shook her head in shame. She had to put her hands on the ground to hold herself up. It took several seconds to regain her composure and sit up straight again.

"I did those things, thinking it was to protect my tribe, the Mokta . . . who, like you, have become my family. I did protect them, but the cost . . . was high. Even now, there are problems I am trying to solve," she said, as her voice broke before softening to a whisper. "I have tried to be a daughter you would be proud of, though I have not always succeeded."

She clasped her hands over one another as they hung down before her lap. Jordan looked down at the gravestones.

"I do not know where your spirits went when you died. That is up to God. I can only hope. I will continue to do my best in the time I have. I still want to make you proud . . . of me and my family. Thank you for bringing me into this world and raising me. Know that you will live on in my children, their children, and future generations. I love you both. Goodbye."

Jordan wiped tears from her eyes as she stood up. Then she walked across the cemetery to where Kayla had shown her Mark's grave. Once there, she slowly lowered herself to her knees again, which had become quite sore. When she got as comfortable as possible, she looked at the tombstone and managed a sad smile.

"I remembered that you never liked flowers, little brother, so I did not bring any for you. It is just me. I had hoped to see you in person, embrace you once more and see if you still played guitar, but—" She couldn't complete the sentence, shutting her eyes in grief. When she spoke again, there were tears in her voice. "I am glad you married Kayla. And you had three daughters. I have only one. But I have two sons. Teesbin, my youngest, reminds me of you. He even has a talent for singing, unlike his mother."

She spoke as if her brother were right there next to her, telling him about Bopol and each of her children and grandchildren.

Jordan shared everything she had hoped to say to Mark, all the while shedding tears. She missed him so much that she ached inside. And when she didn't know what to do or say next, she sang a Mokta dirge:

"Though your eyes have closed

Your spirit shines as the Twin Stars

In the paths of our hearts

The time we shared will continue

In the warmth of our dreams

And the love which endures

Fly beyond the Mountain

Fly unto the sky

Fly beyond the stars

Just fly

Like the birds glide on high

You are so free

So we will let you go

Be free"

By the time she finished the last word, her voice had become hoarse and she was sobbing. She felt cut off. For the first time in so many cycles, she felt lost and unsure of herself.

Then she felt Kayla's hand grab her shoulder reassuringly.

"That was a beautiful song," Kayla told her. "Sad but beautiful. I didn't understand the words, of course."

"The Mokta sing it to cherish our memories and say goodbye to the dead," Jordan replied.

Kayla nodded, helped Jordan stand up, and they both walked back towards the car.

As she clicked her seatbelt into place, Jordan sighed. She had accomplished what she'd wanted, but now she was emotionally drained.

"It—it is hard to accept that they are gone, Kayla."

Kayla nodded somberly. "I know what you mean. I was at the funerals and it's still hard for me to accept. I mean, Mark . . . well, he'll always be with me in a way. I see him in our kids and grandkids. I have so many good memories with him."

"I am glad he had a happy life with you."

"He would be pleased to know about your life, too, Jordan."

Jordan pressed a button to let the car window down. She felt a pang of anxiety as she breathed in sharply. She needed some fresh air. Leaning her head back against the headrest, she sighed deeply.

"I think I need to be among the living now," Jordan considered.

Earlier, Jordan had been disappointed when the calls to Kayla's daughters, Karla and Macy, revealed they had previous commitments to work and family today. She knew it was possible she might see them in the next few days. But even the brief communication with them had made her very curious. She saw some of her brother in their features and mannerisms. It softened the sense of loss she felt. He would live on through them and their children.

"I've already called Jo and asked," Kayla assured. "She and Ethan are waiting for us."

17

ROUGH WATERS

IT HAD BEEN TWENTY-ONE DAYS since Pamela and her mother had left the Mokta village.

Off the Kastadi shore, the storm had begun less than an hour into their voyage in the small but sturdy wooden ship. The waters had already been choppy due to the winds, but the gusts soon grew tumultuous and howled like a frightening creature. Pamela had thought herself ready for almost anything. She had been sailing and fishing many times. But this was the ocean which had a life and strength all its own. Above, bright flashes of lightning were followed by deafening thunder. A noticeable zest stung Pamela's nostrils as she breathed in the air and accompanying ozone. The waves lifted them high like climbing the Mountain back home, only to drop them in freefall until they struck the water once more, rattling body and nerves. With such unrelenting motion, she had no choice but to grab onto the side of the ship and vacate the contents of her stomach. After a while, she felt slightly better.

As the rains lashed at her and the vessel, comforting hands gently grasped her shoulders from behind. When she turned to look at Kacheela, she saw only concern and sympathy on her face.

"Are you well enough to go below?" Kacheela shouted over the tempest.

Pamela nodded in uncertainty. "I think so!"

Kacheela pulled Pamela to her side, helped her cross the deck, and enter the cabin area below. Pamela grabbed a bucket along the way in case her nausea returned. Evtaz joined them while her sons, Holzak and Kizam, maintained the ship's functions on deck.

"This must be her first time on the ocean," Evtaz noted. "We are entering the cold season, when it is like this more frequently."

"I see," Kacheela answered. "We have lived in the Mokta lands for so long, we have never been to the ocean, much less during storms like these."

Evtaz chuckled. "This one is strong but there will be far worse before the season is finished. I am surprised you seem well, Eree-Kah."

"I do not get sick easily," Kacheela replied. "I will be fine. I am much more concerned for my daughter."

"The first time on these waters is the hardest," Evtaz acknowledged. "And we are less than one rotation from the islands. Cheer up, Pamilla, this is probably as bad as it will get."

"Probably?" Pamela repeated.

"Never tempt the sea," Evtaz warned. "It can always deliver something worse."

Three hours later, the storm had begun to relent. There were still strong winds and light showers, but the motion of the ship was steadier. Pamela felt more at ease lying on one of the beds. The smell of the rain was pleasant. She no longer felt ill, just tired. Sleep soon followed.

When she woke up, it was dark, and the motion of the vessel seemed even calmer. She stood up and walked to the deck. On the horizon, she could see the soft pre-dawn glow of the twin stars. Over these waters, it was one of the most beautiful things Pamela had ever seen.

"You live, Pamilla! Good!" Holzak said. "My brother and I were worried. But your kacheela was sure you would be all right."

"Kacheela has known me since I was a small child and raised me since I was ten," Pamela replied. "She knows me well."

"It is strange. She does not look old enough to be your kacheela," Holzak added.

"I know," Pamela agreed. Holzak nodded.

They both turned to look at the twin stars peeking out from the furthest edge of the distant waters, silently marveling at the sight.

"What was it like, growing up among the Mokta?" Holzak asked.

"I spent my earliest cycles in an Ullvarr village, before the Gulstaa attacked," Pamela answered. "It took me a while to learn the Mokta language and their ways, but they were patient with me."

"Then, do you consider yourself Ullvarr or Mokta?"

"I am Ullvarr, but I chose a mate from the Mokta. He is half-Mokta."

"Really? What is he mixed with—if that is all right to ask?"

Pamela smiled. "It is all right. His mother was born on Earth. But like my kacheela, she was changed by SnowFire's blood. My mate has that blood as well. And so do our children."

"Does that ever frighten you?"

Pamela frowned. "Very little frightens me anymore."

A few hours later, Kizam announce that he had spotted the islands.

Erica leaned against the side and gazed across the water towards the lush, turquoise land masses before them. There were at least four islands, each several miles across. Past their beaches, each island had vast fields and tall sloping hills covered with flowers and trees. The largest of them, towards the center, must have encompassed twenty miles from one end to the other.

Evtaz walked up behind Erica. "That one is Marbulua. It is where most of us live. To that side is Kimbyala and Orktim. On the other end is Keeloz and Embaa. Our leader is Valibos. He is an elder who has governed us for thirty cycles. His mate is blind in one eye, but she can sometimes see the future. She has advised Valibos well. And she is the one who told us it was time to trade with the Kastadi. That ended our isolation of hundreds of cycles."

"I would like to meet her," Erica said.

"I am sure she already knows you are coming."

Erica smiled at that. She didn't believe in fortune tellers any more than she believed in gods. But she was curious about this. She just didn't want to be disappointed.

————

After they disembarked from the ship, Erica and her daughter followed Evtaz and her sons into the village on Marbulua. She hoped that this Valibos was not like Daraz, the only Ullvarr leader she had known. Daraz had been overconfident, egotistical, and arrogant. He had led a campaign of deception that had robbed Erica of her free will for years. Daraz had been completely unprepared for the Gulstaa due to his obsession in striking at the Mokta and using Erica SnowFire to do so. That plan had ended as unceremoniously as Daraz.

Erica was distracted from her bitter memories by the beautiful fabrics on display in the marketplace. Males and females were selling clothing in brilliant shades of green, red, purple, and yellow. Others had jewelry made of painted shells and crusted with gem-like stones she had never seen before. And then she caught whiff of fresh and still-baking foods. Was that egisban? She made a mental note to get some of that later.

"—SnowFireChild!" a woman's voice boomed behind her.

Erica turned to see a tall Ullvarr woman in late middle age. Her long green hair, shaved on one side, was sprinkled with strands of silver. She wore a loose sapphire-colored robe and a white metal necklace adorned with small crimson gemstones. The color of one eye was clear, denoting her blindness, and the other was a deep shade of emerald. She had a huge smile. Erica and Pamela stopped and faced her.

"You are the SnowFireChild," she repeated.

"One of them. I am Erica."

"Eree-Kah SnowFire, I am Kaztema. My mate is the village leader, Valibos. I have been looking forward to your arrival."

"You know me?"

The older woman grinned even wider. It made Erica a little nervous. She felt odd being singled out, but as she looked around, no one had stopped to stare. The crowd continued about their business, as though this was just one more conversation in the midst of dozens of others. That was strange, too.

"The SnowFireChild who was not born on Algoran? The one who saved the last of the Ullvarr village and preserves our ways and tongue with her children and grandchildren? Yes, I know you."

Erica was stunned and staggered back a step. "How could you possibly know all that??"

Kaztema lifted her arms up and away from her sides, her smile never faltering.

"You do not believe the incredible, even though it surrounds you," Kaztema answered, turning and making eye contact with those near her. Then she returned her attention to Erica. "You like to understand and control what you perceive."

Kaztema pulled her arms close to her chest and approached Erica. Her expression was sympathetic. "I understand why you were so sad after the death of your mate. He helped isolate and protect you. Now you must face things as they are, and you do not like it."

Feeling exposed and uncomfortable but wanting answers, she demanded, "Who are you that you can know such things?"

"I told you. I am Kaztema," she cupped her hands in front of her, a friendly gesture. "I see things. Welcome to our land, Eree-Kah SnowFire."

Erica broke the almost-mesmerizing gaze of the older woman and looked at her equally surprised and amazed daughter.

"I knew nothing about this, Kacheela," Pamela said softly.

Kaztema walked very close and leaned toward Erica, dropping her voice into a whisper. "You will see something when you return to the Mokta that will make you believe the incredible. Something that even you cannot deny."

Erica looked at Kaztema for a moment, wondering briefly whether the woman was insane. The crisp focus in her good eye gave Erica the answer, even though she didn't like it.

"Come with me, I will take you to Valibos," Kaztema said, walking briskly through the large village. Erica and Pamela followed her. "He is also eager to meet you."

Erica was fascinated by how different this place was from the Ullvarr community she had known for six years. It wasn't just because of the larger population. The people conversed openly and pleasantly with one another while also freely acknowledging and speaking to Erica and Pamela. The children were respectful. It was not out of fear; it was just how they had been raised. Erica was almost shocked to see more than one flirtatious gaze at her, which would have been unheard of in Daraz's village. She actually felt welcome here.

Erica wondered where Kaztema was taking her and Pamela, since they now seemed to be exiting the village and heading towards the beach. Up ahead, she saw a bald and heavyset Ullvarr man casting a fishing line into the water from the shoreline. He did not turn as the three women approached.

"I told you the fish will be sluggish after the storm. They will not bite," Kaztema teased with a smile.

"Just once, I want to prove you wrong," the fisherman replied with some frustration.

"It will not be today." She chuckled. Then she took a more serious tone. "My mate, I have brought the ones from my dreams. This is Eree-Kah SnowFire and her daughter, Pamilla."

Valibos pulled in the fishing line then stabbed the rod deep into the sand before turning to face them. He was also of upper middle age with a weathered face and neck. He bore scars: across his forehead, on part of his chest that was not covered by his vest-like gray shirt, and all down his left arm. The older man studied both Erica and Pamela before responding.

"I have never met a SnowFireChild," he said with a respectful voice, looking at Erica.

"Outside the village we live in, not many have," Erica responded. She and Pamela gave the traditional half-bow of respect to Valibos.

"My mate tells me you rescued this Ullvarr who is now your daughter," Valibos continued. "Is it also true as Kaztema says, that you took an Ullvarr for a mate and had children with him?"

Erica nodded proudly. "We gave Pamela a sister and brother, yes. My mate died several cycles ago."

"Much sorrows, Eree-Kah. We mourn with you," Valibos offered sincerely. He looked back towards the village and extended a hand in that direction.

"What do you think of this place?" he asked.

"It is better than I had hoped to imagine," Erica admitted. "You have a paradise here."

The older man smiled and took the compliment graciously. "You and your family are welcome here, either to visit as often as you like or to stay," Valibos added. "Your heart is as Ullvarr as mine. I do not need a seer's eye to know this."

Just then, Erica heard Pamela gasp. She turned to see her daughter mesmerized by something in the sky. She saw a small silhouette but couldn't make out its details.

"Kacheela, it is the spaceship of the Onchei," Pamela warned. "It has returned!"

18

THE SISTERS' TESTIMONIES

Ethan Carstens was scribbling some notes on an electronic tablet when the doorbell rang. Mom was in the living room already, having finished baking the chicken casserole and blueberry pie.

"I'll get it, Ethan," Mom said.

"Okay, Mom. Do you want me to brew some coffee for them?"

"Would you, please? Thanks."

His mom unlocked the door and greeted his grandmother and Great Aunt Jordan. When he turned his head to catch a glance of them, he almost dropped the carafe. He barely recognized his great aunt! The woman who had looked to be in her late twenties with blue hair and glistening ice blue eyes was now around the same age as Grandma and had gray hair. But the kindness in her gaze and smile were the same. Something extraordinary must have happened to her.

"Ethan, it's rude to stare," Grandma chastised.

"I think it is all right this time, Kayla," Great Aunt Jordan put a hand on Grandma's shoulder. "I look a lot different than when he met me."

Then Great Aunt Jordan looked at him and gave a reassuring smile, which had the desired effect. "It is good to see you again, Ethan. How have you been?"

"I—I'm well, thanks, Great Aunt," he replied warmly. "It's good to see you, too."

The older woman chuckled. "I think you should just call me Jordan. Can you do that, Ethan?"

He really liked the idea of just calling her by her name, but he didn't want to be disrespectful. "I guess so, ma'am."

Mom seemed to be adapting to Jordan's changes as well. Apparently, she was just being quiet about it.

They sat down to eat in the dining room. Grandma asked everyone to close their eyes and bow their heads. Then she prayed a blessing for the food. Following that, Ethan barely noticed how his supper tasted, though he consumed it all. He was too captivated by his now-human relative. His mind burned with questions, causing him to harbor imaginary scenarios like his Great Aunt being cursed with immortality. And now, she had somehow freed herself. Or had she fought a powerful mage and lost? Everything about this relative was a mystery to him . . . except how she felt about him, Mom and Grandma. She definitely loved them, looking happy to be surrounded by family. But sometimes, he saw her look sadly towards the window. Was she thinking of her own family and home?

Grandma shared with them how she and Jordan had spent their day. Both she and Jordan complimented Mom on the meal, which pleased her. Then they all headed back into the living room and sat down on the couch.

"Would either of you like some coffee? Water?" Mom nodded at Ethan.

"Some coffee would be lovely," Grandma answered.

"I will have some coffee also," Jordan added.

Ethan went back into the kitchen. He returned a few minutes later with several mugs of hot java. After he served his family, he sat down to join them with a bottled water for himself.

"I feel like I should tell you, this happened to me once before, many years ago on Algoran," Jordan said. "I turned human, but it was for only a few minutes."

"Could you tell us about that? What caused it then?" Kayla asked.

Jordan sighed and lowered her head, dealing with unpleasant memories. "It was six years after I had returned to Algoran from Earth, after I met you, Kayla. A war had broken out on Algoran. My tribe, the Mokta, were pulled into the conflict to defend our allies, the Kastadi. Our enemy was a people called the Gulstaa. They attacked in overwhelming numbers, killing anyone, even the sick, elderly, children. I made a new alliance with some intelligent creatures called Deathwings."

"Deathwings? What kind of creatures are those?" Ethan interrupted.

Jordan smiled but her mood was bittersweet. "The closest comparison I could make would be like dragons, although they are not dragons," Jordan continued. "They have wide wingspans and breathe black fire that can destroy almost anything."

"Whoa! How did you talk to them?" Ethan inquired.

"My gems allowed me to speak to them. The Deathwings told me that SnowFire gave them the ability to breathe fire. That helped them defend themselves when they were hunted almost to extinction. Since they acknowledged me as SnowFire's daughter, they felt obliged to hear me out. They agreed to follow . . . my commands."

Jordan went silent then, and a tear fell from her right eye. She harbored so many painful regrets. Kayla wrapped her arms around

Jordan and leaned against her. After taking several deep breaths, Jordan was ready to continue.

"I was enraged with the Gulstaa for their atrocities against the Kastadi and others," Jordan told Jo. "To save Erica—your mother's cousin—I even killed one hundred Gulstaa by myself . . . some with my bare hands."

Neither Jo nor Kayla made a sound but were clearly shocked by this confession. Ethan was frozen in place.

"The Deathwings knew how I felt about the Gulstaa, that a part of me wanted them dead." Jordan paused. "So they flew to the Gulstaa lands and . . . ended the war for me."

"What do you mean, the Deathwings ended the war for you?" Jo asked.

Jordan gazed at her for a few seconds before answering. She had hoped to avoid explaining further. "They massacred the Gulstaa people and destroyed their buildings, land, everything."

Jo covered her mouth as she gasped. Kayla shut her eyes, horrified. Ethan looked down, gripping his tablet with both hands. There was a brief pause.

"As Chieftess, I was responsible for all of it," Jordan resumed, her voice heavy with sorrow. "Every death was on my conscience. The few Gulstaa who survived that devastation had to rebuild from almost nothing. They may never fully recover. And that tore at my heart as well. I nearly lost my mind from grief and regret."

"I—I can't even imagine," Kayla said softly.

"In the midst of my misery and despair, I had questions that only God could answer. One night, despite there being a raging thunderstorm outside, I climbed to the top of the Mokta Mountain and cried out to

God. I asked why He had saved my life only to let me become a child of SnowFire, the Chieftess of the Mokta Mountain Village and . . . a killer."

Jordan looked down, her shoulders slumped, immersed in memory.

"At first, there was no answer. But then everything became still. I was instantly inside an invisible space where the storm could not reach. The snow was gone, and grass and flowers bloomed on every side of me. A glowing man appeared, not too far from me. He was so bright; I could not look in his direction and I felt like all my strength abandoned me in his presence. He did not speak, either. But an angel I could not see spoke from near him. The angel had such a strong voice. It sounded like deep crashing waves."

"What did he say?" Jo asked, fascinated.

Jordan stood and looked upward, hands clasped together, and then closed her eyes for a moment. When she opened them again, she peered at Kayla, then Jo, and then Ethan. She noticed he was writing something on his tablet, but she didn't ask him about it.

"It has been a long time since then, but I made myself remember the words: 'Shadrach, Meshach, and Abednego, answered and said to the king, O Nebuchadnezzar, we are not careful to answer thee in this matter.'"

Kayla nodded in recognition of the words. Tears began to well in her eyes.

"'If it be so, our God whom we serve is able to deliver us from the burning fiery furnace, and he will deliver us out of thine hand, O king,'" Jordan quoted.

Kayla looked amazed, still tearful, as if she was hearing these passages for the first time. Jo seemed to be searching her own memory. Ethan was listening intently.

"'But if not, be it known unto thee, O king, that we will not serve thy gods, nor worship the golden image which thou hast set up',"' Jordan continued. "'Then was Nebuchadnezzar full of fury, and the form of his visage was changed against Shadrach, Meshach, and Abednego: therefore he spake, and commanded that they should heat the furnace one seven times more than it was wont to be heated. And he commanded the most mighty men that were in his army to bind Shadrach, Meshach, and Abednego, and to cast them into the burning fiery furnace.'"

"'Then these men were bound in their coats, their hosen, and their hats, and their other garments, and were cast into the midst of the burning fiery furnace',"' Jordan continued. "'Therefore because the king's commandment was urgent, and the furnace exceeding hot, the flames of the fire slew those men that took up Shadrach, Meshach, and Abednego. And these three men, Shadrach, Meshach, and Abednego, fell down bound into the midst of the burning fiery furnace. Then Nebuchadnezzar the king was astonied, and rose up in haste, and spake, and said unto his counsellors, Did not we cast three men bound into the midst of the fire? They answered and said unto the king, True, O king.'"

Kayla seemed really happy and excited, almost girl-like, as she listened. Jo appeared surprised and even impressed. Ethan continued writing on his tablet, looking up occasionally. Was he taking some kind of notes about what she was telling them?

"'He answered and said, Lo, I see four men loose, walking in the midst of the fire, and they have no hurt; and the form of the fourth is like the Son of God. Then Nebuchadnezzar came near to the mouth of the burning fiery furnace, and spake, and said, Shadrach, Meshach, and Abednego, ye servants of the most high God, come forth, and come hither. Then Shadrach, Meshach, and Abednego, came forth of the midst of the fire.'"

Jordan stopped and closed her eyes. She felt tired but also relieved. She turned and sat back down next to Kayla.

"After I heard that, the glowing man was gone but the angel was still there. I was in the field and it was calm," Jordan said. "I asked if his words were from the Bible because they sounded like they were. And he said yes."

"That's right," Kayla smiled serenely. "It is from the third chapter of a book in the Bible called Daniel."

"He told me someday, I would understand what those words meant," Jordan added. "I asked the angel if I was like one of the three men being put in the furnace."

That intrigued Jo. "How did he answer that?"

"I'd like to know that, too," Ethan added.

"He told me that the Holy One had come to protect those men. So, I asked was He there, on the mountain, to protect me? If so, I wondered why—because I had done awful things. I felt like I was an awful thing."

Jo's eyes conveyed her heartfelt sympathy. She started to speak but stopped herself.

"But the angel questioned that. He asked if I was a child of SnowFire right at that moment," Jordan added. "And when I looked at myself, I saw that I was as human as I am now."

Kayla's eyes brightened even more. "Jordan, that's your answer! God made you human before, to show you that He could. And He did it again, when you asked for a sign."

She smiled at that before continuing. "The angel told me that I have a purpose in this life and that I am loved."

Kayla took Jordan's hand and gently squeezed. "That's so true, Jordan."

Jo looked astounded, almost dumbfounded. But Ethan smiled in relief.

"He told me to acknowledge the Most Holy in all my ways and that He would bless me and my people. That is what I have tried to do all this time," Jordan said. "And we have had peace in our land for over four decades . . . until now."

Jordan had just answered an unspoken question, reminding Jo of a time when she was at her lowest. She had tried so hard to hold her marriage and family together through sheer force of will. Yet in doing so by herself, she had failed. She knew that perhaps nothing would have made a difference. She felt some accomplishment in attaining sole custody of her son but still felt broken inside. Half of her heart had figuratively and literally moved out and divorced her.

She didn't know what to do, so she had turned to her mother. Mom had done her best to console her. But in time, she told Jo that someone else could do a far better job restoring her heart and soul. She needed Jesus. Truly at her wits' end and wanting to provide a stable home for her son, Jo let go of her pride and turned to the Lord for His Salvation. It was a feeling she would never forget.

Suddenly, Jo came to an inescapable conclusion. She looked at Jordan, feeling pure astonishment and wonder.

"Aunt Jordan?" she said.

"Yes, Jo?"

"You were in the presence of Jesus."

Aunt Jordan seemed to recognize the name but still looked confused. Looking at Ethan, Jo saw him mouth the word "wow" in amazement. He stopped writing on his tablet. Mom repositioned herself on the couch and leaned forward attentively.

"I have heard that name before, when I was young," Aunt Jordan replied. "I know he was from the Bible, too. But I have never read the Bible, so I do not know who Jesus is."

Mom nodded at Aunt Jordan. "I'll tell you. Jesus is the Son of God. He sent Jesus to Earth to be born through a virgin woman that God chose. When Jesus was born, He was human but also the Son of God. He felt everything we feel and lived as we humans do, with one exception: He never sinned throughout His entire life."

Aunt Jordan appeared intrigued to hear this.

"What is sin?" she asked. "I do not know that word."

Mom blinked a few times but said nothing while Ethan's eyes briefly widened. Jo was not entirely surprised at this, since Aunt Jordan had been away from Earth for so long.

"Sin is the bad things people do or think about doing, Aunt Jordan," she interjected. "Hate, envy, violence, stealing, lying, and murder are all sins. Plus, many other things that cause harm to others or yourself."

"This Jesus did not do or feel any of those things? How?" Aunt Jordan inquired.

"He is holy. He . . . shares the power of God," Jo replied, finding it difficult to relay what she knew in layman's terms. She also found it ironic, since she was a professor who gave lectures on the intricacies of historical data to hundreds of students. But now she was relaying something deeply personal. "He is One with God."

Aunt Jordan looked down for a moment and then returned Jo's gaze. "I believe you, but I also do not understand," Aunt Jordan said.

Jo was quiet as Jordan then excused herself to the restroom. She looked at her mother, still feeling tense and inadequate in some ways. She silently asked for help communicating with Aunt Jordan through a slight turn of the head and a subtle shrug. Mom smiled and nodded her assurance that Jo was doing fine. A couple of minutes later, Aunt Jordan returned and sat back down on the couch.

"As I said before, I do believe you. I want to understand what you are talking about," Aunt Jordan said. "Can you help me?"

Still sitting next to Aunt Jordan, Mom put her arms around her sister-in-law and hugged her happily.

"Yes, Jordan. I think we can help," Mom replied.

Mom stood up and stretched for a moment. Ethan had returned to writing something, almost feverishly, in his tablet. She didn't want to disturb him but would definitely ask him about it later.

Jordan was pleased when Kayla led them in short prayer before they continued their discussion. Then Kayla put a book in Jordan's hands.

"Jordan, I want you to have this Bible," Kayla said. "Read it while you are here. And when you go back to Algoran, please take it with you."

"But this is yours," Jordan started to protest, but Kayla smiled and shook her head.

"That's all right. I can get another one," Kayla continued. "For now, I would like to read a bit of it to you, if that's okay?" Jordan nodded in response.

Kayla opened up the Bible and read from Matthew in the New Testament. When Jordan asked her, she explained who the Jewish people were, their special relationship with God and a bit about the Old Testament of the Bible. Through reading the Scriptures, Kayla shared who Jesus was and is, the role God had and has for Him. She conveyed that Jesus also suffered and died, bearing the punishment for the sins of the whole world in the place of all mankind. Then Kayla explained that God resurrected Jesus from the dead, giving His Son power over sin and death—and that presently, Jesus is in heaven, sitting at the right side of God.

Jordan listened both patiently and with growing interest.

"This is all incredible, Kayla. I believe you. Everything you have told me about God, Jesus, and the Holy Spirit, I believe these things," Aunt Jordan replied. "I have never seen God, but I know He is real. He has responded to me and my prayers—not through words, but in things that have happened all around me. He has protected me, my family and the Mokta people. I believe that He loves me because I have experienced these things. However, there are still some things I do not yet understand."

"It is a lot to take in," Kayla acknowledged. "What don't you understand?"

"These things you told me from the Bible, they happened thousands of years ago," Jordan added. "Did they reach out to you, too? Tell me what they mean to you."

Kayla looked both surprised and pleased to hear this. She smiled with contentment.

"God is—I don't know if I have the words to properly explain what God is to me," Kayla replied. "But . . . God is the Heavenly Father of all of us. And Jesus is our Savior."

Jordan leaned closer to Kayla.

"What did Jesus save you from—and how did He do it?" Jordan asked.

Kayla took in a breath through her mouth and exhaled through her nose. She nodded thoughtfully at Jordan.

"Myself. He saved me from myself, from the person I had become," she said. Then she sighed. "You didn't have time to get to know me well when we first met, not like now. My father died right before my tenth birthday. My mother did her best to raise me by herself. I leaned on my art and creativity to keep me focused and sane. But I had anger problems for a long time; I struck out at people with my words and my actions. There were times when I just couldn't control myself. I resented my father being taken from me. And I resented him for dying."

Jordan nodded. What Kayla was describing reminded her of Erica's pain and bitterness since her mate Vakar died.

"I met Mark a few years later in high school," Kayla continued. "He was having a hard time adjusting to school since he'd been out for a year."

"Why had he been out of school for so long?" Jordan asked with concern.

Kayla looked at Jordan sadly for a moment.

"Your brother was very traumatized by the loss of you and your mother," she answered. "He thought you were dead, and he couldn't deal with it. He told me he stayed in his room for weeks. It got so bad, Mark was diagnosed with severe depression and put on medications. It took almost a year of therapy for him to face the rest of the world again. He was hurt, sad, and angry."

Absorbing those words and their meaning, Jordan slumped forward and put her head in her hands. Fresh tears fell down her cheeks.

"The last time I saw him, he mentioned needing a psychologist," Jordan said. "But . . . he made it sound like it did not last that long. He said he recovered."

"You can heal but you never completely recover from something like that," Kayla replied. "You just get to where you can move on. Mark did that through music. That's how I met him. I got to know Mark Lewis and he got to know me."

"You fell in love. You found something in each other that you needed."

Kayla nodded.

"Yes, we fell in love," Kayla said softly. "Mad, deep, wonderful love. Unfortunately, that didn't solve our problems. That love just gave us a temporary source of comfort and release. We dated and married young, moving into our first apartment. But when we disagreed, it was fierce. Your brother didn't like confrontation, so he would go quiet and walk into another room. I would follow him and keep it going. And . . . though I'm ashamed to say it, when I got too angry, I hit your brother."

Jordan abruptly lifted her head in dismay. "What did you say?"

"I wasn't good to him then," Kayla admitted somberly. "I knew what he had been through . . . but when I got angry, I didn't know how to stop myself. I can't tell you how many times I apologized to him since those days. And Jordan, I am so sorry for how I treated your brother."

Jordan had to work hard to restrain her anger for a minute or two in silence.

"What happened?" was all she could eventually say in a strained voice.

Kayla took a moment to gather her thoughts before continuing.

214   JORDAN'S DELIVERANCE

"One of Mark's co-workers was named Jack. He let Mark confide in him about why he was stressed out. Jack invited us both over one evening. He and his wife—they're both deceased now—were Christians," Kayla said. "Jack quoted a verse from the Bible, from the book of John, chapter three, and verse sixteen. 'For God so loved the world that he gave his only begotten son, that whosoever believeth on him should not perish but have everlasting life.' That gave me hope for the first time since my father died. I knew I was sabotaging our relationship, but it wasn't on purpose. I knew we needed help."

Kayla picked up her cup and took a sip of water.

"We didn't make any decisions that night," Kayla continued. "Mark later told me he believed them, but he was too scared to change at the time. He thought it would be too hard and he'd have to give up too much. I felt differently. I was tired of the way things were, I didn't like who I was."

Kayla shifted again on the couch, uncomfortable with her position and apparently the memories, too.

"Mark and I had started talking about having kids, but I didn't think I'd be a good mother. I already wasn't a good wife or friend to him," Kayla added. "So, I called Jack's wife on my own. We met and talked some more. She took me to their church a few times and I heard more about Christ's love. I learned about salvation."

"Salvation?" Jordan repeated. Kayla nodded matter-of-factly in response.

"I prayed to God and gave Him my confession of faith: that I believed Jesus was His Son, that He lived, died and was raised from the dead. I admitted to all my sins and asked Jesus to forgive me and send

His Holy Spirit into my heart. And He did. I became a changed person, a new person. He soothed my pain and anger."

Jordan nodded slowly. "And Mark, did he find this salvation also?"

Kayla smiled. "Yes. It took a little longer. But when he saw how the Lord had really changed me, he wanted that change for himself."

"I am glad that you both found peace," Jordan added.

Kayla looked at her with an encouraging smile. "You can, too, Jordan."

Jordan considered all she had heard and experienced this evening. It was a lot to take in. However, she felt close to an answer she hadn't realized she was seeking.

"I do not know about you, Kayla, but I am very tired," Jordan shared. "Can we talk about this some more tomorrow?"

"Of course," Kayla replied, pleasantly tapping on Jordan's leg. "I'm tired, too."

19

AN OLD WOUND REOPENED

THIS WAS ONE DAY THAT Erica wished she had even greater abilities than the ones she had received by SnowFire's blood. She knew Pamela was terrified for her children and the rest of the Mokta, even though her daughter worked hard to mask her emotions. Erica wanted to magically wave her hands and make them both appear in their home village in an instant. But she couldn't. The best they could do was ride the ever-changing ocean waves in Evtaz's ship, proceeding however fast the winds allowed. At least the weather had been better on the return trip.

They were still half a day's journey from the Kastadi lands, surrounded entirely by water and a misting rain that had not let up since they'd left the islands. Pamela stayed below to reduce the chance of another bout of seasickness. Kizam was also there, catching some sleep before taking the night shift at the helm. Erica remained on-deck with Evtaz and Holtaz, noting the daylight was almost gone.

Evtaz walked over to Erica while Holtaz remained at the helm. She looked surprisingly pleasant, considering the circumstances.

"Eree-Kah, you continue to fascinate me," she said.

"How so?"

"I have never seen someone so calm on the ocean, you almost seem born to it," Evtaz continued. "If you decide to move to the islands, I

216

think you would make a fine sailor. I would be honored to have you as a member of my crew."

"That is a kind offer, Evtaz. But I do not know what our plans will be. We may have a serious fight ahead of us . . . or we may have reason to mourn. I don't know."

Evtaz reached out and clasped Erica's shoulder. She had a sincere gaze that reminded Erica of Jordan.

"My sons and I are not many, but if your family is threatened, we will join your fight," she added. "And if there is cause to mourn, we will mourn with you."

"I thank you," Erica replied. "For accepting me and my family as Ullvarr. Time will tell what is needed."

"Come below with me to the galley, Eree-Kah. I was about to make a hearty stew and would like some company."

Erica nodded.

The galley was an extra room for crew quarters that had been cleared out. Evtaz lit both lanterns in the room. Several barrels stored ingredients Holtaz and Kizam had brought aboard that morning. Next to them was a large metal pot held up on a tripod over a box filled with sand. There was also a small table opposite the stove. A cutting board hung above it on the wall, along with a spice rack of some kind. Evtaz opened the nearest barrel, revealing several vegetables.

"Nothing but the best for new kin," Evtaz said with a smile. "Do you cook?"

"Yes, but this is your ship, your galley. I'll be happy to chop the vegetables and help however I can," Erica replied.

Evtaz slapped Erica on the back and laughed. "I like you, Eree-Kah!"

An hour later, the vegetable stew was ready. In one of the lantern-lit crew quarters, Holtaz served it in bowls to Erica, Pamela, and his mother at a small wooden table that had been secured to the floor. Then he made a serving for himself. He filled a pitcher with fresh water from a nearby barrel and poured some into their cups before joining them at the table.

Erica lifted the bowl and slurped down some of the stew. She was impressed with its slightly spicy heat. It was savory but not overly-salty nor bitter. The vegetables retained some of their crispness and while it was a thin broth, she enjoyed it.

They shared stories with each other during the meal. Erica talked about Pamela's childhood with her siblings as well as her beloved Vakar. Pamela talked about her own children and mate. Evtaz had plenty to say about her sons but was reluctant to speak of their father. Before things got too awkward, Evtaz pulled out a wooden bottle from a box next to the barrels. Without asking, she poured it into Erica and Pamela's near-empty cups.

"What is this?" Erica asked, more intrigued than anything.

"This is klentuth, a special recipe passed down through my family. Please believe me when I say it's a very rare treat!" Evtaz replied with a giddy look. Holtaz nodded in agreement, gazing hungrily at the bottle. "I was keeping it for just such an occasion. It goes well with this stew. Please, drink and enjoy!"

Erica and Pamela turned their heads to face each other then back at Evtaz. Understanding the honor being bestowed upon them, they smiled and lifted their cups to their lips. It had a bitter, burning taste initially, and then it tingled briefly and became much sweeter, almost like it evaporated before it went down her throat. She downed the rest of the cup's contents with a few more gulps. Seconds after that, she felt a strong swirling sensation in her head which alarmed her.

"This—is liquor?" Erica growled, leaning forward slightly, putting her hand to her forehead and closing her eyes.

"Yes. Is something wrong?" Evtaz replied, sounding worried. "It can be . . . strong if you have not had it before."

Erica forced her eyes open, even though her vision was slightly blurred. Her daughter was even more affected than she was. Pamela's head drooped, and she blinked several times in a row, appearing disoriented. She tried to shake it off but that wasn't possible.

Pamela cleared her throat before she spoke. "Kacheela was drugged by Ullvarr villagers for several cycles. They did it to control her," she told Evtaz woozily.

Before Evtaz could respond, Erica had grabbed her by the shoulders angrily. When Erica spoke, it was with more than one voice. Evtaz's face was illuminated by the glow of Erica's eyes and the flames in her hair. Evtaz's eyes widened in momentary terror.

"Never again!" Erica exclaimed.

"Kacheela, stop!" Pamela shouted. "She didn't know!"

To Erica, these few seconds felt like minutes. She was fighting the effects of the liquor, but it was difficult, especially while she was trying to suppress her own rage. She knew Pamela was right. Evtaz could not have known about Daraz and Kalami's deception. Moreover, she needed Evtaz and her sons to safely reach the Kastadi lands. But the intoxicant had lowered her inhibitions and heightened her emotions, stoking fears she'd thought forgotten.

Evtaz's gaze narrowed in anger and outrage. She snarled, knocking aside Erica's arms with her own before shoving her away. Erica landed on her back unharmed. She struggled to get to her feet, since her sense of balance was still compromised. The best she could manage was getting on all fours, which still left her vulnerable. When she looked up, she saw the dagger Evtaz gripped tightly in her left hand.

"Think, Eree-Kah! You and your daughter are my guests," Evtaz barked, barely restraining her own rage. "Why would I be stupid enough to provoke a being like yourself?"

She put the dagger back into its sheath on her belt.

"But let me tell you: if you were my enemy, I could kill you easily right now."

Erica eyed Evtaz. "I am sorry, Evtaz. This was all . . . unexpected."

Evtaz stretched out a hand to help Erica stand up. "That is how this life is. We all make mistakes, even me. I should have told you how strong the drink was. I am sorry that I did not."

Erica took the outstretched hand. Once on her feet, Erica still felt slightly wobbly. She sat back down next to Pamela, who hugged her.

"If you both finish your stew, the effects will fade more quickly," Holtaz suggested.

Evtaz sat back down and exhaled through her mouth. She poured some more of the klentuth into her cup and downed its contents quickly, still irritated. Then she peered at Erica again.

"Who drugged you before?" she asked. "And why did they want to control you, Eree-Kah?"

"It was Kalami, Pamela's first kacheela," Erica replied. "She was following instructions from Daraz, her mate and Pamela's first asta. He knew I was a SnowFireChild and wanted to harness my power."

"To what end?" Evtaz wondered aloud.

"My mate Vakar told me once. Daraz wanted to attack the Mokta. This was because my sister, Jordan, had killed Daraz's kacheela in a battle before I came to Algoran. Daraz wanted vengeance, but the Ullvarr village did not have enough warriors for the task. During the time I lived in the Ullvarr village, he told neighboring tribes about me. He tried to use the legend of SnowFire to rally support for his cause. And he was evidently succeeding. He even planned to convince the Kastadi Chief, but the Gulstaa attacked before he could attempt that."

When Erica finished speaking, Evtaz slammed her fist on the table. Holtaz looked incensed. Pamela ate her stew, all the while keeping her head lowered.

"This Daraz was cunning . . . but he had no honor," Evtaz replied derisively. "He put his own interests above those he was supposed to protect. The community you lived in was very different from ours."

"That is true," Erica said as she lifted her bowl to her lips once more. The stew was still warm and tasted just as good as before.

"What role did your mate have in the village, Eree-Kah?" Evtaz asked.

"He led the warriors," Erica responded.

Evtaz nodded. "I see. So, as Master Warrior, he would not have ascended to Chief."

"No, I suppose not. Why do you ask?"

Evtaz took one more sip from her cup and smiled at Erica.

"Did you know that, once Daraz and so many others in the village perished, you became Chieftess of that Ullvarr tribe's survivors?"

"What? Wouldn't that title go to Pamela, if anyone?"

"You said she was a child below the Age of Emergence," Evtaz replied. Then she shook her head. "She could not have become Chieftess."

Erica was confused by this revelation. "How could we be a tribe of three?"

"A tribe can be two or sometimes even one. But it will not stay that way. You are no longer a tribe of three. You and your mate had two children. Do all of your children have children?"

Erica nodded.

"Eree-Kah, you taught your children the Ullvarr language and culture," Evtaz continued. "You could have taught them the ways of the Mokta or even the world you came from. Whether you meant to or not, you fulfilled your role with your small family tribe. You created an Ullvarr legacy to be proud of."

20

SERENITY

PASTOR IAN LANCASTER ENJOYED THE leisurely drive to Kayla Lewis' house. He was tall with broad shoulders and an average build, receding black and silver hair and small, rectangular spectacles with thin wire frames. He wore a light brown long-sleeved dress shirt, black tie with black slacks and dress shoes. Mina, his wife of twenty-eight years, sat in the passenger seat of the truck as it glided down the neighborhood streets. She was shorter and heavier than him, wearing a tan dress and black jacket that matched her husband's attire. They were in their late fifties.

It was cool outside, and the sky was overcast this late morning. Raindrops were occasionally sprinkling onto the windshield. Traffic was increasing as the lunch hour approached.

The pastor eased the vehicle to a stop before turning right onto the next street.

"Wait a moment," Mina urged. "I remember her late husband did have a sister, but didn't something happen to her?"

"She can tell us her story—whatever she's ready to share," he replied. "Sister Lewis says her sister-in-law's been through a lot and is seeking the Lord."

Mina nodded and then closed her eyes. Ian heard her whispering a prayer.

Soon, the pastor pulled into Kayla's driveway and parked next to her car. He grabbed a blue umbrella from the back of the cab and extended it upwards as he walked around the truck to open the passenger side door for his wife. They walked up the driveway towards the front door and he rang the doorbell. A few seconds later, Jo happily invited them both inside and offered to store the umbrella for him. She looked relieved to see him and his wife.

Ian appreciated the warmth and coziness of the house. It was an immediate and pleasant refuge from the damp chill outside. He could smell a hint of cinnamon in the air. Was that from tea or maybe a candle? Soft instrumental classical guitar music was playing at a low volume as they passed through the hallway towards the living room.

Kayla and a woman he'd never met sat on the couch in the living room. Both women stood up and walked over to greet him and his wife. Kayla's eyes were filled with pride and excitement. He assumed Jo's son, Ethan, was at school.

"Brother Lancaster, thank you so much for coming," Kayla said warmly as she shook his hand. "This is my sister-in-law, Jordan Lewis."

Ian immediately noticed the resemblance between Jordan and her brother, mostly in the eyes and cheeks. He was slightly surprised to see that hers bore scars, as did her hands. A great sadness radiated from her, despite her attempt at a smile. She had a unique presence, silent yet powerful, like a figure of authority. Her gaze was humble and inquisitive at the same time.

"Hello, Miss Lewis," he made eye contact and shook hands with her. She seemed like she was unfamiliar with the tradition. "I'm Ian Lancaster and this is my wife, Mina."

Mina shook Jordan's hand as well, after greeting Jo and Kayla.

"I'm the pastor at Agape's Promise, a church here in Chase Creek," he continued. "I understand you're Mark's sister?"

"I am Jordan Lewis. Mark was my brother, yes."

"He was a faithful Christian and a good friend. I miss him a great deal."

"Thank you," Jordan replied.

"How about we sit down? Could you tell me about yourself and why you wanted to meet with me?"

"All right." Jordan replied as Jo received a text and stepped out of the room to respond.

"Why don't we sit down in the living room?" Kayla suggested. "Would anyone like some water, tea or coffee?"

"Could I have some tea?" Mina asked.

"I would like some water please," Ian replied.

Jordan shook her head at Kayla.

Ian and his wife sat on the couch with Jordan. After Kayla returned with the drinks, she pulled up a chair. Jo joined them around the same time, grabbing another chair for herself and sat by her mother.

Ian couldn't help but notice the strange-looking metal box on the coffee table in front of the couch. Jordan opened it and removed some thin metal tablets.

"Before I begin, I wanted to show you these," she said. "This box and its contents are why I first came to see Kayla."

Jordan offered one of the tablets to the pastor. He was reluctant to receive it at first. It gave him an odd feeling, even before he touched it. He didn't recognize the writings on it, which seemed almost like a form of hieroglyphics but in a language he had never seen before. It looked incredibly old.

"What is this? It looks like something from a museum."

"That box has been in our family for generations," Jordan responded. "My mother once said that her father gave it to her. Kayla told me that after my mother passed away, Mark gave it to her. I believe it was sealed at least one thousand years ago. I recently discovered a way to open it and found these tablets inside."

"That . . . is fascinating. But I don't understand; why are you sharing this with us?" Ian interjected.

"I shared it with you because this is proof that what I am about to tell you is real and not imagination," Jordan replied. "Both Kayla and her daughter also know my truth. They have witnessed it with their own eyes."

"We did, Brother Lancaster," Kayla confirmed. "Jo and I can vouch for Jordan."

"Yes, sir," Jo added with a nod.

The conversation was getting stranger and more interesting by the moment, Ian thought. Inwardly, he prayed for guidance and wisdom.

"Please continue," he added. "What is your truth, Jordan?"

"I was born on Earth and Mark was my brother. But when I was seventeen, my mother and I were abducted by what you would call space aliens. We were stranded on a faraway world called Algoran, an Earth-like planet. My mother lost her sight there from an illness."

"I met your mother once or twice, when Jo was still little," Ian said. "I thought she had always been blind. How did she come back?"

"The same beings who took her returned her as well."

"Did they also bring you back?"

"No," Jordan replied. "I came back on my own, months later."

Kayla's eyes brightened at that and she fidgeted with her bracelet, whispering some quick commands to it. A moment later, a still image flickered into existence several inches above her wrist. She turned so everyone could see it.

"Mark insisted on taking pictures while Jordan was with us again!" Kayla near-gushed in excitement. "I made sure to make permanent digital copies. These are from fifty years ago!"

It took a moment for the pastor to realize that the young woman was Jordan and the teenager arm-in-arm with her was a grinning Mark Lewis. The Jordan in the photo had striking long blue hair and icy blue eyes. She was also wearing some kind of animal skins and furs that made her look like a warrior. But the scars on her face and hands were the same. Somehow, this was the same woman.

That picture faded and another one appeared. This one included a teenaged Kayla, Mark's parents and a plump young woman with dark hair that Ian didn't recognize. Kayla showed them a few more images and then turned off the holo-display.

"Jordan only stayed for a couple of days," Kayla clarified. "Then we all watched her walk through a portal of light to go back to Algoran."

The pastor looked upward for a moment and closed his eyes.

"Canst thou bind the sweet influences of Pleiades, or loose the bands of Orion? Canst thou bring forth Mazzaroth in his season?" Ian said. "Or canst thou guide Arcturus with his sons? Knowest thou the ordinances of heaven? canst thou set the dominion thereof in the earth?"

Jordan looked at him quizzically.

"Is that also from the Bible?" she asked.

"Yes, it is, from the book of Job," Ian replied. "God was reminding Job that He—that God was the one who created and has power over everything in the Earth and the heavens, even the constellations in the sky. God is everywhere. If He wished for there to be life on some other world, it is within His power to do so. And if He wanted to allow travel between two worlds, then it could happen."

Ian glanced at his wife, who appeared somewhat pale and astonished.

"Are you all right, Mina?" he asked.

"Yes," she replied. "This is just a lot to take in."

"I am sorry, Mrs. Lancaster," Jordan said. "I wish I could make this easier for you."

Somewhat recovered, Mina lifted her hand as if to deflect the notion.

"It's all right, Jordan. You've been through much more than I have. I'll be fine."

Jordan nodded. "Okay."

"Could you tell me about your experiences on that other world, Jordan?" Ian asked. "I would really like to know."

———

For the next hour and forty-five minutes, Jordan told the pastor about her life on Algoran, the influence of SnowFire and the ways that God had blessed her, her family, and the Mountain Mokta tribe over the last forty years. She also admitted her mistakes and terrible failures. And then she explained about the return of the Onchei. She shared how, in looking for a way to save the Mokta, she learned the old story that led her back to Earth. And finally, she related the miracle that God did in restoring her humanity. When she was done, she looked emotionally spent but also relieved.

"Thank you for being open to me about your life, Jordan," Ian said. "By faith, I believe that you're telling me the truth."

Jordan smiled and then looked down. "Thank you."

The pastor grabbed his Bible from the coffee table and opened it.

"In Second Peter, the Word of God reads 'The Lord is not slack concerning his promise, as some men count slackness; but is long-suffering to us-ward, not willing that any should perish, but that all should come to repentance,'" Ian said. "Jordan, the Lord has allowed you to make a home on Algoran, but He made a way for you to come back here to hear the Gospel and learn about the salvation He offers."

"Yes."

She had no reason to disagree with what he said. It sounded like truth. She didn't know much about pastors or church. But she instinctively wanted to hear what this man had to say. He had a kindness in his eyes and a compassion that reminded her of Dad. He spoke convincingly without seeming imposing.

Pastor Lancaster quickly flipped through the pages to another location.

"In Romans it is written, 'But what saith it? The word is nigh thee, even in thy mouth, and in thy heart: that is, the word of faith, which we preach; That if thou shalt confess with thy mouth the Lord Jesus, and shalt believe in thine heart that God hath raised him from the dead, thou shalt be saved. For with the heart man believeth unto righteousness; and with the mouth confession is made unto salvation. For the scripture saith, Whosoever believeth on him shall not be ashamed. For there is no difference between the Jew and the Greek: for the same Lord over all is rich unto all that call upon him. For whosoever shall call upon the name of the Lord shall be saved.'"[2]

2 Romans 10:8-13

He looked at Jordan. It seemed like he wanted to confirm that she understood what he was saying. She nodded happily. She had never heard anything like these words before, but she accepted them. She scooted closer to her couch seat's edge, wanting to hear more.

"'How then shall they call on him in whom they have not believed?'" the pastor continued. "'And how shall they believe in him of whom they have not heard? and how shall they hear without a preacher? And how shall they preach, except they be sent? as it is written, How beautiful are the feet of them that preach the gospel of peace, and bring glad tidings of good things!'"

Pastor Lancaster gazed at Jordan sympathetically. "Jordan Lewis, what is it that you're seeking right now?"

He did not have to wait long for her answer. She was calm. She felt like the words were already inside her, waiting to be spoken.

"I want this Jesus to save me," she said.

The pastor relaxed and smiled. He explained a few things to her and then she got down on her knees in front of the couch, resting her elbows on the couch pillows. The pastor prayed aloud next to her and encouraged her to do the same. Jordan noticed Kayla, Jo and the pastor's wife looked like they were already silently praying. She closed her eyes and began her own prayer.

Jesus, I know now that You are the Son of God. You were in heaven with God, but You were born on Earth long ago. You lived a sinless life, yet You died for my sins and were brought back to life by God. You were the one I saw on the Mokta Mountain, the One Who made me human again the first time. You and Your Father have saved my life many times. Even though I have anger and hate, even though I am a killer, You watched over me and took care of me from across the stars. You are everywhere and can do anything. I am so sorry for all I have done wrong, all my sins. I ask You to forgive me and send Your Holy Spirit into my heart. Help me, please!

A span of heartbeats passed. She could feel herself starting to shake from fear and worry.

But then a stillness descended on the room. All talking and movement stopped. And for the first time in over forty years, Jordan felt that peaceful calm from the mountain. There was no glowing man this time, no voice of an angel. Instead, the serenity she felt all around her became a part of her, enveloped her in love and joy, and began healing her from the inside.

She opened her eyes in amazement, no longer feeling weak at all. She laughed giddily as she stood up, almost like the teen she had been before ever leaving Earth.

"Jordan?" Kayla asked. She had been quietly standing close by.

"His spirit is here!" Jordan exclaimed, her eyes warm, soft and tearful. She pointed at her heart and smiled. "I feel it!"

21

FAMILY OF TWO WORLDS

When the dust settled and he'd recovered his senses from the eighteen-foot drop straight onto his back, Arrow saw the light of the twin stars and was overjoyed. He sat up and looked for his traveling companions. Maska was getting to her feet already but Zeetra looked like she was in some pain. Arrow stood up and went to help her.

"Are you all right?" he asked, extending a hand to her.

She grimaced as she forced herself to sit up and take his proffered hand. He helped her stand, but she started limping with her left leg as they moved forward a few steps.

"Somewhat. My hip is not well-padded," Zeetra remarked with a self-deprecating expression. "Hopefully, it is just a bruise."

They were towards the edge of the Mountain Mokta village, its familiar huts within sight and their neighbors approaching, looking amazed and excited. He was momentarily delighted to see the Mountain itself, the familiar greenery and the tisa birds in the air. The chill was almost as intoxicating as it was welcome.

"We will get you to the healer," Maska said, concerned.

"First, we must get to the Chieftess," Zeetra interjected. "I have important information for her."

Jasta cleared her throat nearby. "Then tell me, Zeetra."

Arrow understood Zeetra's confusion when she saw his sister. She had not been told of her rise to Chieftess yet. His torkomm, Bopol, was standing at her side, both as advisor and protector. Arrow could see the pride in the man's eyes, the subtle smile that conveyed his satisfaction that Arrow and Maska had returned safely.

Many villagers had now gathered around, but Jasta held up a hand, silencing them. She turned with hand still extended and gave a gentle pushing motion once, indicating that this conversation was private. The bystanders walked away and went about their business. Arrow was impressed with the respect his sister now commanded as Chieftess. Clearly, Maska and Zeetra were as well.

"Jasta? I do not understand," Zeetra asked. "Where is your gemta?"

"She needed to go to Earth to retrieve something. She made me Chieftess in her absence," Jasta replied. "And she has not returned yet."

That alarmed Arrow and Maska. "It is well past the deadline she told us!" Arrow interjected. "Something must have gone wrong."

Arrow could see the deep worry now showing in Torkomm's eyes. Then Arrow turned to the Chieftess.

"I agree, brother. We should hear what Zeetra has to tell us, then you should go to Earth and bring Gemta back."

Arrow nodded enthusiastically. "I will bring back Gemta!"

"And I will go with him," Maska insisted.

He looked at Maska quizzically.

"You know that your mate will blame me if anything happens to you," Maska added. "Besides, I care for your gemta also!"

"Of course," Arrow agreed. Then he turned to look at his sister. "Maska and I will do as you have commanded, Chieftess."

"Good," Jasta said. "Now Zeetra, tell us your news. Then I will take you to the healer."

Arrow noted that Torkomm appeared briefly pleased that Arrow and Maska were finally getting along.

Zeetra explained to Jasta what she had learned while on the Onchei spaceship. She told her about the colony's population and their current level of technology. Then she informed them about the political leader she had met, her conversation with him and the true threat her race posed to the Mountain Mokta.

"By now, the Ruling Council will have contacted the second ship, the one that was already on its way here," Zeetra continued. "It has powerful enough weapons to destroy the mountain itself and us on it."

Hearing these words, Jasta clenched her fists and raised them to chest level. She looked fierce and determined, possessing a confidence that surprised Arrow. Then he noticed a slight glow to her eyes and felt raw power emanating from her. He had to step back—it was a little troubling to see this manifested. Part of him wondered if she was ready for such a responsibility. But he knew that now was not the time for second guessing. She was Chieftess and he needed to believe in her. He made effort to put his doubts and worries aside.

"The Qui Tol can come to our land, but they will not step foot on this Mountain or harm one person," Jasta declared, sounding as though she had more than one voice. "Or I will finish what Gemtabana started!"

"Chieftess," Torkomm said as calmly as he could. "I suggest you conserve your energy until the Qui Tol arrive."

Jasta closed her eyes and mastered her emotions once more. She took in several deep breaths and released them slowly. Soon she opened her eyes and looked at Arrow.

"Arrow, you and Maska should leave at once to retrieve Gemta. I will put our scouts on high alert. They will tell me when the Qui Tol are approaching. I will do what must be done here. Find and protect Gemta and bring her back to us as soon as you can."

Arrow bowed respectfully. "You have my word, Chieftess. We will do as you have said."

Jasta turned to her torkomm. "Since Arrow is taking the only teleport device, we do not have time for a full evacuation. Our javelins will be of no use against the Qui Tol ship, so have the warriors bring the people to the nearby caves for shelter and guard them as best they can. I will defend the Mountain itself."

"Yes, Chieftess," Torkomm replied.

———————

Zeetra tapped on Arrow's shoulder. He turned to see what she wanted.

"I would ask you this, Arrow: How did you and Maska find me and work the device to bring us back home?"

"Maska woke up the device." His reply prompted a confused expression from Zeetra. "She talked to it for three days until it began to respond to our questions and commands."

"I was bored," Maska half-jested. "I borrowed it from Arrow and pretended like it was my friend. I named it Giskol."

"Shy?" Zeetra repeated, translating the word.

"It did not respond at first, so it seemed shy, yes," Maska said.

"You have a healthy imagination," Zeetra retorted.

"You are just now learning this?" Maska laughed, patting Zeetra on the back a few times. "We will speak about that someday soon, friend Zeetra!"

While Maska and Zeetra had been talking, Arrow had told the device to locate Earth and scan for his gemta's lifesigns. The device was having trouble locating her, based on previous readings of Jordan SnowFire. He told it to locate the position she had traveled to three weeks ago instead and the device succeeded. On his command, the device opened a portal to that destination.

"Maska, we have to go!" he shouted.

Arrow waited until Maska sprinted right up to him, then they both entered the portal together.

The pastor and his wife had left a few hours earlier. Grandma and Mom were talking in the kitchen. Ethan walked up to Great Aunt Jordan, who was looking at the framed photos on a nearby wall.

"Excuse me . . . um, Jordan?" Ethan said sheepishly. "Can I talk with you a minute?"

His great aunt turned and smiled warmly. "Of course. What did you want to talk about?"

He stretched out his hand to her, clearly nervous. She took it calmly.

"It will be easier for me to show you, okay?" he replied. She nodded.

He led her back to his room. On his study desk were two thin electronic tablets. One was larger than the other and had some kind of artwork displayed on its screen. The other was the one he had been writing so much on before. Peering at the large tablet, she lightly gasped when she saw the artwork.

"You have drawn the SnowFire gems—and me when I was a young woman?"

"Yes."

"You are very talented, Ethan. But why did you do this?"

He took a deep breath and mustered his courage. "It's because I want to tell your story to the world. I think you have had an incredible life, a powerful testimony—one that people could learn from. And I—I'm a writer. I know I'm young and I'm not very good right now. But if you give me your permission to do this, I'll take my time and get it right. I won't release it until the Lord shows me it's good enough."

The older woman seemed moved by his words and more than a little embarrassed. She looked into his eyes for several seconds. Then she smiled again.

"You believe what you're saying," Jordan responded. "You have a lot of faith. I have witnessed that God honors such faith. And I believe He will honor your intent. So yes, I give you my permission. I wish I could read it when you finish."

"You could always come back?" Ethan suggested. But Jordan shook her head.

"When I go to Algoran this time, I will not be back. Also, I am old now. Each new day I see will be a cherished gift. You should take your time with this and enjoy it. I believe in you."

Her words made him happy and sad at the same time. He wasn't sure what else to say.

"Storytelling among the Mokta is a precious skill taught to all," Jordan added. "They have no written language, so they have preserved their history and culture through stories and songs. You would be very welcome in my tribe, though your place is here. I want you to know that."

"Thank you!"

She hugged him and then kissed his cheek. "And you have my thanks as well, Ethan. I will let your mother and grandmother know that I approve of your book."

It was night when Maska and Arrow fell from the opening in the sky. Instinct kicked in and she landed in a crouching position, like a feline. She was relieved when Arrow also alighted without harm. She thought this place was not as cold as Algoran but had a far better atmosphere than the blazing temperatures of the Qui Tol colony. There was only one moon in the evening sky. She noted that there were avian, insects, and other forms of animals around them.

She and Arrow stood on a wide road made of some kind of dark, hard rock material and they were surrounded by strange-looking buildings that had oddly-placed, colored lighting. She saw humans nearby pointing at them and speaking in an unfamiliar language. No doubt they were alerted by the shining portal before it closed. And there were rounded objects floating above the ground which had lights of their own, making an odd humming sound as they moved.

"We must find shelter before we find Gemta," Arrow advised.

Maska's eyes darted around and she spotted a two-story building made of bricks with metal steps decorated by a metal fence which led to the roof. She nodded at Arrow and pointed towards the building before dashing in that direction. They were better able to observe the area without further detection from this vantage point.

"This was a good choice," Arrow whispered.

"But how will we find your gemta?" Maska whispered back.

"The SnowFire gems! The device should be able to easily find those; there should not be any here besides hers."

Maska was impressed with his reasoning. "Giskol, find any SnowFire gems near us."

"Working," the device announced in a male voice speaking Mokta.

Several seconds later, Giskol made two quick beeps, indicating it had results.

"Two SnowFire gems are located two-point-seven baas from here," Giskol reported, using the Mokta word for mile. "This map will take you there in the shortest amount of time."

"Thank you, friend Giskol," Maska said. The machine beeped once in response.

They had to avoid being seen, but their night vision was excellent and both were fast and agile. They had gained a lot of practice at prowling and avoiding detection by the Qui Tol over the last few weeks. This world had many more places to hide and hardly anyone knew they were here.

———————

Jordan had just finished setting the dinner table while Kayla prepared salad in a large bowl in the kitchen. Through the large window nearby, she observed Jo and Ethan grilling burgers and hot dogs in the backyard. Jordan smiled at the sight of them. The aroma of cooked meat, spices, and burning charcoal were also appetizing. Jo had some music playing that Jordan didn't recognize, but the words of the songs were about God and Jesus. Jordan vaguely recalled that this kind of music was called "country." It seemed to fit the mood of their gathering.

"Remember the last time I was here, Kayla? It was me and Dad cooking the food on the grill," Jordan said. "This time I get to see your daughter and grandson doing the same."

Kayla chuckled without looking up. "Thanks for reminding me how old we are . . . again."

"We have a saying in my village. In English, it would be 'The generations are joyful.' By that, it means we can take pride in our family, knowing we will go on. All of us have limited time on our worlds."

"Are you sure about that?" Kayla asked with some amusement. "Until the Lord's miracle, you seemed like you were immortal."

Jordan considered Kayla's point a moment.

"I do not think I was immortal," Jordan replied pleasantly. "It is true that I could have lived a long time, even two or three hundred years. But that is not immortal. I would have eventually grown old and died. But I am glad for the Lord's miracle. This is my age. It is who I am supposed to be."

Kayla nodded. "I'm glad for both of the Lord's miracles."

"Both?"

"God made you human again and He gave you salvation."

"I see! Yes, you are right, Kayla."

―――――――

An hour later, Arrow and Maska located the large wooden hut where Giskol had indicated the SnowFire gems were. They were across the road from that domicile, hiding in the shadow of another large residence. Arrow was using Giskol to take additional readings while Maska studied their surroundings. She smelled meat being cooked near the rear of their destination, which was surrounded by a wooden fence and grass that was a sickly deep green. There were a few trees with the odd verdant leaves in the front and one in the back. One of the round objects was at rest on the ground in front of that hut.

She heard several voices talking, sounding jovial. There was also some kind of music being played, but she didn't recognize the style or understand the words being sung. But one thing she could pick out among the sounds was the voice of Arrow's gemta.

"Arrow, listen! Your gemta is over there!" she whispered.

She watched him close his eyes and concentrate. Then his eyes popped open. He immediately darted towards the hut. Maska spotted one of the strange round objects moving towards him. If it struck him, she did not think he would survive. So, she got a running start and hurled herself towards Arrow with all her might, propelling them both towards the other side of the road. The round object came within inches of them. It screamed at them with a shrill noise. As they hurtled through the air, she pulled Arrow into a protective embrace. But his head briefly scraped against the road's surface before they landed in the grass.

Maska shook off her disorientation and wanted to make sure Arrow was okay. He was bleeding from a small gash near his right eye, but not badly. Lying on his back, he looked stunned and barely conscious. He was breathing normally. She had scrapes on her arms and face that she knew would quickly heal.

The object they had avoided had stopped and there were people inside. Maska could see them clearly and they sounded concerned.

"I wish I could understand them," she whispered. Immediately, she heard Giskol beep.

"Are you two all right?" Giskol said, repeating the words of the human woman in the Mokta language.

Would it tell them what she said?

"We are okay," Maska said. A heartbeat later, Giskol repeated her words in English.

Maska could see an adult woman and a girl in her teens inside the object. They both had similar skin color to Arrow's gemta and Eree-Kah SnowFire. They looked alike in their faces and hair color. Perhaps they were gemta and daughter? Maska realized that the object seemed to be for their transportation.

Maska sensed movement behind her. As she turned her head, she saw several people approaching the street from the destination hut. Most of them kept a safe distance but an older woman with long gray hair started running towards them, a look of alarm on her face. She looked familiar somehow. When the woman reached them, she fell to her knees next to Arrow and gently, even lovingly put her hand to his head.

"Arrow? Maska, what happened to my son?" she exclaimed in Mokta.

Maska's jaw dropped.

"Chieftess? Is that you?" Maska could not believe her eyes. "We—we were sent to bring you back. Arrow did not see the object with the people inside, so I—protected him. I do not think he is badly injured."

"Thank you, Maska! Thank you so much!"

The former Chieftess cradled her son's upper body in her arms, crying from relief and joy. Arrow stirred; no doubt jostled by his gemta's movements. He opened his eyes.

"Gem . . . ta? What happened to me?" His eyes widened and his face seemed more alert. "And what has happened to you?"

"Maska saved your life. I am so happy to see you both! I will explain in a minute."

The adult female stepped out of the object, which was still hovering above the ground with her daughter inside. The short and stout woman had shoulder-length hair the color of grain. She wore thick blue clothing and a matching head covering. The human woman approached them cautiously. She held both arms close to her chest and took small steps forward. Her eyes were apprehensive, made moreso when she got a close look at Maska and Arrow.

"What's going on here? Are you two really okay?" the woman said.

The daughter exited the object then. She was tall, thin and wore much brighter clothing. She was not scared, and her eyes were riveted on Maska.

"Don't you recognize her, Mom?" the teen said. "She's dressed up like Mikoto from 'Super-Advanced Monster Racing Squadron Gamma!'"

"That's one of the anime holos you watch, Carolyn?" her mother asked.

"It's only the most popular anime in the world right now!" Carolyn insisted, sounding insulted. "She's even imitating speaking in an alien language—because she's an alien, duh. And she's even got a working mega-translator!"

What is this child talking about? Maska frowned at them.

Carolyn walked up to Maska, completely awed and unafraid. Maska decided to remain perfectly still, unsure what to do or say.

"You are so tomorrow! How did you get your make-up so perfect?" Carolyn asked. "And your eyes—are they holograms or some kind of whole eye contact lenses? They should utterly give you the role for the live action holo!"

Maska waited for the translation to finish. She made what she hoped was a calming smile as she looked right at the teen.

"Thank you. But I . . . cannot reveal my secrets," Maska said.

Carolyn thought about Maska's words and then nodded before she winked. "Right! I understand."

Inwardly, Maska sighed with relief.

"Can I give you some advice?" Carolyn asked.

"Yes?"

"Your clothes don't really match Mikoto's. Your colors are reversed, and she wears a skirt," Carolyn asserted. "But everything else is freeze and sky!"

"Freeze and sky?" Maska considered with a raised eyebrow.

The former Chieftess helped steady Arrow as he stood up. Then she approached the driver.

"I am sorry for this. My son did not see your vehicle. But he will be fine. We should not take up anymore of your time."

Jordan's words were correct. Arrow's SnowFire blood could heal almost any injury at an extraordinary rate.

"It's okay. I'm just glad I didn't hit him and that everyone's okay," the driver replied. "And Carolyn, my daughter, is clearly fascinated with your son's friend. But are you sure we don't need to take him to the hospital? I'd be glad to—"

"Thank you but that really is not necessary," the former Chieftess interrupted with a sweet voice. "He just needs some rest. He'll be okay by tomorrow."

"A-all right," the woman replied. "Then we have to go."

The woman dragged her daughter away from Maska and they drove off.

Jordan motioned to Arrow and Maska to come to her and they did.

"We need to go inside before anyone else sees you," Jordan urged, looking at each of them. "You were fortunate this time. Humans do not know there is life on other worlds yet."

"Why were they not scared of us?" Arrow asked as they began to walk towards Kayla's house.

"And what is 'ah-nee-may'?" Maska wondered, following them.

Jordan motioned to Kayla, Jo, and Ethan to come closer. They had been standing by patiently but looked unsure of what to do or how to help. Jordan allowed herself a sigh of relief, knowing things could have gone considerably worse. Ethan stared in amazement and perhaps a touch of fear while Kayla and Jo were clearly curious now.

"This is my son, Arrow, and his friend, Maska," Jordan announced in English. Then she turned to Arrow and Maska and spoke in Mokta. "This is my brother's mate, Kayla Lewis, her daughter, Jo, and grandson, Ethan."

Maska and Arrow looked somewhat nervous around the family members they had never met before. Jordan ushered everyone inside the house, being both pleasant and insistent simultaneously. Once they reached the living room, Maska spoke up.

"Giskol, will you translate for us again?" Maska asked, holding the teleport device in her hand. Giskol beeped in response. "I think it would be good if we could understand each other, yes?"

After hearing the translation, Kayla nodded. "Yes, it would. We are family after all."

"So, he got the blue hair, too—sort of?" Jo said nervously, looking at Arrow. "Definitely has your eyes."

"He has SnowFire's blood in his veins. So does Maska," Jordan added.

"Is she related, too?" Jo asked.

"Well, she is like family," Jordan replied with a maternal smile. "But my son gave her a blood transfusion as a child. The SnowFire blood saved her life . . . but it made her like us . . . like I was."

Jordan half-collapsed to a sitting position on the couch. Her adrenaline-fueled strength was fading fast and the collective stress of the last few minutes pressed down on her like a weight. Arrow was right there with her, offering emotional support while physically steadying her. He looked fearful for her, deeply concerned.

"I was so worried for you. I forgot I am not as strong as I used to be," she admitted.

"Gemta, what has changed?" Arrow asked. "In all my life, I have only noticed subtle changes in your appearance from the passage of time. But now, this is . . . it is hard to see you so changed, so frail. Is your life force fading? Are you going to . . . die?"

Jordan put her arm around her son, leaning into him. As tired as she felt, it was wonderful to have him at her side again. But she couldn't fully indulge those feelings.

"A miracle, Arrow. I can only call it a miracle. The God I pray to, He took the SnowFire blood from my veins and restored me to how I was before. I look and feel like a woman my age now. I am mortal again, like your torkomm. But I will continue living awhile longer, just as he will."

Arrow stared at her in disbelief, his mouth gaping for a moment. "You told us that even SnowFire could not restore you!" Arrow asserted. "Your—your God is that powerful?"

Jordan smiled at him. "Oh yes! There is nothing He cannot do. He has even given me peace in my soul, a peace I never could have imagined."

Arrow nodded slowly. "Then I am happy for you, Gemta."

"I am happy, too. I want to get back home to see your children. And be there when your first grandchild is born."

Arrow blinked a few times in surprise. "What?"

"Meespa and her mate are expecting, my son," she said with a grin. "I am so happy for you!"

Jordan noticed Maska smile briefly but kept her attention on Arrow. He smiled very briefly then became serious again.

"Thank you. But before we return home, I must ask: Did you accomplish your task here on Errrth?"

Jordan nodded. "I did. I have the Qui Tol artifact. I opened it and have seen its contents. It is everything we need to stop them."

Arrow now looked even more delighted than before. "That is great news!"

"And Zeetra?" Jordan asked, looking concerned.

"She is at the village, reunited with her family," he confirmed.

She put her hand to her chest in relief. "Also good news."

Then Arrow looked nervous, as if recalling something important. A somberness descended on him. "The Qui Tol have another spaceship, Gemta. And they are sending it to destroy the entire Mountain."

Jordan stood straight up, despite her exhaustion. "Then we must go back now! I can stop them—and I will stop them!"

ACT FIVE

DELIVERANCE

22

PROTECTING THE VILLAGE

THE *AMZATAR* ARRIVED AT THE Mountain Mokta village faster than the scouts could. Within seconds, its shadow had covered the entire mountain and part of the valley. Chieftess Jasta SnowFire stood outside the Chieftess' hut, her torkomm a few feet away, staring skyward. His face was unflinching, but his eyes were wide in astonishment as he clenched his fists. Was that frustration or terror? This massive vessel was horrifying. Her neck was beginning to strain from stretching backward as she peered up at it.

Many of the villagers were frozen in dread, gazing helplessly at the spaceship. No one spoke. What was there to say or do? It was clear that their javelins could not be thrown high enough to reach it. And even if they could, what harm could they inflict?

Zeetra walked closer to the Chieftess, accompanied by one of her younger grandsons. They stopped and looked up at the ship, then Zeetra glanced fearfully at Jasta, embodying the growing sense of despair that had filled the community. Villagers began to point, gasp, and scream when what appeared to be the vessel's weapon ports, clearly aimed at their village, started to glow with white-hot energy.

Seeing Zeetra's forlorn and powerless expression helped snap Jasta out of her momentary stupor. Peering at the similar expressions on everyone gathered outside reminded Jasta that her people needed her.

Had she not vowed to protect them as the Granddaughter of SnowFire? Where had her confidence and resolve gone? She felt ashamed for being so quickly petrified by an enemy.

I am Chieftess! I am the only one who can defend the Mokta.

With new determination, Chieftess Jasta instinctively lifted her arms at her sides. Her hair began to flicker like blue flames and her eyes glowed brightly.

I will protect my people! I will—PROTECT!

From every corner of the mountain, SnowFire gems ranging in size from pebbles to small boulders flew into the air. They converged into one solid blue shell above the mountain mere seconds before the spaceship fired its energy weapons.

When twin beams struck on opposite sides of the SnowFire gem barrier, the force cracked but did not penetrate the shield. The ship fired again and again, splintering the shell, sending shards flying in all directions like shrapnel. But at Jasta's mental command, those pieces slowed in mid-air, never endangering her people or their homes. The fragments flew back together to reform the protective screen over the village repeatedly each time.

Mentally, that effort was painful for Jasta. She squinted and clenched her jaw in response to her efforts. But the enemy's persistence was not wearing down her resolve, it was increasing it. It began to make her angry.

Enough defensive tactics! I will see how you deal with this!

With a turn of her right wrist and a slashing motion with her left hand, she intentionally shattered the SnowFire Shield into hundreds of thousands of pieces. Then those shards flew upwards in a frenzied blur towards the Qui Tol ship and smashed into all the weapon ports simultaneously in a barrage. Then Jasta directed them to shear away sections of the outer hull by battering them mercilessly. She soon determined that kind of attack would take hours. So, she pulled a portion of the gems into a massive spike and sent it through one of the six vital spinning parts, causing it to spark, spit fire, and belch smoke as it ceased to work.

She felt a surge of triumph as the battered ship began to very slowly retreat upwards towards the atmosphere.

"Chieftess!"

The voice belonged to Zeetra.

"Yes?" Jasta answered, not sure what to expect next.

Zeetra was excitedly pointing at something behind them. Jasta and her father turned and saw a teleportation portal shining and pulsating with energy several hundred feet away. Seconds later, she saw her brother and Maska emerge. There was also another woman, a silver-haired human who was carrying a gray rectangular object and wearing a brown satchel bag attached to a strap over her left shoulder.

I sent them to find and bring back Gemta! Who is this elderly human female? Why would they—

Jasta gasped. As the trio got closer, she recognized her gemta even though she had drastically changed. Gemta looked decades older, tired, even somewhat frail. Jasta espied her torkomm next to her, squinting to look at the trio. A second later, he clearly identified Gemta as well, blinking several times in confusion. Then he ran in her direction.

The villagers were talking among themselves, some cheering at the Chieftess' actions while others held their loved ones close. Some seemed to be waiting to see what the Chieftess would do next, including Zeetra and her grandson.

Above them, the crippled ship continued to sluggishly ascend. Jasta ran and embraced Gemta as well, who welcomed her affection.

"I see I was correct to make you Chieftess," Gemta said proudly. "I do not know how you did so much damage to that giant ship, but I am impressed. You have done well!"

"Gemta, I am so pleased you are alive! But how—why—are you like this?"

Gemta briefly lost her footing. Jasta moved to help her but Torkomm was already there. He picked up Gemta in his arms, equally concerned. Gemta looked at him lovingly for a heartbeat then focused on Jasta again.

"It would take time we do not have for me to explain, Chieftess," Gemta said. "We can discuss this more after the crisis has passed. Somehow, I have to talk with the Qui Tol in command of that spaceship."

Zeetra cleared her throat and stepped forward. "I think I can help with that, Jordan. Arrow, could you hand me your teleporting device?"

Arrow had been holding onto the small metal mechanism since they arrived. He gave it to Zeetra.

"I can adjust this machine to let us speak with the spaceship," Zeetra continued. "It will just take me a few minutes."

———————

Jordan nodded at Zeetra and let her friend begin her adjustments to the device.

She looked up at her mate of forty-eight cycles and smiled. She reached out and touched his cheek with her hand. "I am home now," she said with great satisfaction.

Bopol held her closer to him, leaning his head forward to be near hers. His breathing told her that he was very emotional. His smile showed her how happy he was. It was invigorating just to experience this after being apart for weeks.

But then her sense of duty reasserted itself and Jordan peered over at Zeetra, who was waiting patiently.

"I did not know if I would ever see you or this world again," Zeetra stated. "Thank you for sending Arrow and Maska to bring me back."

"I would have gone myself if I could have," Jordan replied. "But I had to retrieve something from Earth."

Zeetra nodded. "I am glad you were successful. And I have configured the teleportation device to communicate on the same frequency as the *Amzatar* above us."

"Good," Jordan answered. She motioned for the Chieftess to join them, which she did. "Chieftess, here is what I need you to say to the Qui Tol on that spaceship . . . "

———

Commander Vizyel Agandif was having a terribly difficult time managing an impossible situation. Her ship, the *Amzatar*, was falling apart around her and a quarter of her crew was already dead. An untold number were injured, and the rest were frantically looking to her for answers when she had none. How did one of these Mokta brutes possess either the technology or the apparent supernatural power to take simple stones from the planet's surface and forge them into both an effective shield and offensive weapons? How could they do any damage at all to Zarmandoz's flagship, much less maul it like a wild animal, leaving it barely functional?

The control deck was in complete chaos. Half of the consoles were shorted out but there were not enough personnel to attend to the ones that were still operational. Most of her crew were putting out fires or trying to move the wounded to the medical bay. The air had an acrid tinge to it, quickly becoming toxic.

"Life support is damaged," Agandif told herself. "We cannot stay in orbit for long or head into space again without repairing it."

She fought a sense of anxiety that threatened to become a panic attack. Observing how badly her ship was damaged, it was a wonder that it was still airborne. She looked to her Mydzah, the Onchei second-in-command position.

"Mydzah, are the emergency teleport pods still functional?"

He checked his data pad and inputted several commands. The older man did not look pleased with the results. He looked at the Commander with regret.

"No, Commander. That system is offline."

"I see. What is the condition of our engines?"

"Faster-than-light is offline. Standard is operating at one-third capacity."

"Can you give me ramming speed?"

Her subordinate's eyes widened for a fraction of a second before he mastered his emotions, stiffening to attention.

"Yes, Commander. I can operate the engines myself if necessary."

"I may ask that of you. We will complete our mission, even if—"

Just then, one of the communications consoles sprung to life. An Onchei female appeared on the screen.

"Commander of the Onchei vessel," the woman said. "I am Zeetra Ketranos of Algoran. Please respond if you are able to."

Agandif seethed. Was a fellow Onchei responsible for their current crisis? Had they been betrayed by the person the *Kildee* had been sent to rescue?

"I should kill you and all of the filthy Mokta with what is left of this ship!" Agandif roared, no longer able to restrain herself.

"Your mission is a mistake, Commander. The Mokta did not slay our people here. They are not responsible in any way."

"I know the story you told them, traitor! Someone has to pay for murdering our people. The Mokta are clearly the ones who did it."

"You are wrong. We have proof that my fellow Onchei brought this on themselves."

Agandif wanted to laugh but she was too angry. All she wanted to do was smash something or have the satisfaction of wringing the neck of this arrogant woman on the screen. But her centuries of training pushed to the surface. She closed her eyes and attempted to calm herself once more.

"What proof?" Agandif demanded. "Show me."

"I will come to your vessel with one of the humans our people took from Earth," Zeetra replied. "She will show you our proof. We can teleport to your location shortly."

"Be warned, Zeetra. If I am not satisfied with your proof, I will kill you both myself."

"No. You won't. If you harm us in any way, the Chieftess of the Mountain Mokta has said she will finish what she started. Believe me when I say this: if she attacks, no one on your ship will survive. And neither will the ship itself."

By the time Zeetra finished speaking, Agandif hated her and the Mokta with all her heart. She could not stand feeling so strategically weak and defenseless. There was no way for her to take control of this situation with the resources she had.

"Bring your proof" was all she could manage to say in a low growl.

"Of course," Zeetra responded.

Then the screen went black. Commander Agandif closed her eyes, clenched her jaw, and tightened her fists at her sides with supreme effort.

23

BLAME

"WITH ALL DUE RESPECT, YOU are not going to that place unpro-
tected," Arrow insisted to his gemta.

"I am not going alone," Jordan answered with mock seriousness.
"I will have Zeetra."

"You will also have Arrow," Bopol interjected, his eyes most insistent towards Jordan.

"And me," Maska added as a fact, not as a suggestion, with her arms
crossed.

Jasta had led them here, inside the Chieftess' hut, mainly for
privacy but also to calm down and discuss the situation. The mid-
afternoon sunlight illuminated the room through its doorway.

Jordan wanted to embrace each of them. They were just as protective of her now as when she was Chieftess. Between Arrow and Maska,
she and Zeetra would be well-defended.

Jordan noticed Zeetra staring at the lid of the box brought back
from Earth, appraising it carefully.

"That box has Onchei symbols, though they are very old. Is that
what you went to Earth for, Jordan?" Zeetra asked.

"Yes. Have you ever heard any tales about 'The Disgrace of the Qui
Tol?'" Jordan replied.

Zeetra's eyes peered upward, reviewing her memories. Then she focused on Jordan and shook her head. "No, I have not."

"It is an ancient story about an artifact from the time of a Great War. No one knew what was inside the artifact, but it was hidden away and passed down from family to family for generations," Jordan continued. "Its contents were considered forbidden and the artifact's handlers were not allowed to know what was inside. What it contained was so dire that your people wanted to get rid of it, to the extent that they developed scanning equipment and teleport technology to send it to Earth about one thousand cycles ago."

Jordan took the lid off the box and showed the metal tablets inside to Zeetra and the others.

"This is that box," Jordan asserted. "And it was passed down through my family. My gemta was the last one to receive this."

That revelation was met with a mixture of amazement, fear, and some skepticism from those gathered.

"What do the tablets say?" Zeetra asked.

Commander Agandif felt as if she was wearing down the deck plates with her pacing. She grew more impatient and aggravated by the minute. The alarm klaxons were silent, but the operations deck was barely illuminated by the pale blue emergency lights. The temperature had risen even higher and the leftover smoke still made the air hazy and hard to breathe. She did not know how long they could remain aboard if conditions did not improve. And where was the Onchei woman who called herself Zeetra?

"'Shortly,' that traitor said. It feels like one-quarter dayturn!" Agandif grumbled.

"We have two of the strike fighters repaired and fueled, Commander," Rodim reported.

She thought about it for a moment and then shook her head. "No. I know it is a good plan. The fighters might even inflict significant losses," Agandif acknowledged. "But that sorceress of the Mokta would tear us to pieces in retaliation. We can't risk it. We have an uneasy truce and we should abide by it."

As she spoke, there was a brief flash on the other side of the room. When Agandif's vision focused again, she saw an old human woman with Zeetra and two strange-looking Mokta, probably warriors.

"You just saved your crew's life," the gray-haired woman said in Mokta.

"You are human," Agandif noted, also replying in Mokta.

The older woman began coughing from the tainted air. The male Mokta warrior immediately handed her the small satchel bag she'd brought with her. She breathed into it, which helped filter the harmful elements. After taking in several deep breaths, her coughing lessened. Agandif wondered why the fragile human was here. Why were they being so protective and even respectful to her?

"And you are observant, Captain," the other woman responded after a moment, her voice somewhat hoarse.

"Actually, she is a Commander," Zeetra whispered.

Agandif stiffened. At least Zeetra knew something about her people.

"I am Commander Agandif. Who are you?"

"I am Jordan Lewis. The Onchei took me from Earth fifty-two cycles ago."

Agandif knew the Onchei faction that remained on Algoran had a practice of experimenting with humans. She had believed such efforts were wasted but she had never openly opposed them prior to leaving to establish Zarmandos. Now she was facing one of the results of that Onchei faction's hubris.

"That is unfortunate but also irrelevant to our discussion," the commander rebuffed. "What is this proof you spoke of?"

Jordan glanced at Zeetra, who pulled a flat, tablet-shaped device from a small bag attached to her belt. Zeetra inputted a command. A second later, a hologram of the ancient box appeared above them, enlarged to show full detail. The hologram rotated to give a complete view of the object.

"This object is Onchei," Jordan declared. "It was created around the time of Algoran's Great War. It contained secrets so critical that some of your people hid them from the rest of Onchei society for over nine thousand cycles. They looked for another world and invented teleportation just to send it away . . . to Earth."

Agandif was skeptical. And yet, if any of Jordan's words were true, the implications they held could radically alter Onchei history. She decided to listen further.

"This was delivered to Earth one thousand cycles ago," Jordan continued. "The Onchei who took it there somehow managed to get a human family to guard it and pass it down to their descendants. My family. I brought this back here."

"What?" Agandif gasped. Then she calmed herself. "You . . . used our technology to go to Earth and back?"

"Yes," Jordan replied.

Agandif turned her gaze to Zeetra, who had clearly been sharing Onchei technology with these lesser species. She felt nothing but contempt for the traitor.

"So what?" Agandif said, still staring daggers at Zeetra.

After several seconds, Agandif returned her attention to Jordan, who crossed her arms. She returned Agandif's look with determined eyes that did not convey deception. If she was lying, she was quite accomplished at the skill.

"When your forces returned and took Zeetra to learn what had happened to the other Onchei on Algoran, I knew you would blame and threaten the Mokta." Jordan continued. "I searched for answers from the ancient stories and I learned about The Disgrace of the Qui Tol. I recognized the object described in the story, since it was in our home during my childhood. So, I went to Earth, located the box, and was able to open it. I now know its secrets."

From Agandif's experience, the Mokta were grand storytellers. Obviously, this human woman had learned how to weave a few tales herself. Yet there seemed enough truth to her story that she could not dismiss it outright. She needed to know more.

"The markings on this ancient container are clearly Onchei. And I know my own people's history well enough, human. Yet I have never heard of the Onchei sending anything to Earth," Agandif studied the markings some more. "What are these secrets you speak of?"

Jordan nodded at Zeetra, who pressed a button on the device. An image of one of the metal tablets replaced the one of the box. Jordan walked around to the right of it and pointed at the top of the vertical-facing tablet.

"This tablet contains the first of the forbidden knowledge that had to be sent away," Jordan told Agandif. "Ten thousand cycles ago, your people knew a way to extend their own lives. They would perform a particular method based on alchemy from that time. They would kill a victim and then incorporate their . . . vital fluids."

Agandif felt nauseated and disturbed by the very thought of this supposed practice. It went against everything she had been taught since her youth. How could any Onchei come up with such an unspeakable idea? And yet, here was a tablet with Onchei engravings that showed exactly how her people did this terrible thing.

"By the look on your face, you can understand why your people would want this knowledge suppressed," Jordan said.

Agandif slowly nodded.

Suddenly, an alarm klaxon made a shrill noise. It came to an abrupt stop as another console erupted with sparks and smoke. The lights on the console flickered before going dark. The woman who had been operating it stood up quickly but not fast enough to prevent burns to her right hand and arm. She cupped her injured hand and moved back.

"Assist her!" Agandif barked in the Onchei language to another crewman. "Re-route scanning operations to another station."

"Yes, Commander!" the crewman replied.

Agandif took in what breath she could, still fighting a sense of being overwhelmed. Then she looked at the human again.

"Even if what you say is true, what does this have to do with the attack that slaughtered the Onchei on Algoran?" Agandif asked.

"Zeetra, move to the next one," Jordan said.

Zeetra did as Jordan requested, though she had to wipe sweat from her forehead. Agandif was also perspiring and mentally noted how everyone on the *Amzatar* was suffering from the conditions on the ship.

"This should begin to explain that. Your people were thorough even back then," Jordan said. "They had rejected the forbidden ways but were still obsessed with extending Onchei life. They devised alternatives to pursue that same goal."

"Why?" Agandif asked. "We already live for nearly one thousand cycles."

The lighting flickered and went off for a few seconds. Agandif heard two of her crew frantically pushing buttons as they moved quickly across the operation deck. Soon, the emergency lighting resumed.

"Why does anyone want to live longer than their normal lifespan?" Jordan continued. "They were not satisfied. And learning the legends of SnowFire seemed to have started that particular fascination."

"SnowFire? She was just a Mokta story. You are saying my people were that superstitious?"

Jordan looked at her with a mixture of restraint and sadness. It was baffling to Agandif.

"SnowFire is real. She infused a portion of her own blood to me to keep me from an early death. So, in a sense, I became her daughter," Jordan said.

A metal object fell to the floor behind Agandif. When she turned, her Mydzah stood mid-deck, staring at Jordan in fear and awe. When he noticed Agandif peering at him, he quickly picked up the tool he'd dropped and went back to attempting repairs.

When Jordan had Agandif's attention once more, she pointed to the male warrior.

"Arrow is my son and SnowFire's grandson. The Mokta Chieftess who damaged your vessel is my daughter. She wields the power of Snow and Fire, which you have witnessed firsthand."

That is the source of her power? SnowFire? Agandif's thoughts raced. *Did the Onchei witness such power from her as she walked the land back then?*

She clasped her hands behind her back and looked downward.

I can see how they might have become obsessed with her!

She returned her gaze to Jordan. "The old stories said SnowFire was immortal."

"That is correct."

"You are not immortal."

"No," Jordan answered, shifting her weight with mild awkwardness. "Not anymore."

There was much more that Jordan was not telling her.

"Are your children immortal?" Agandif asked.

"They are long-lived. Arrow has seen forty-six cycles."

Agandif thought he barely looked twenty cycles.

Jordan turned her attention back to the hologram of the ancient metal tablet.

"Those Onchei words at the tablet's center declare that the key to extending their own lifespan was found in the genetic lineage of the Mokta."

The Mydzah walked over to the commander.

"Our life support is critically compromised, Commander," he told her. "At this rate, there is no way we can sufficiently repair it before it becomes completely nonfunctional. I have been getting reports of personnel losing consciousness in other, more heavily damaged, parts of the ship."

"Very well. Have those parts evacuated to less damaged sections," Agandif replied. "I will issue new orders shortly."

"Yes, Commander."

Agandif's options were extremely limited now. "We will need to finish this quickly, human," she said to Jordan. "Before we run out of air."

Jordan nodded. "I will keep this brief. Below this line in the center, you will see the description takes a strange turn. The Onchei planned to experiment with interbreeding the Mokta with other races on Algoran and eventually races from other worlds."

"What? Why? That would violate one of our most fundamental beliefs!" Agandif fumed in dismay. "Onchei do not believe in interbreeding, so why would our people impose it on other races? It is worse than hypocrisy!"

Zeetra shook her head in disapproval.

"You disagree?" Agandif scoffed.

"My mate is Mokta and my offspring are a blend of our races," Zeetra replied, holding her head up with pride. Her eyes seemed to challenge the Onchei commander.

Agandif's eyes narrowed as she looked at Zeetra with disgust. "Then you are even more of a traitor than I thought!"

Jordan cleared her throat loudly, getting both women's attention. Arrow and Maska, who had been watching the exchange with intrigue, also looked her way.

"These Onchei knew about SnowFire and her biological tie to the Mokta," Jordan added. "Old Mokta stories do tell of the Qui Tol taking Mokta from their homes. They say that some of those Mokta returned with bizarre stories about what happened to them. And there are many tales about when the Qui Tol started bringing humans to Algoran several hundred cycles ago. I am living proof of that."

Agandif leaned against one of the walls, feeling the effects of the lowered oxygen. She lowered her head in some small expression of shame at the tarnished and distressed state of her vessel. She motioned for her Mydzah to come over.

"Prepare the crew for evacuation to the surface," she said, leaning close and speaking for only him to hear. "It may be the only way to save the crew, if not the ship. And it will be more productive than these repairs."

"Yes, Commander. What will happen to the ship?"

"I cannot let any of its technology be taken. I will activate the disintegration protocols when the time comes."

"Yes, Commander."

Wistful at the necessity for such orders, she watched her second-in-command leave the operations area. Then she faced Jordan once more.

"The Onchei have been divided for a long time. There are those of us who believe in Onchei purity and self-reliance," she said. "The Purists, like myself, do not think the Onchei need any improvements."

She sighed. "Our differences became so strong that the Purists located a new world to colonize: Zarmandos," Agandif continued. "Everyone who stayed behind on Algoran did not support our views."

"They did more than that," Jordan interjected. "Zeetra, show the last hologram."

Zeetra entered a command to her device and the hologram shifted, changing to a different metal tablet. Agandif studied the markings on it while Jordan remained silent. It was baffling. She squinted and tilted her head as she gazed at the hologram, trying to verify that her eyes and understanding of the Onchei language were not deceiving her.

"You are not misreading the symbols," Jordan finally said. "The Onchei's last plan, if all else failed, was to gather SnowFire gems. They wanted to use them to call SnowFire herself and request her presence. They wanted to make her do their bidding."

"But—why?" Agandif wondered.

"Your people followed every other step in these tablets. Perhaps one of them still remembered this information, I do not know," Jordan answered. "If they somehow managed to contact SnowFire through the gems . . . well, knowing her as I do . . . "

Jordan closed her eyes and appeared on the verge of passing out from exhaustion. Her son quickly helped steady her. She took a few deep breaths and looked at him assuredly, smiling weakly. The heat was now becoming oppressive and the air even thinner. Everyone was perspiring and visibly more sluggish, bordering on miserable.

"What would SnowFire do if my people did try to contact her through those gemstones?" Agandif asked.

"Zeetra, you were there after it happened," Jordan said as she looked down at the floor. "Can you tell the Commander what you saw?"

Zeetra coughed a few times and had a look of dread on her face. It took her a few seconds to begin speaking. "Many were burned, most had been stabbed," Zeetra answered, her voice tear-filled, heavy with loss and pain. "Others had been shot with their own weapons while some had limbs torn from them. When I saw them, it had not been that long since they died but no one had been spared. And there were no survivors. It had been a massacre."

"I know this is difficult, Zeetra," Jordan soothed. "But did you notice anything unusual besides the dead themselves?"

Zeetra took in a shallow breath and Agandif heard her sob. This was not acting. Zeetra had been there. The traumatized look in her eyes seemed genuine to Agandif. And for the first time, Agandif's heart felt a sympathy and kinship with the woman she had labeled a traitor.

"There were blue gems scattered all around the city, especially near the bodies," Zeetra answered. "I would soon learn that they were called SnowFire gems."

Agandif's breathing quickened and a sinking feeling began to fill her stomach. She wasn't sure whether to be shocked, angry—or even both.

"Those fools tried to harness something they did not understand," Agandif realized.

"There is a saying from Earth: 'They signed their own death warrants,'" Jordan replied.

Agandif sighed heavily. "Then you are correct. The blame for their deaths does not fall on the Mokta. But on themselves."

She walked slowly and unsteadily around the damaged operations deck. She wanted to rage or cry, but neither would be appropriate for her position. It was a struggle to contain her grief.

"My crew, my ship . . . none of this had to happen," Agandif said softly. "This was a meaningless confrontation."

Zeetra turned off the holographic projector. Then she looked at Jordan, who was nearly unconscious, still being tended to by Arrow. Zeetra steeled herself and walked over to the ship's commander.

"It can have meaning, Commander," Zeetra offered in a sympathetic tone. "Have one of your engineers salvage some communications equipment and let us take your crew to the Mokta village. No one else has to perish today."

Agandif began to protest with her eyes and drew in a breath to disagree. But Zeetra held up a hand.

"You can contact Zarmandos to send a ship to retrieve you," Zeetra assured. "But first, you must tell them that our people have no conflict with the Mokta."

Agandif couldn't argue with Zeetra's logic. But she still despised her.

"Your plan is sound," Agandif conceded. "But they are my people, not yours."

Zeetra shrugged. "If that distinction pleases you."

———

Jasta hated this idea. Her gemta, having just returned from a stressful time on Earth, had insisted on leading this mission to the damaged Qui Tol vessel. Even with Arrow and Maska's protection, there was no guarantee of her safety. She was an elder now and obviously spent from her journey. How could she even consider doing this?

She shook her head. She knew why. Even though Gemta was no longer Chieftess, she still felt the responsibilities of that position. Gemta had created this plan and was determined to see it through to assure the safety of the Mokta.

Jasta understood. She just didn't like it. She glanced at Torkomm, hoping for some reassurance. He looked worried, too.

Then she gazed around. She was still near the center of the village. People were gathered near her; some had asked if the danger was over. Others murmured among themselves, taking brief glances at the vessel or Jasta before resuming their conversations.

I do not have the luxury of being a child concerned for my gemta's and brother's lives. I have to console the tribe first. But what do I tell them? What would I like to hear, if I were them?

She stepped forward with her SnowFire Gem javelin and struck it against a nearby rock three times to get the tribespeople's attention. She steeled herself inwardly before speaking.

"I know that my gemta and those with her have been away for some time," Jasta said, raising her voice for all to hear. "But you trusted her before. Trust her now. My brother, Arrow, and Maska are with her and Zeetra. They will keep them safe until they return. And I will not let the Qui Tol ship harm us, if it has any fight remaining within it. We must be patient . . . and calm."

Just then, a portal of light flashed behind Jasta. Arrow was carrying their unconscious gemta while Maska kept a protective stance near Zeetra. Jasta and her torkomm rushed over to Arrow and Gemta.

"What happened?" Jasta's heart seized with worry. "What is wrong with Gemta?"

"The air was poor there and she is very tired," Arrow replied. "She will be fine now that she is home."

"Maska, you have healer skills. Do you agree with my brother?" Jasta inquired.

Maska smiled, appreciating the recognition. "Yes, Arrow is correct. Your gemta needs time and rest. But she should fully recover."

Jasta nodded. She looked to Zeetra and then her brother, who was handing their gemta over to Torkomm. "What happened on that ship?"

"After Gemta showed their commander what she found on Errrth, Gemta made a deal with her," Arrow replied. "The Commander agreed that the Mokta are not to blame for what happened to the Qui Tol in the Southlands. She will try to convince her government of that. And we will let them wait for a rescue ship here."

"Why must they come down here? I do not like that idea," Jasta insisted.

"If they remain in their vessel, they will die," Arrow replied. "The air is bad, and the ship is damaged beyond their ability to repair. It would only be for a short time."

"How short is a short time?" Jasta asked with a hint of irritation.

24

INTEGRATION AND DISINTEGRATION

AGANDIF HALF-EXPECTED ZEETRA NOT TO keep her word to return. But there she was, standing in front of the open portal. She did not look smug or aggressive. Her only expression seemed to be one of concern for the Commander and her crew.

"Commander, please have your people escape through this portal. I will keep it open as long as you need," Zeetra said in Onchei. "It can accommodate everyone. The exit point is at the village center below."

The Commander searched for any sign of deception from Zeetra, still not trusting her, but she found none. Despite her reluctance, she decided to put her crew's welfare ahead of her misgivings. She turned to her second-in-command, who was at her side.

"Commence the evacuation through this portal," Agandif told him. "Keep it orderly but get as many through as quickly as you can, Mydzah."

"Yes, Commander, at once."

He turned and walked briskly just outside the operations area to where the evacuees were waiting. He briefly explained their orders and they proceeded to depart the ship. It took several minutes for the personnel, who numbered one hundred and forty-five, to make it into the portal. Only the Mydzah, Commander, and Zeetra remained.

The heat was steadily rising, and the air was continuing to become toxic. Smoke had caused a haze to settle over the operations deck, which looked odd with no personnel walking about.

Agandif looked at her second-in-command and put her arm close to her chest in salute. "You go with Zeetra. I need to activate the disintegration protocols, then I will follow."

He returned the salute. "Are you certain, Commander? I have authorization as well."

She relaxed and smiled at her fellow soldier. "You know I cannot do that. But thank you for the offer. I will handle it."

He nodded and then made a half-bow. After a final salute, he went to Zeetra's side.

"It may take me a few moments to do what I need to do, Zeetra," Agandif said. "I must destroy this ship."

"Won't its destruction damage the valley below?" Zeetra asked.

"There will be no detonation. So no, it won't."

"I can stay behind until you are done?" Zeetra offered.

"That is not necessary," Agandif responded, resolute.

Zeetra lingered several seconds, as though giving the Commander a chance to reconsider. Agandif kept her expression neutral until Zeetra left, accompanied by the Mydzah. The portal remained open.

Agandif went to one of the still-functioning terminals to input several commands. Various warning beeps sounded in response. She stared at the digital readout with dismay, as it read in her language:

AUTOMATED DISINTEGRATION PROTOCOLS CANNOT BE INITIATED. DAMAGE TO SECONDARY RELAYS AND PROCESSORS. FOR MANUAL PROCESS, PROCEED TO ENGINEERING DECK.

The manual process was complicated. In fact, it usually took two people and a considerable amount of time. However, she had sent the Mydzah to the surface to keep order with the surviving crew, so she had neither at the moment. She checked the sensors for the ship's location in proximity to the Mokta village, where her crew now had temporary residence. She verified that it would be far less difficult to cause the engines to overload and accomplish the same task. But the debris and radiation would threaten everyone in this region of Algoran, which she could not allow. That was not the fate Agandif wanted to give her crew nor the legacy she wanted to leave for her family on Zarmandos.

With her mind made up, she rushed to the engineering deck and began to work. After a few minutes of re-routing circuit paths, pressing buttons, and briskly walking from one end of the deck to the other, making adjustments and restoring power to key systems, she felt some sense of accomplishment. She was at least halfway to her goal.

Then the room began to spin. She felt flush and weaker than expected. Agandif checked her wrist-unit. Daestano particle levels on this deck were far above nominal. There was a leak from one of the still-functioning engines. She could stop the leak but that would require turning off the equipment. That would cause the ship to drop dangerously low in the sky or possibly even crash. The adjustment thrusters would not be sufficient to compensate, even briefly.

Agandif took a deep breath. In the next handful of minutes, she finished the bypasses and re-wirings that needed to occur to access the Disintegration Protocols. No longer needing to look at her health indicator, she pressed a final button.

In the midst of the village, Zeetra was growing restless and increasingly concerned as she looked at the vessel above. She turned to the Mydzah.

"I thought she said she would only be a few moments?"

As his eyes met hers, she noticed he was already grieving. "The ship was too badly damaged, Zeetra. The Commander is doing her duty."

"What?" Stunned, she returned her gaze to the vessel.

"You should close the portal," he added.

Zeetra tensed and appeared ready to run through the opening. "I could go get her. It's not too late—"

The second-in-command put a paternal hand on Zeetra's shoulder to gently restrain her, shaking his head. "You would only waste your life," he said sadly. "And tarnish the Commander's efforts."

Crestfallen, Zeetra pressed a symbol on her device to close the portal. She noticed that other crewmembers, the ones who weren't injured, had gathered next to their Mydzah. They were watching the final moments of the vessel they had called home. Some appeared curious to see what would happen next while others saluted in its direction, paying their final respects to it and their Commander. All were equally silent.

Zeetra noticed the ship's bow began to sparkle and glow. The effect was ironically quite beautiful. During that time, Jasta and Arrow walked over to Zeetra.

"What is happening now?" Jasta asked her.

"The Commander of the *Amzatar* has done as she said she would," Zeetra replied. "The ship is being destroyed in a way that protects the Onchei and our world."

"I do not see the Commander," Arrow interjected.

Zeetra nodded somberly. "She . . . stayed aboard to oversee the process."

Over several seconds, Jasta's eyes widened and her expression saddened in realization. Then the Chieftess clasped her hands together and half-bowed in the direction of the shining vessel.

"Thank you for your sacrifice," Jasta said humbly. "You have proven your honor. And your death allows us all to live. We will remember you."

Bopol, Arrow, Maska and Zeetra all repeated "thanks for sacrifice" and made half-bows towards the ship. The rest of the gathered villagers did the same.

This was very moving to the Mydzah and the rest of the crew of the Amzatar. They did not speak, but they collectively made a half-bow in the direction of their ship.

Over the next few minutes, the glimmering effect enveloped the entire vessel. Then it winked out of existence in a flash. Zeetra felt a pang of regret that she had not been able to make peace with Commander Agandif.

Meanwhile, the Mydzah clasped his hands behind his back, blinking back tears while trying to maintain composure. He faced the crew, who had lined up in an orderly fashion in front of him. Out of respect for their loss, the Chieftess and the rest of the tribe stayed back and remained silent to allow him to address his people.

"You have all seen what just transpired. But do not despair. Commander Agandif's actions have allowed us to salvage communications equipment to contact Zarmandos. They will send our sister ship to return us home," he told them. "In the meantime, you will address me as Acting Commander Intoth. I cannot replace Commander Agandif. But I will fulfill my duties in her absence, and you will follow my orders now."

The assembled Onchei all saluted and said "Yes, Commander!" in unison.

Some of the passing villagers gave the Onchei odd or confused stares but said nothing. They did not know the Qui Tol language and were not used to the military attire of the crew. However, Jasta had told them that these strangers would be with them for a short time, so the Mokta held their peace and went about their business.

Intoth briefly surveyed the surrounding village with his eyes and then returned his focus to his soldiers.

"These people, the Mokta, whom we fought against—are no longer our enemy," he said. "In fact, they have opened their village to us, despite our actions towards them. Whatever your feelings towards them and what happened to our vessel and crew, you will make no efforts to antagonize or provoke them during our stay. If I see or hear of any such behavior, I will deal with it immediately . . . and severely."

He narrowed his gaze at his soldiers. "Is that understood?"

Their unified response was immediate. "Yes, Commander!"

Intoth made his way over to where Jasta and Bopol were already talking, close to the Chieftess' hut. Zeetra followed.

"May I speak with you on behalf of my crew, Chieftess?" he asked respectfully in Mokta.

She nodded.

"Including myself, we are one hundred and forty-six people," Intoth continued. "I can attempt to contact Zarmandos soon."

"And what will you tell Zarmandos?" Jasta inquired, her arms crossing over her chest. She peered at him with distrustful eyes.

"I will report what we have learned here," Intoth replied. "With the holographic copies of what Zeetra and your gemta demonstrated onboard, I can prove that the Mokta were not responsible for what happened to the Onchei who remained behind. And you Mokta are more than capable of defending yourselves, should anyone try to press this matter further."

Jasta allowed a smile to briefly cross her face. Then she reasserted her somber air.

"I believe you. However, I will have Zeetra monitor your communications with Zarmandos."

"A sensible precaution, Chieftess."

"How long will it take one of your ships to reach here and retrieve your crew?"

"At least—how do you Mokta put it?—at least seven moonturns, perhaps more."

Jasta turned her head and made eye contact with Bopol.

"We can set up enough tents on the north side of the village," Bopol offered. "And the sentries can accompany them."

Jasta nodded. "Good. I will address the village at the evening community meal. I do not want them to fear the Qui Tol or act against them."

"Yes, Chieftess," Bopol replied.

She focused on Intoth again. "Let Zeetra know your people's needs and she will bring them to my attention. I will do whatever I can to make your brief stay with us hospitable. And we will protect you. On that, you have my word."

Intoth gave a half-bow. "On behalf of my crew, I am grateful, Chieftess."

25

RECOVERY

JORDAN DRIFTED IN AND OUT of consciousness as day progressed into evening. Too weak to open her eyes, she could hear her own breathing and felt someone wipe her forehead occasionally with a damp cloth. She recognized the tender touch of Bopol's weathered hand now and then, either against her cheek or stroking her hair. When she felt strong enough, she opened her eyes and tried to focus on her surroundings.

She was in the hut she'd shared with her husband for many cycles. She inhaled more deeply and enjoyed the familiar chill of Algoran's early morning air. She was laying in her kelkono. As she lowered her gaze from the roof to the rest of the room, she recognized her son Teesbin's pleased face. Under slightly furrowed brows, his eyes were filled with relief. He looked like he had not slept.

"Gemta! How do you feel?" Teesbin asked tenderly.

"Groggy . . . and a little weak . . . thirsty," Jordan replied.

"Your fever left you not long ago. I feared you might not survive," he added. Then he smiled. "But I think you fought death, even in your sleep. I watched it. I have not left your side since Torkomm brought you home a moonturn ago."

Jordan wanted to reach up and touch her son's face, but she lacked the strength. He reminded her of herself at that age, taking care of her

281

Shilvaba-stricken gemta, always attending to her needs. Jordan smiled at him with pride.

"I missed you terribly, my son," she said, her voice raspy from dehydration. "I missed everyone while I was away. It is good to be home."

"I will get you some water, Gemta."

"Your torkomm is with the Chieftess?"

"They are talking with the healer," he answered. "They check on you often."

Jordan relaxed and nodded. Teesbin dutifully poured some liquid from a nearby pitcher to a cup. He helped his gemta sit up and sip as much as she needed, which was considerable.

"The healer said you could eat if you are hungry," Teesbin suggested.

"Perhaps later," she replied.

In the doorway, a woman cleared her throat. Jordan looked in that direction.

"I had to see this with my own eyes," Zoska announced, looking both pleased and intrigued. "Welcome home, Jorr-Don."

"Zoska!" Jordan answered with delight. "Come in! I would stand to greet you, but I am still recovering."

"I would not ask that of you anyway," Zoska replied with a wry grin. "Since you are as old as me now."

Jordan raised an eyebrow at that.

"I am two cycles younger than you," Jordan rebuffed.

"Is that supposed to make a difference?" Zoska chuckled.

Jordan started to laugh but felt too weak and needed to stop.

"I tried to ask Arrow and my daughter what had happened to you," Zoska continued. "But what they told me did not make much sense. How did the SnowFire blood leave you?"

"Straight to the point as always, eh, hoszab?" Jordan replied, using the Mokta word for sister.

"Always."

Jordan turned her head to look at Teesbin.

"Teesbin, could you go outside for a few minutes?" Jordan asked. "I would like to talk with Zoska alone."

"Yes, Gemta," he replied.

As Teesbin exited through the doorway, Zoska came over to Jordan's side. She took Zoska's hand in hers, gripping as tightly as she could. She hoped Zoska could sense the wonder and awe she was trying to convey to her.

"It will be difficult to explain . . . but something wonderful has happened, Zoska. More than just the transformation of my body."

Zoska's gaze narrowed in response. "What do you mean?"

Jordan took a few seconds to decide how she wanted to begin this discussion. "Do you remember right before Bopol and I became mates—"

"That long ago?" Zoska interrupted, jesting. "You ask much."

Jordan just stared at her with an irritated "are-you-finished-yet?" expression.

"What were you going to say, Jorr-Don?"

Jordan reminded Zoska of the time she was separated from her, Reiban and Bopol on their trek to the Southlands, when she almost died from the Mosdon poison except for the intervention of the one she called God. Zoska acknowledged that as well as the fact that Jordan had made the Observance Torch for the times Jordan spoke alone to God.

Jordan let Zoska's hand go, but she maintained eye contact.

"That is all true," Jordan replied confidently. "Your mind has remained as sharp as ever in my absence."

"That will never change," Zoska assured.

Jordan couldn't help but laugh at that. Fortunately, this time it held its strength. "That is a bold statement, hoszab," Jordan added. "What do you base that on?"

"I am Zoska. That is all that needs to be said."

Both of them laughed together. Jordan was starting to feel better. Zoska pulled a chair close to her kelkono and sat down.

"It is good to see you laugh," Zoska said. "You looked like you needed it."

"I did," Jordan acknowledged, nodding. "Listen, my friend: God removed the SnowFire blood from me. My teleport machine was destroyed when I arrived on Earth. I was cut off from Algoran. And while I met some of my family from Earth and was able to stay with them, days were passing, and I had not heard from Arrow. I was starting to despair. So, I asked God to show me a sign that Arrow and all of you were safe. And He did this for me. I went to sleep one night as I was and awoke like this."

Zoska looked quizzical.

"Did it hurt, Jorr-Don?"

Jordan smiled at Zoska's question. It was a reasonable one.

"I felt nothing as I slept," Jordan answered. "I did not even know anything had changed until I started moving the next morning and noticed how difficult that was. Then I saw my reflection."

Zoska stared intently at her. She knew Zoska was extremely curious, but her friend was also being respectful. She could have uttered some truly vicious jokes by now, but she hadn't. In fact, she looked concerned.

"You were cut off from your people, this world, and went through this change without warning," Zoska said slowly. "I am glad that it did not kill you."

"I was not alone," Jordan replied softly. "My brother's mate and her family supported me. God's actions showed me that He did not want me to die. He freed me from all that had been burdening me for so many cycles. Now I can live the rest of my life with Bopol. When it is our time, we will die like everyone else."

Zoska took in a deep breath and released it, considering Jordan's words. "I know how much that means to you, hoszab. I am happy for you and Bopol."

Jordan smiled at that. But she could sense that Zoska was withholding something. She waited a moment to see if Zoska would continue, but she didn't.

"Is something wrong?" Jordan asked.

Zoska looked uncharacteristically reluctant to speak her mind.

"Tell me," Jordan insisted.

Zoska sighed. "It is a small thing, hardly worth voicing." Zoska looked slightly embarrassed.

"Then it should be easy to say, yes?" Jordan prodded.

"It sounds foolish, even in my thoughts. It—it is nothing. Forget it."

"You cannot seem to forget it," Jordan continued, now more curious than anything. Zoska was rarely embarrassed by anything. "So, I must know what it is."

Zoska gazed downward briefly. When she looked up at Jordan again, her expression was apologetic. "I was feeling a regret, I suppose," Zoska finally answered.

"Regret? About what?" Jordan wondered.

"Well, you are old now, and . . . "

It was strange to hear Zoska utter those words, even if they were the truth.

Jordan's curiosity was increasing but her patience was starting to wear thin. "And what, Zoska?"

"I cannot encourage you to have children anymore. That time is clearly past," Zoska added. "And I think I will miss that."

Jordan blinked at that several times. Then she chuckled and relaxed.

"This may surprise you, but I think I will miss it, too," Jordan replied.

Zoska stood up, leaned over, and briefly kissed Jordan's forehead.

"As long as I breathe, Jorr-Don, I will help you however I can."

"Thank you, hoszab. I love you, too."

Zoska nodded with a satisfied smile. "I will tell your son I am leaving. I will return tomorrow."

"How is your daughter?" Jordan asked suddenly.

Zoska hesitated before responding. "Maska is Maska," she said. "She is alive and seems in good spirits. Beyond that, I do not know yet."

"We will talk more on this tomorrow?" Jordan asked.

"Yes. Now rest, Jorr-Don."

Jordan snickered. "You still act like my gemta."

"You still need one."

Zoska waved as she left the hut. And Jordan felt fortunate to have such a friend.

26

THE ART OF MAKING PEACE

SEVERAL MORE DAYS PASSED, AND Jordan fully recovered from her symptoms. She was somewhat surprised to be invited to a formal meeting between Chieftess Jasta, Zeetra, and Commander Intoth. Sitting on the floor next to her daughter and Bopol, they faced Zeetra and the Commander, who were sitting several feet apart from one another. All were silent and there was an air of tension in the Chieftess' hut.

"I am glad we are all here," Jasta began. "There are some things I would like us to discuss together. Commander, can you share with everyone here what you told me?"

"Yes, Chieftess," he replied. "Based on my report to Zarmandos' ruling council, they have unanimously agreed to end hostilities against the Mokta. They have already dispatched our sister ship to pick us up. It should arrive in eight moonturns."

Jasta nodded. "Thank you. As I look at each of you, I see something special: I am the Mokta Chieftess. Zeetra and Commander Intoth represent each of the Qui Tol factions. And there is my gemta, a woman from Errrth taken by the Qui Tol who remained on Algoran. Of those Qui Tol, Zeetra is the only pureblood still living. Yet she chose to forsake her own faction, join our tribe, and have family from among the Mokta."

Jasta noted the Commander clenching his jaw in apparent distaste at that description, but he remained silent.

"I know that the Qui Tol of Zarmandos find such actions distasteful," Jasta continued. "But Zeetra also thought she was the last of her kind. She had very few options."

"The Council has pardoned Zeetra Ketranos of all offenses," Intoth stated stiffly. "On the condition that she never set foot on Zarmandos."

"Gladly, Commander," Zeetra interjected.

Jasta's irritation grew and Jordan understood it. Zeetra could unintentionally derail the entire conversation with her remarks. So, the Chieftess intervened.

"I feel there is one more matter that needs to be handled," Jasta said in a presiding manner. "And it involves you and your people, Commander."

Intoth's eyes brightened with intrigue. "Yes, Chieftess?"

"Do you think your ruling council could issue a formal apology to my gemta, Jordan Lewis of Errrth?" Jasta asked. "I know the Qui Tol of Zarmandos did not abduct her and her gemta, but—"

"But the ones who did relocate them were of our race," Intoth acknowledged.

"That action is not necessary," Jordan interrupted. "I have already forgiven the Qui Tol—the Onchei who took us from Earth."

Intoth peered at both the human woman and the Chieftess, pondering his response.

"It is a reasonable request," he determined. "I will convey it to the ruling council."

"My thanks," Jasta replied.

"Do not thank me yet. I do not know how they will respond."

"I thank you for your wisdom and the effort, Commander."

Intoth stood up and gave Jasta another respectful half-bow. "Very well, Chieftess."

Then he left the hut.

"You really did not have to do that, Chieftess," Jordan insisted. "I do not require it."

"Perhaps you do not, Gemta. I can respect that. But what about the voices of all the ones the Qui Tol took before you and Gemtabana over the many cycles?" Jasta countered. "Do you not think they require it? Should the Qui Tol not at least admit their wrongdoing and apologize?"

"I do not know," Jordan answered. "I cannot speak for them."

Jasta stood up and offered her hand to her gemta, who took it and also rose. "When their ship attacked the Mountain, I could have destroyed them."

"I saw that," Jordan replied.

"After that, no doubt they would have sent more ships. And I would have destroyed those."

Jordan felt both sadness and understanding.

"I would have destroyed them all to protect the Mokta, Gemta. But I did not. It is not a light thing I ask of them in return for their continued existence. I will have this concession from the Qui Tol or I will not be satisfied."

"You are Chieftess, my daughter," Jordan said with her eyes lowered. "Do as you must."

———

Maska had been perched in a tree, keeping a keen eye on the Chieftess' hut, for the last hour. Now, she watched as the Qui Tol exited, soon followed by former Chieftess Jorr-Don and Zeetra.

"What have you learned?" a voice boomed from below, almost causing her to fall from her spot.

She looked down and spotted Foonta. In the decades since their childhood, they had become friends. He was no longer the rude little boy who insulted her, the one she had beaten up and humiliated at Arrow's fifth birthday celebration. And their friendship had grown closer after the death of his mate ten cycles ago. Foonta was taller than Maska, wide and heavy but equally muscular. He had shaved his head when his mate died. Since then, he had let it grow some, but never as long as it had been. Foonta had not chosen another mate, raising his four children alone during that time. Maska respected the man he had become.

"I believe Chieftess has made new demands of the Qui Tol," Maska replied after a moment. "But I do not know any details."

"As long as they leave and never come back, I will be happy," Foonta added gruffly.

Maska leaped to the ground effortlessly, landing in a feline pose in front of Foonta. Then she stood up and slapped him across the back. "Well said, Foonta! I agree."

"What now then?"

Maska shrugged. "I have no plans."

"Join me and Antol at the community supper then."

She nodded agreeably. "Your daughters all have mates. And your son has almost reached The Dawning Time, yes?"

He grinned. "Yes, in forty moonturns."

But his grin soon left him, leaving Maska concerned. They began to walk together.

"What is it, Foonta?"

He tried to reclaim his smile. "I should not feel this way. I should be happy for Antol. He has strong feelings for Shelima—Kortai and Lotah's daughter. I think he will ask her to be his mate."

"That is good, yes?"

"Yes . . . but then the hut will be empty. I will be alone for the first time," he replied. "And I do not like to think about that. I do not know how I will fill the days."

"You are the finest weaponsmaker in the village!" she interjected. "You will always have work."

He nodded, still unconvinced. "A man must be more than his work. He needs someone to work for. When my children are gone, I will have no one."

Maska paused and looked at him as if that was the stupidest thing he could have said. "Really? You will have no one, Foonta? Who am I then?"

"What? I do not understand."

"In all the cycles since your mate passed, have I let our friendship drift?"

"No."

"Have I ever ignored you?"

"No, you have not. And why is that?"

A few steps away, Maska sat atop a large rock. Foonta remained standing, curious.

"I chose not to take a mate," she told Foonta. "And you are one of the few who remained friends with me after I began to care for my torkomm."

"After he was stricken with the Shilvaba, yes."

"Then your mate died from the Shilvaba—and I understood your pain."

Foonta nodded slowly. "You encouraged me. You gave me hope that I could be a good torkomm to my children, even without my Eleesi."

"And you have been a wonderful torkomm to them. You have made me proud of you, Foonta."

"It is strange. You still look half my age, but I feel we are the same inside."

She was moved by the gratitude in his eyes, which were near tears. "I know I age much slower, but what do you mean about being the same inside?"

"I feel like we are family, Maska. You were there for me and my children, when you were not caring for your torkomm," he said. "You did not raise my children, yet they think of you like another gemta. They have all told me so. And I agree."

"You exaggerate my role," she replied, a slight heat rising in her face. "But thank you. If I helped, I am glad. That is an honor."

A tear dropped onto her cheek as she looked at the ground. Why was she so touched by his words? She knew the role she had taken, but had it not just been as a good friend? Why did it feel so good to be called family? Was it because her torkomm was gone and her gemta was old? Her twin brothers had added more than one generation to their families already. She had thought she'd gotten used to the idea of being alone, of waiting for Arrow as long as she needed to.

But what about now? What about in the meantime? Was it some cruel trick of the twin stars? Did some invisible law somewhere state, "Maska must be alone and miserable?"

"Are we not family, Maska?" he asked sincerely, yanking her attention away from her inner turmoil. "Have I misunderstood you? If so, forgive."

At that moment, it hurt her heart to think of these feelings as a mistake. They weren't in error. She just hadn't known they were real. She hadn't acknowledged them. She feared what they might mean. But holding onto them felt more important than giving them up or giving in to fear again.

She looked up at Foonta and smiled, not bothering to wipe her tears. "You are not wrong, Foonta. We are family. Of course, we are family!"

He extended a hand to help her stand up. She took it.

"Come," he said pleasantly. "We will get Antol and go to the community supper."

She nodded and they walked towards the western side of the village.

———

The Zhizhal had never seen this Mokta Chieftess before nor the human woman next to her. But through the image screen, he thought this Chieftess was most striking. Was she really his diplomatic counterpart from his former homeworld, a queen amongst these luddites? Then he reminded himself that those same Mokta had learned Onchei technology and outwitted the security of two Onchei starcraft. In that light, he knew he should probably revise his opinion of this tribe of Algoran.

"I am Meylor Oztan, Zhizhal of the Zarmandos colony."

"I am Jasta, Chieftess of the Mountain Mokta."

"And I am Jordan Lewis," the human said.

"She is my gemta," Chieftess Jasta clarified.

Oztan reacted to that with some surprise. The Mokta Chieftess was a hybrid of human and Mokta? Then he observed Jasta's hair, a unique mixture of Mokta white and the deepest blues. And her eyes were the color of ice. He now recalled certain details of Commander Intoth's report.

He suddenly comprehended that this Chieftess was the grand-daughter of SnowFire. And yet, how could that be possible? She claimed the human woman was her mother. Wasn't her mother the daughter of SnowFire, a human who had been made immortal through a blood transfusion? And wasn't that woman the Mokta Chieftess?

He was distracting himself and made himself refocus on the task at hand. If there was time and opportunity, he would get answers to his questions later.

"I have been made aware of what you want, Chieftess."

Jasta crossed her arms and slightly tilted her head to the left. "And?"

That was a bold tactic, the Zhizhal mused. Even Jordan looked at her daughter with some bewilderment. But she said nothing. Oztan figured her silence was probably done out of respect for the Chieftess' position.

He smiled. "I see we can dispense with the niceties and get straight to business."

Jasta began tapping one of her fingers on her arm impatiently, raising an eyebrow in irritation. Oztan had to restrain the urge to laugh. Jordan looked uncomfortable.

"We are prepared to offer the apology you have asked for," Oztan continued. "Would you prefer that in writing or for me to say the words only?"

"We have no written language, Leader of the Qui Tol," Jasta answered. "But my gemta will accept your words on behalf of herself and all the humans taken from Errrth by your people. And I will commit your words to memory. They will become our stories and songs."

Jordan finally spoke up, now given the opportunity by Jasta. "I will accept your words, Zhizhal, as my daughter the Chieftess has said. Your efforts at reconciliation are welcome and appreciated."

Oztan smiled. Whatever had happened to her over the cycles, this human was a seasoned fellow diplomat. And though she would be justified in despising the Onchei, she humbled herself and was making more efforts towards peace than the sitting Chieftess. That was admirable.

Now he felt comfortable proceeding with a long and sincere apology to the humans and Mokta, on behalf of the Onchei. Jasta held her authoritative stance but as Oztan continued, he saw her relax and even show hints of warmth and something resembling gratitude. Or maybe it was just happiness for her mother, who listened quietly. She occasionally nodded. Like the Chieftess, Jordan had looked guarded and almost defensive when he began the acknowledgment of the Onchei's misdeeds. But as he progressed and he could tell she had determined his sincerity, her tough facade crumbled, and she became teary-eyed.

Oztan was moved by that. He had long regretted his people's one-sided interactions with humans. He had fought against it by supporting the faction separation and move to Zarmandos. Now he had the chance to make some small measure of atonement, to declare that the unsound practices of the past were finally over. He suddenly realized that this was just as important to him as it was for Jordan and the Mokta.

27

HOMECOMINGS

THE PRESENT, JUST OUTSIDE THE MOKTA VILLAGE

As they arrived, Erica was just as stunned as her daughter to see the massive spacecraft above the Mokta village. It was even larger than Pamela had described.

"That is a vessel of the Heelos?" Evtaz asked from behind them, her sons close to her.

"Yes," Pamela answered. "That is what took my friend, Zeetra. She sacrificed herself for the rest of us. But was it for nothing? Why are they here?"

Erica's jaw tightened and she could feel her hair starting to flicker with her anger. "If they are here to cause trouble, they will regret it. And if they have taken lives, I will avenge them!"

They all began to run in the direction of the Mokta mountain. But as they grew closer, the ship ascended skyward. And by the time they reached the village gates, the spacecraft could no longer be seen. Erica and her companions were simply relieved to see the village more or less undisturbed.

Pamela tapped her mother's shoulder and pointed towards some of the villagers. Almost immediately, Erica spotted Zeetra and her mate Jaidos. She called out to them and jogged over to talk with them. Pamela joined her while the other Ullvarr cautiously stayed back to observe.

"Zeetra, it is wonderful to see you again!" Pamela exclaimed, giving warm embraces to her and Jaidos. Erica stood close by and nodded in agreement. "What happened?"

"The Onchei sent a second ship, the *Amzatar*, to attack. But Chieftess Jasta badly damaged it, protecting us all," Zeetra replied, sounding gratified but weary. "The *Amzatar's* captain negotiated with your sister and Zeetra. She sent her surviving crew to the village and destroyed the ship in mid-air. The ship that just left, the *Kildee*, is taking the survivors back to their Zarmandos colony. We will have no more trouble with the Onchei."

"You are right," Erica replied. "A lot did happen!"

"And from what I can see of your traveling companions, you have a story as well," Zeetra added.

"Indeed," Erica replied.

"Tell me, has everyone returned?" Pamela asked, looking Zeetra in the eyes, clearly wanting to know about her mate.

Zeetra nodded. "Yes. I saw Arrow walking towards your hut a moment ago, Pamela. And Jordan is spending time with her granddaughter, Kalta, at Jasta's hut."

Pamela excused herself quietly and began a mad dash towards her hut. Erica smiled, happy for her daughter.

"How is my sister?" Erica asked Zeetra.

"She is well. But she has changed much since you last saw her," Zeetra replied.

"What does that mean? Was she injured on Earth? What happened?"

"I am not sure I can explain what happened." She paused. "But the SnowFire blood has left her. She is a normal human woman again."

"How can that be?" Erica exclaimed. "All her blood has been SnowFire blood for over forty cycles!"

Zeetra nodded. "I know that. But it is true. As I said, I cannot explain it. Jordan no longer has the SnowFire gems, her hair and eyes have reverted to what is normal for humans. And she is mortal."

Those words hit Erica like ice water. They were impossible. They didn't make sense. "Did Jordan say why this happened?"

"She said that God made her this way," Zeetra replied. "She called it a miracle."

"God?" Erica repeated softly, stunned.

"That is what she said," Zeetra had confirmed.

Woodenly, Erica walked over to Evtaz and her sons. She felt surreal and out of place from this news.

"What is it, Eree-Kah?" Evtaz asked, concerned.

"I need to check on my sister," Erica said. "The danger to the Mokta has passed. You and your sons should return home."

"All right, Eree-Kah," Evtaz replied. "Will we see you again?"

Erica clasped Evtaz's shoulder with her hand. "Of course! When next we visit, I will bring more of my family. I am sure they will be as delighted to meet their fellow Ullvarr as my daughter and me."

Evtaz smiled at that. "I hope your sister will be well."

"Thank you, my friend."

"We are more than friends now, Eree-Kah SnowFire," Evtaz said as she turned to leave with her sons. "We are Ullvarr, so we are kin."

After Evtaz and her sons departed, Erica rapidly crossed the village until she reached the doorway of Jasta's hut. She knocked on the door.

"Jordan?"

She heard scampering footsteps that she recognized as belonging to young Kalta. As she opened the door, the girl smiled brightly at the sight of Erica.

"Eree-Kah SnowFire! Welcome back!" she said slightly above a whisper. "Gemtabana is sleeping right now. Do you need me to wake her?"

That puzzled Erica. It was the middle of the afternoon. "No, do not wake her," Erica replied, matching the girl's volume. "But may I come in and see my sister? I will not disturb her."

Kalta nodded happily. "Would you like some tea? I can make some."

Erica couldn't help but smile in response. "Thank you, Kalta. That would be nice."

Erica followed the girl into the hut and almost immediately heard Jordan's soft snoring. She followed the sound and found Jordan napping in a chair next to one of the walls. But could this really be Jordan? Erica had become so accustomed to seeing Jordan with blue hair. It was jarring to see silver locks instead. Erica was equally fascinated and horrified to follow the new lines and wrinkles on Jordan's slumbering face and neck. And yet, her scars were still present. This was the same woman.

Erica was reminded of the words whispered to her by the Ullvarr oracle, Kaztema: "You will see something when you return to the Mokta that will make you believe the incredible. Something that even you cannot deny."

Was this what Kaztema was talking about? Erica had no way to explain Jordan's transformation. SnowFire herself had said she could not reverse what she had done to the two of them. At the very least, this did qualify as incredible. It was real. It had happened.

But did that have to mean there was a God? Was this something only He could do?

Erica had believed in God as a child. Her father had taken her to church now and then. But he had also been unfaithful in his marriage. And her mother had grown cruel in response. It had led to verbal and physical fights, and Erica had been caught in the middle. She loved them both. She couldn't understand why they couldn't get along. Why couldn't they be good to her? Wasn't she their only child? The tension was always in their home, forcing her to walk an emotional tightrope. Each day, she felt like a part of her was dying inside.

She'd had one escape, whenever she went to see Jordan. And then Jordan was gone. None of Erica's friends were as close as Jordan, so she couldn't help but feel abandoned.

By the time her mother had been tried and convicted for the murder of Erica's father's lover, Erica had given up on almost everything and everyone, including the idea of God. Her depression further isolated her.

Even after Jordan re-appeared and Erica saw a glimmer of hope, it was dashed upon her journey to Algoran. She was separated from Jordan again, this time on a completely different world. She endured the betrayal of the Ullvarr villagers. And then all but two of them were massacred by the Gulstaa, taking away even the fake comfort she had grown used to.

She did find solace in taking Pamela as her daughter. Then having and raising two more children with Vakar, in whom she found love and security, was the most profound and rewarding time of her life. That is, until he died. Spending time with her children and grandchildren brought her temporary peace these days. But she also knew that, with the SnowFire blood in her veins, she would outlive generations of the family she had helped create. It felt profoundly cruel.

But here was Jordan, her sister by blood for decades, now free of that curse. Jordan had achieved what Erica had hoped for ever since Vakar's passing: mortality.

Yet even SnowFire had believed in God, whom she called the Father of Spirits, speaking with reverence. To Erica, SnowFire was the closest thing she had ever seen to anything resembling a god. SnowFire had such power and strength that most of Algoran knew who she was, generating legends, awe and fear.

Erica would give up all her special abilities for the chance to grow old and die someday. Jordan proved this way existed. However, Erica wasn't sure it was possible to lay aside a lifetime of doubt, loss and mistrust to embrace that chance.

Then she remembered how Jordan had said she'd actually sought God on the Mokta Mountain, not long after the end of the Gulstaa war. And Jordan told Erica what had happened to her there. Erica had done her best to be supportive of her sister but had not believed the story. Perhaps it had merit even now. It was worth pondering.

Shaken, she walked out of the hut and sat down. A few moments later, Kalta sat down beside her.

"All morning, Gemtabana and I made sweetbread and irta fruit pies," the girl said with excitement that trailed off in regret. "I wanted to make a lot, so we did. But I think I made Gemtabana tired."

"Baking is a lot of work." Erica gave a slight smile.

"We used to do this before and it was easy for her," Kalta replied, her brow furrowing in confusion. "But since she returned from Errrth, it is not so easy. She tries anyway though."

"That sounds like my sister," Erica said.

"You have not changed, Eree-Kah, and you two are sisters." Kalta paused. "Are you not the same age? Why do you two look so different now?"

Erica had to chuckle at the earnestness in which Kalta asked her questions. She sincerely believed Erica would have all the answers. In truth, Erica probably knew less than the girl.

"Your gemtabana is human now, little snowflower," Erica answered sympathetically. "And I am not. That is the difference."

"Am I human? Will I be old like Gemtabana someday?"

"No, you are not human, Kalta. Someday, you will grow old . . . but it may be a long time from now."

The girl nodded as if she understood, even though Erica knew she didn't. She went inside to check on the tea she was brewing for them. Erica enjoyed the aromatic liquid and some more conversation with Kalta. Then she asked the girl to let her gemtabana know that Erica had been by to see her.

All Pamela wanted to do was run over and kiss Arrow. But she was enjoying watching him chop wood in front of their hut. He was working earnestly to slice the timber and looked like he had been at it for a while. She liked it when he tied his long hair into a loose ponytail. His arm and back muscles tensed as he took another swipe with his axe. After allowing herself another moment's satisfaction in observing her mate, she cleared her throat, smiling all the while. He turned around quickly and grinned from ear-to-ear.

"Pamela! I did not know you had returned," Arrow exclaimed, dropping the axe.

He ran over and embraced her, kissing her the way she had hoped he would.

"What is the wood for?" she asked him.

"Ah! I was told that Meespa is pregnant, so I wanted to make a cazta for the baby," he replied.

"That is very thoughtful of you. I am sure your daughter will be pleased."

"Do you think your kacheela could paint it? She is very good with colors."

Pamela nodded. "I will ask her. I am sure she will agree."

She looked away a moment, still in his arms, then looked up at him expectantly.

"What is it?" Arrow asked.

"Are you going to tell me what happened with Maska or do I have to drag it out of you?"

There was a smile on her lips, but she made sure her eyes told him she was serious. He pulled her closer to him and kissed her neck.

"We talked," he replied. "We finally had a chance to talk. We moved past a lot of the old hurts. I do not think everything was resolved, but we were able to work together. We accomplished what we set out to do."

Pamela breathed in deeply and released it slowly. "I am glad you were able to talk. I am even more pleased that you were able to bring back Zeetra and your gemta."

"But . . . ?"

"Can you tell me what you two said to each other—in as much detail as you can recall?"

Erica had remained unsettled after seeing Jordan in Jasta's hut. She went to visit her other daughter, Izikaa and her grandson, Shamol. But the imagery of the Mokta Mountain continued to pervade her thoughts. She still needed answers. As wonderful as it was to see her family, it was difficult to fully enjoy when she was so troubled. She felt strongly compelled to ascend the mountain, so she set off to do so. She reached a high enough elevation to view the entire Mokta village below. The winds were stronger and near-constant there, making it difficult for the tisa birds to get close. She had long grown accustomed to the temperatures. Yet her thoughts continued to haunt her.

Sometime later, as the twin stars were beginning to set and Erica was peering at the mountain's peak in the distance above, there was a crunching of footsteps in the snow below her. When she turned to look, she saw Jordan making her way towards her. Even using a sturdy walking stick, the strain on Jordan's face was evident, from the physical effort she was making. Jordan was wearing thick furs and when she got closer, she could see the older woman was shivering.

"I used to come up here many times to think," Jordan said, still breathing hard. "Especially when I was troubled, before I made the Observance Torch."

Erica offered her hand to Jordan to steady her. She pulled her towards the flatter area she was standing on. Jordan looked both grateful and embarrassed.

"I am sorry I was not awake when you visited earlier," she continued. "I am still not used to being human again. I overexerted myself."

"So now you nearly kill yourself to come see me here?" Erica was not jesting.

"I may be my real age now, but I can still make it up this mountain," Jordan answered. "At least this far."

"That is your pride talking," Erica quipped. "Or maybe you think you are still invulnerable."

"I was never invulnerable, and neither are you. We just healed fast."

Erica sighed in concern. "And now, you do not. You should not have come up here."

"I am here. That is what matters," Jordan added. "So, talk to me."

Erica crossed her arms and continued to stare at Jordan in disapproval. But she knew Jordan was right. "You have told people that God did this to you, took away the SnowFire blood?"

"I do not know exactly what God did, whether He took away the SnowFire blood or just reversed its effects," Jordan replied. "But I know it was Him."

"How? How do you know it was God?"

Jordan told Erica an abbreviated version of what she'd experienced on her return trip to Earth and the miracles that took place, including her physical and spiritual transformations. Out of respect, Erica listened patiently. It was intriguing. Erica could tell that Jordan believed what she was saying.

"Can I ask you something, Jordan?"

"You can ask me anything, Erica."

"Are we still sisters?"

That question seemed to shock Jordan, whose eyes widened, and her mouth gaped momentarily. But she quickly recovered. "You were like a sister to me, even when we were kids," Jordan answered. "Then we became biological sisters through SnowFire's blood. We have lived as family for more than forty cycles. How can you ask me whether we are still sisters? Do you not already know?"

"I know in my heart, we are sisters. The rest is hard for me to grasp."

Jordan nodded. Then she pulled out a small device from her furs. Erica recognized it as the remaining Onchei teleport device.

"Perhaps on Earth, they could take blood samples from each of us," Jordan said. "Or run a DNA test and verify what you want to know."

Suddenly, Jordan turned and threw the device down the mountain at a particularly rocky precipice about one hundred feet below. They both watched the device shatter on impact, its tiny pieces flying downward in all directions as gravity took hold. Erica was stunned.

"Why did you do that?" she exclaimed.

"If we cannot go to Earth, I guess we cannot run those tests, can we?"

Erica did not understand Jordan's reasoning.

"Zeetra could always build another?" Erica said.

Jordan shook her head slowly and defiantly. "I have advised Jasta and Zeetra to let knowledge of the teleport devices be forgotten. The threat from the Onchei is over. We can let their technology go as well. The Chieftess and Zeetra agreed with me."

Erica nodded, still surprised. "So, it is truly over?"

"Well, the Onchei still have the technology. But these Onchei have no quarrel with the Mokta. They have made peace with us. They will never come back here."

"I suppose you are right," Erica said.

"Erica?"

"Hm?"

Jordan smiled. "We will always be sisters, and nothing can ever change that."

Those simple words brought a great peace to Erica's heart. And yet, she could see from how Jordan was still shivering and the way she spoke that she was getting much too cold. She doubted Jordan would be able to descend the mountain by foot anymore. So, without asking, she picked up Jordan in her arms and began walking down the ridge. Jordan gave her a severe look but held her tongue, finally sighing in defeat.

"I will get us back to the village safely," Erica confirmed. "Had we walked back, you could have caught a cold or gotten the Shilvaba. You are not immune to those things anymore, you know."

"I know, all right? You do not have to remind me."

"Says the woman who climbed the mountain at evening in the cold months."

"Thank you for not saying old woman."

Erica grinned. "You said it for me."

———

Thirty minutes later, Erica entered her own hut and placed Jordan on her bed, covering her in heavy blankets she had sewn cycles earlier. She knelt beside her and stroked Jordan's hair.

"Rest, sister. I will send word to Bopol that you are here."

"Erica," Jordan said weakly, looking up at her. "I know you want to be human again."

Erica softly patted Jordan's hand. "More than anything."

"Then . . . open your heart to God."

Erica kept her hand on Jordan's but pulled her head back a little. "I do not know if I can, Jordan."

"You opened your heart to me, to Algoran, Pamela, Vakar . . . even to SnowFire," Jordan replied. "Why not God?"

"I can see you, this world, my family. I even saw SnowFire, felt her blood in my veins. I have never seen God."

Jordan smiled and gripped Erica's hand with her waning strength. "Yes, you have. When you have seen me."

Erica felt her brow furrow in confusion. "I do not understand?"

"Many cycles ago, on the journey to find the Qui Tol, I took a Mosdon strike and should have died."

"I remember you telling me about that."

"God reached out to me when I was dying. He offered His help and gave me a choice."

"You could have been delirious from the poison, Jordan."

"Do you know anyone else who has survived the Mosdon?"

Erica considered that. "Perhaps the SnowFire blood—"

"That had not happened yet. I was still human when its stinger pierced my leg."

Erica felt a chill descend her spine. "I did not know that."

"I am alive because of God," Jordan added. "And I am human again because of His mercy and power. He asked me to trust in Him and His power. And I am asking you to do the same."

Erica felt frustration build within her until it nearly erupted. "Why? Why do I have to do that?"

"Ask yourself this, Erica," Jordan said, her voice just above a whisper. "Why is it so important that you do not trust God? What . . . do you have to lose?"

With that effort accomplished, Jordan lost consciousness. Erica checked Jordan's forehead and confirmed that she had no fever. She watched her a few moments longer, glad Jordan had no signs of seizure or anything indicative of the Shilvaba. She sat down on the floor next to the bed and sighed in relief.

"What exactly am I fighting so hard for?" Erica whispered in Ullvarr. "I've known her my whole life. Shouldn't I be able to trust what she's telling me?"

She leaned forward, resting one arm on her belly and the other at Jordan's side.

"Jordan, your life is incredible to me. You were just an ordinary girl like me. Then after you were taken, you adapted here, took care of your mother and became a good huntress," she said. "You chose to marry and have a family, but you were thrust into the role of SnowFireChild and Chieftess. Now you've passed on that role to your daughter and you can be a normal woman again.

"Is it possible that there is a God and He protected you all this time?" Erica considered. Then she gasped in realization. "Did He protect me, too—and this whole village—as a result of Jordan's—"

She shook her head abruptly, astonished at her own behavior.

"Erica, now you are acting like there is a God . . . "

28

TO WHOM HONOR IS DUE

SEVENTEEN MOONTURNS PASSED BEFORE JORDAN was well enough to speak to the rest of the tribe, who had gathered together near the center of the village. The Chieftess stood beside her, poised to help keep her steady, and Bopol was just as close. Jordan was not fully recovered but grateful her voice was strong enough to carry her words. She had been fortunate, avoiding the Shilvaba this time. The Healer had used many herbal remedies to alleviate her symptoms. But more importantly, Jordan had earnestly prayed and knew that the Lord was the main source of her strength. He had healed her.

The cold season had begun, and the winds stung, even through her thick clothing. She could see strands of her smoky gray hair blowing in front of her eyes and over her shoulders. She smiled at the strange comfort that brought. With all its positives and negatives, this was who she was, who she was meant to be. Time was not an enemy but merely a companion on her journey through life. Before she spoke, she turned to look at her mate and then her daughter, the Chieftess. She saw her family, including Erica, and all the friends she had made over the many cycles. Then she took in a breath and focused on the people instead of her own thoughts.

"Thank you all for your love towards me and my family since my return from Earth," Jordan began, her voice loud but raspy. "Many

310

of you have wondered what happened to me—why my appearance has changed so much. You all know of the Observance Torch I had made during my time as Chieftess and how I would take time to be alone. I called out to a Being higher than the stars, to the One who made the stars themselves. God is Holy. His heart is pure and clean with perfect power. Even SnowFire submitted to Him. She honored Him, calling Him the Father of Spirits. I honor Him as well. I asked this Being to watch over us as a tribe, the Mokta as a people, and Algoran, our world. He is the One who changed me, not just physically. God has changed me from within. I may no longer possess the power of SnowFire, but that is fine. He has given me the strongest power there is: His own Holy Spirit, which is now in my heart."

Jordan smiled but she had to pause. She felt an overwhelming joy in sharing these words, her experiences, with the tribe. She turned her head and saw that her daughter was listening intently and in awe. So was Bopol and their sons. Jordan returned her gaze to the rest of the villagers.

"God has taken away my rage and the desire to commit actions which are against His perfect nature," she said. "He has removed my sorrows and regrets. Instead, He has brought peace to my spirit.

"I am glad you have my daughter, Jasta, as your Chieftess. She has already proven that she will lead and protect this village. She directed the rebuilding efforts after the Qui Tol attack and caused all the SnowFire gem shards to depart to the far side of the mountain. I feel comfortable spending my remaining cycles with my family before I—"

Just then, there was some commotion from the western end of the crowd. Jordan stopped to see what they were reacting to, but her farsight was blurred. Seconds later, she heard the trees rustling and saw some kind of movement. Tall, gray-skinned people emerged from the forest into the village. It was the Kastadi, an entire delegation of them. One of the sentries ran ahead of them to address the Chieftess.

"Chieftess, Hakorth of the Kastadi has come to pay respects to your gemta," the young man said.

Jasta grinned and nodded. "Let the Kastadi Chieftess come. I have been expecting her."

Jordan turned her head, semi-stunned. "You knew about this?"

"Know about it? I planned it," Jasta replied, putting her hand on her gemta's shoulder lovingly.

"Bopol, did you know as well?"

"I was sworn to secrecy by my Chieftess," he replied with mock-seriousness.

It was tremendously rare for the Kastadi leader to travel outside their own territory. Surrounded by no less than fifty people in her entourage, she was fully adorned in a brightly colored robe made from something similar to snakeskin. She wore a silver headband with a deep red gemstone fastened to its center. To Jordan, the middle-aged Kastadi woman looked remarkably like her father, the late Chief Teebor the Mighty, when Jordan had met him nearly fifty cycles earlier. Like Teebor, she was thick-bodied and brawny. Her long, silky red hair had beautiful white highlights throughout. Her face was round with smooth and beautiful features for a woman of her years. Only the wrinkles at the corners of her eyes revealed her age. When she looked at Jordan, Hakorth smiled and Jordan could feel the Kastadi Chieftess' respect for her.

"Mokta Chieftess, may I address your gemta?" Hakorth bellowed pleasantly from one hundred feet away.

"You may," Jasta responded with equal volume.

The villagers parted to allow the Kastadi leader and her people through. Hakorth stopped at about ten paces from Jordan and gave a full bow. Her entourage did the same. Jordan was astonished. Even Teebor had not shown her such respect in his time. When Hakorth raised back up, so did the other Kastadi.

"Jorr-Don of the Mokta, it is good to see you again," Hakorth said warmly, her smile radiant.

Jordan bowed her head slowly and raised it back up. This felt partly like the many diplomatic visits she had received over the cycles during her time as Chieftess. Jordan had worked with both Teebor and Hakorth to forge the trade authority and financial system which had replaced traditional bartering and allowed Mekit, the capitol of the Kastadi lands, to become a prominent city in the region. But it also felt personal. Even though Jordan knew Hakorth was only a few years younger than her, she felt like the Kastadi's respect was more towards a mother figure than a sister.

"Welcome, Hakorth. I am honored by your presence."

"I see that the rumors I heard are true," Hakorth continued. "You are no longer a SnowFireChild. You have become as one of the people again."

"Yes, that is true," Jordan replied. "The explanation for that is—"

"The explanation is not needed, Jorr-Don," Hakorth interrupted, raising a hand but keeping her manner respectful. "The Kastadi have come to celebrate your return from Errrth as well as your victory over The Ones Who Bring! I was pleased to receive that news from your daughter, the Mokta Chieftess."

Jordan felt slightly overwhelmed. Wasn't it a bit drastic of the Kastadi to come to the Mokta village to celebrate this? Then Jordan peered at her daughter. The love and pride in the Chieftess' eyes were unmistakable. Then Jordan saw the same emotions on the Kastadi Chieftess' face as well. Peering over the crowd, Jordan couldn't help but notice the reverence on the faces of everyone gathered. She knew she was outnumbered, so she quelled her resistance to the honor they were intent on giving her.

"Almost fifty cycles ago," Hakorth resumed. "You and your fellow Mokta hunters entered Mekit and fought three Deathwings beside our warriors. I was in my fifteenth cycle, but I took up the sword when I saw you riding a Deathwing, trying to kill it."

Hakorth pulled up her right arm sleeve, revealing a long-since-healed burn, wide and coarse, etched from her shoulder to just above her elbow.

"I still proudly carry this scar from that battle," Hakorth beamed. "It reminds me of who I am and who gave me the courage to fight. I would not have become worthy to lead my people if not for you, Jorr-Don of the Mokta. You will always have my gratitude and respect."

"It was your torkomm who saved my life that day," Jordan replied. "If not for him, this day would not be possible."

"Well said!" Hakorth replied. "The Kastadi have brought gifts for you and your tribe. And we shall make a feast today worthy of your finest stories!"

"We have many fine stories, Kastadi Chieftess," Jasta interjected teasingly. "I look forward to your challenge! Join me and Gemta at my table!"

"Of course!" Hakorth delighted in response. "We shall dine and sing songs!"

"I do not think you want me to sing songs, Hakorth," Jordan warned with a wry grin. The Kastadi Chieftess laughed heartily at that.

The festivities began and went well into the night.

29

RECONCILING WITH THE PAST

IN ALL HER YEARS, JORDAN had never been on a boat ride exclusively with her daughter. Those rides were originally between Jasta and Bopol only. And because of his paternal role in raising Jasta's daughters, Bopol occupied a place in Jasta's heart that Jordan never would. She didn't mind that. She respected her mate for offering their granddaughters stability during their childhood in a way only he could provide. So, she had been surprised at the previous night's community supper when Jasta asked her to join her on the lake today. Delighted, Jordan had immediately agreed.

This was the warm season, early afternoon. The weather was peaceful and serene. The clouds were light and scattered in the green-hued sky, and a soft breeze was at their backs. Jordan closed her eyes and leaned her head back slightly, breathing in with immense satisfaction.

"I am so glad you are enjoying this, Gemta," Jasta said.

"I feel honored. The Chieftess is taking me on a trip along the lake," Jordan replied, almost giddy. She was facing sideways, looking out at the water.

Jasta exhaled sharply through her nose. "Right now, I am not Chieftess. I am only Jasta, your daughter."

Jordan raised a finger in protest. "Much as that pleases me to hear you say, you are always Chieftess."

Her daughter sighed. "I know that as well as you, but can we not pretend otherwise for now?"

Jordan turned her head and saw that Jasta was serious, her eyes conveying her need to shed the responsibilities she always carried, if only briefly. Jordan nodded. Those burdens had been hers for most of her life; she knew them well. Occasionally, a respite was not only desirable but imperative.

"What does my daughter want to talk with me about?" she asked.

"Can we just talk like we used to, before I took a mate and became a gemta?"

"Of course. Have you seen Meespa recently? I think she could give birth any time now."

"Is it twins? She looked like it could be twins."

"I think so, but I have been . . . hesitant to bring it up."

"You think Karfoz may have indulged her much during this time?" Jasta inquired, her eyes slightly widening in surprise and amusement.

"I think it would be rude to ask," Jordan answered. "Either way, we will know soon."

Jasta laughed, sounding carefree. "My brother is about to become a torkommta! That should make me feel—"

"Old?"

"I was going to say strange, Gemta."

"I am surprised Kaltisa has not made you a gemtabana yet."

"She and Antam are having . . . difficulties. They have been apart for some time."

Jordan shifted her position in the wooden boat slowly, so she could turn to face Jasta without losing her balance.

"Is it because of her or because of him?" Jordan asked.

"It is both. Kaltisa can be demanding. At first, she was afraid to have a child so young, so she made him wait almost a cycle," Jasta said. "But now that she is ready, he is still angry and makes her wait."

Jordan chuckled for a moment, then allowed herself a good laugh. Jasta seemed perplexed at that.

"Do not worry, Jasta, they will be fine," she told her daughter. "They have not seen twenty cycles yet, but they love each other. I saw that the day they became mates."

"I know. It is just hard to watch them be unhappy right now."

Jordan waved her hand slowly and dismissively. "It is all right. I assure you, by this time next cycle, they will give you a grandchild."

Jasta blinked a few times at that, looking unsure how to respond.

"Do you not want to be a gemtabana?"

"Kalta has barely seen thirteen cycles and Altisa seventeen. It seems too young for either of them to have children yet."

Jordan empathized with her daughter.

"Then again, I had my first child at seventeen," Jasta continued, sounding wistful. She paused and looked like she might begin crying. "Had Kenjel survived the Shilvaba, this would have been the twenty-sixth cycle since his birth."

Feeling past grief resurface within her, Jordan tenderly laid her hand on her daughter's. Jasta wiped her tears from her cheeks with her other hand, allowing the boat to flow with the gentle current.

"Kenjel was a wonderful child, Jasta. You and Kabi—"

"Six cycles, Gemta," Jasta interrupted, desperate and heartbroken. "We only had six cycles with him!"

Jordan realized this was the real reason Jasta had wanted to spend time with her. Only she would understand this kind of terrible sadness and loss. Jordan recalled Bopol telling her about Jasta's experience in the Chieftess' hut, where she felt the presence and power of the Lord. Within herself, Jordan knew another way she could be a help to her daughter. With all her heart, she wanted to show Jasta how to seek the comfort that only the Lord and His Holy Spirit could provide. Jordan knew that would take time. But Jasta was grieving now and Jordan needed to allow for that. She embraced her daughter and let Jasta express her bereavement.

Bopol had been standing at the shoreline near a tree, close enough to intervene, should a threat arise but far enough to allow the Chieftess her privacy with her gemta. He also knew the significance of this day and how urgently Jasta needed Jordan's compassion and love.

His granddaughters both called him Torkomm. He was the only torkomm either of them remembered. Jasta had expressed her unending gratitude and respect for him on many occasions. He was thankful she had emotionally recovered from her losses.

It had been a couple of hours since they had left in the boat. He could see now that they were returning to the shore. Jasta exited the craft first and then helped Jordan onto dry land. He waited a moment before approaching them.

Bopol and Jordan entered the village with the Chieftess. Maska ran to meet them. She appeared both excited and concerned.

"What is it, Maska?" Jasta asked.

"Chieftess, I went exploring this morning, as I often do, and I found something incredible!"

"What did you find and where?"

Maska turned towards the Mountain and pointed.

"I was training some of the young hunters and took them to the base of the mountain when one of them noticed an opening that had never been there before," Maska continued. "It was like a jagged scar on the rockface. I think it may have happened during the battle with the Qui Tol ship. The hunters volunteered to go explore the opening with me."

"Tell me more," Jasta insisted.

"We entered a long passageway that led to a cavern inside the mountain," Maska added. "It was large enough to house many villagers. There was a column of crystal which reached to the top of the cavern. There was a shallow pool of water and—"

Jordan's eyes widened and she stepped forward, gently touching the arm of the Chieftess to get her attention.

"I know this place!" Jordan interrupted. "Long ago, I saw it in a dream. And I think I have been there once, the first time I returned from Earth."

"What is its significance, Gemta?" Jasta inquired.

"That chamber belonged to SnowFire."

Both Jasta and Maska gasped at that revelation. Bopol's eyes narrowed in apprehension and his stance tensed but he remained silent.

"What else did you see there, Maska?" the Chieftess asked.

"That was the most unusual part, Chieftess. I saw many lines and symbols carved onto the walls of the cavern. It may have been some kind of language, I think."

"I wish to see this place, Maska," Jordan said sternly, almost a demand.

Jasta turned to face her gemta. She looked worried.

"Gemta, the last time you ventured up the mountain, you nearly perished. I know this is important to you, but I will not risk your health and life," Jasta insisted. "It may take time, but we will learn what Gemtabana wanted."

"Do you think SnowFire intended for us to find this place?" Bopol asked.

"SnowFire was very deliberate in everything she did," Jordan stated. "And as her descendants, the Mokta were always in her thoughts."

"Then the answer is yes, Torkomm," Jasta said. "Gemtabana wanted us to find this one day."

It took a team of twenty Mokta elders, as well as the Chieftess, nearly six months to catalog and interpret what was found in the mountain chamber. During that time, Mokta builders inserted wooden support beams inside to secure the passageway. It was already frigid and made damp by the circular pool at the center of the massive room. Lighting the cavern with multiple torches, they still had to look closely to decipher its contents, as the orange flames and the blue-hued surfaces nearly cancelled out one another. The team was relieved to find that the markings had been deeply etched into the walls, making them somewhat easier to discern.

The chamber was separated into three sections: On the far-left end of the cave, there were images of various common objects, each with a single syllable representing them. On the far right of the cave, there was a list of the symbols only. They were grouped two or three at a time. When the team sounded them out, they were the names of well-known Mokta people, foods, tools, and items. This made it easier to recognize the relationship of the symbols with the objects.

In the center, using what they had learned, they interpreted phrases pertaining to the history of SnowFire's ten children plus Jordan and Erica. Maska had been correct: this was a language.

The Chieftess had included Jordan, Bopol, and Erica in all discussions about their discoveries within the chamber. Presently, they sat in the Chieftess' hut. It was early evening and quite cold outside.

"The interpretations are complete," Jasta began. "We now know what SnowFire intended for us with this chamber."

Bopol stayed silent, as he often did. But it surprised Jordan that Erica was equally quiet. The Chieftess appeared fatigued yet excited.

"SnowFire has honored us with a dual inheritance: a written language and a partial history of Algoran," Jasta continued. "The right side of the chamber contains letters and, on the left, common words side-by-side with drawings explaining their meaning. In the middle is a dedication to each of SnowFire's children, including Gemta and Eree-Kah. There is also a tale of the Great War which changed the face of Algoran forever."

Jordan's jaw dropped and Erica gasped. Even Bopol blinked several times and shifted positions at that news.

"So . . . will you have this written language taught to the tribe?" Jordan still reeled from the enormity of this news.

Jasta nodded. "There is no harm that will come from learning it. Gemtabana meant it for our good."

Erica brightened at that. "Chieftess, I volunteer to help teach it. Although it has been many cycles, I was once a teacher of children among the Ullvarr. It would please me to do so again."

Jasta smiled. "Good! Thank you, Eree-Kah. We need more teachers, especially now."

It pleased Jordan to see Erica take an interest in interacting with the tribe again. And yet, Jordan was still concerned by questions she had about the writings in the chamber.

"What can you tell us about Algoran's Great War, Chieftess?" Jordan inquired.

"It began around seven or eight thousand cycles ago. A kingdom called Jai-Teyn had a conflict with its neighboring kingdom, a people called the Eenstatt. They shared a border with the Gulstaa, who were a great power in this world," Jasta answered. "After several dozen moon-turns, the Gulstaa were drawn into the conflict and it escalated to involve almost all of Algoran, including the Onchei, Kastadi, Ullvarr, and Mokta. Entire populations of other races were wiped out. And every race's numbers were severely thinned. Machines and structures which were once common were destroyed. The knowledge of how to build them was lost. The history was almost entirely eradicated. The world had to start over again. And only SnowFire, being immortal, knew the truth."

"Incredible," Jordan said in amazement. "A world war on Algoran, one so devastating it changed everything!"

"It . . . explains so much," Erica said, clearly stunned. "That was why so many of the Ullvarr set out for the islands they occupy now. Evtaz did say there were stories of the Ullvarr settling there after a Great War."

"This is also why the populations have taken so long to recover," Jordan pondered.

They did not speak for a few minutes. Then Jasta turned to Bopol with a look of intrigue.

"Torkomm, what are your thoughts regarding this new information?" she asked.

He nodded. "I would like to know about SnowFire's children."

Jasta grinned. "Certainly! It all began with her firstborn, a son named SkyWings."

EPILOGUE

THE NEXT MORNING, JORDAN AWOKE early, as had been her habit
for so long. She still enjoyed the brisk air, sounds, and smells of the
village before daybreak. The twin stars' warm glow inched over the
hills in the distance. She stood by the stream's edge near the village,
leaning on the sturdy walking stick she now relied on. She had recovered from her last illness, but her body had been badly weakened by it.
She was blessed to still be alive and accepted that this limitation was
the trade-off. It would be with her the rest of her days.

Presently, her thoughts were focused on SnowFire's written words
concerning her and Erica:

"Jordan, my first daughter of Earth, joined to me by blood and
not through birth. Nevertheless, you are mine. You have shown me a
different kind of strength and passion. You have defied every obstacle
in your way and opened your heart to the Father of Spirits. You are a
worthy Chieftess, the gemta of leaders."

*SnowFire learned something from me? I am not sure what she meant by
"a different kind of strength and passion." But it is comforting to know she
thought well of me.* Jordan smiled. *Well, I am the gemta of at least one leader.*

"Erica, my other blood daughter, your heart was forged in the fires
of your past. My hope for you is that you can find peace in who you
have become. Break your own chains with the strength I have given

you and share the love you have always carried within. Believe in things you cannot see but know are true."

She knew us so well. How long was she watching us before we met her? I wonder.

"My only living offspring, be well. You are my legacy and my love."

I have known the love of so many mothers: my birth mother, Kitranor, Zoska and then SnowFire. Perhaps Zoska was right. She chuckled. *Maybe I did need that many.*

Jordan walked over to a grassy mound not far from the stream and sat down. She pulled her Bible from the knapsack she had brought with her. The stars were now in full rise, so she could more easily see its contents. She had been reading from the New Testament since her return. She opened it to where she had bookmarked a page in the third chapter in John.

"Verses sixteen through twenty-one. 'For God so loved the world, that he gave his only begotten Son, that whosoever believeth in him should not perish, but have everlasting life. For God sent not his Son into the world to condemn the world; but that the world through him might be saved. He that believeth on him is not condemned: but he that believeth not is condemned already, because he hath not believed in the name of the only begotten Son of God. And this is the condemnation, that light is come into the world, and men loved darkness rather than light, because their deeds were evil. For every one that doeth evil hateth the light, neither cometh to the light, lest his deeds should be reproved. But he that doeth truth cometh to the light, that his deeds may be made manifest, that they are wrought in God.'"

She looked up from the Bible to contemplate those words.

I did a lot of wrong over the cycles and caused death and suffering, but Lord, You helped me come to the light. And You forgave me. You sent Your Holy Spirit into me. Someday, this body will die but my spirit will live with You forever.

With some difficulty, Jordan stood up using her walking stick. Then she let the stick drop, clasped her hands together, closed her eyes, and made a half-bow.

"Thank You for Your sacrifice, Jesus," she said softly. "You honor us all."

Jordan straightened her posture, took in a deep breath of the morning air, and slowly released it. She remembered the words the Lord had spoken to her many cycles ago, when she was so young and dying from the Mosdon poison: "Would you be willing to spend the rest of your life on this world?"

Jordan opened her eyes, spread her arms out, and slowly turned around to see the entire landscape before her. Aside from the Mokta Mountain and the village, there was the forest, fields, hills, and of course, the skies. Everywhere was teaming with life and, to Jordan, so much beauty.

"I have never regretted it, Lord, not even for one moment." She grinned as the wind gently blew through her gray hair. "Thank You!"

THE END

ACKNOWLEDGMENTS

I must first thank God and His Son, Jesus Christ, for Their eternal love and power in my life. I could not have written this trilogy without Their inspiration. Through Their salvation and grace, I am the person I am today.

"For God hath not given us the spirit of fear; but of power, and of love, and of a sound mind. Be not thou therefore ashamed of the testimony of our Lord, nor of me his prisoner: but be thou partaker of the afflictions of the gospel according to the power of God; Who hath saved us, and called us with an holy calling, not according to our works, but according to his own purpose and grace, which was given us in Christ Jesus before the world began" 2 Timothy 1:7-9.

I also thank my wife, Angel, for her ceaseless love, support, patience, and encouragement. She is my first editor, gets to see the unbridled rough drafts and listens to me talk about these stories and characters at all hours of the day and night. Kudos to my sons and daughter for their love, support and patience in overhearing some of those conversations.

I am grateful for the support of the rest of my family and friends, including those from social media (Facebook, Twitter and Instagram), during this endeavor. Special mentions to my Pastor, Eddie E. Willis, as well as Mary Sue Morris, Michael Bridges, Lacey Bridges, Larry Walker, Jeff VanMeter, Harry Hardcastle, Anjelina Hernandez, Allyssa

Maldonado, Alexzander Maldonado, Glen Kuykendall, Desda Ravanesi, Bobby and Leslie Sahlen.

I am thankful for my entire family at Ambassador International. Everyone from the publisher himself to the staff, editors, and authors have been wonderful, helpful, and encouraging.

ABOUT THE AUTHOR

Allen Steadham created comic books and webcomics before he started writing novels. He has been married to his wife, Angel, since 1995 and they have two sons and a daughter. When not writing stories, Allen and his wife are singers, songwriters and musicians. They have been in a Christian band together since 1997. They live in Central Texas.

For more information about
Allen Steadham
and
Jordan's Deliverance
please visit:

www.allensteadham.com
allen@allensteadham.com
www.facebook.com/jaspecfiction
@Mindfirenovel
www.instagram.com/allensteadham
www.bookbub.com/profile/allen-steadham
www.goodreads.com/allensteadham

For more information about
AMBASSADOR INTERNATIONAL
please visit:

www.ambassador-international.com
@AmbassadorIntl
www.facebook.com/AmbassadorIntl

*If you enjoyed this book, please consider leaving us a review on
Amazon, Goodreads, or our website.*